THE MIRROR OF DIANA

♦　♦　♦　♦　♦

A Novel of War and Love

A. R. HOMER

Requests for permission to make copies of any part of this work should be mailed to Permissions Department, Llumina Press, PO BOX 772246, CORAL SPRINGS, FL 33077-2246

ISBN: 1-932560-63-7 Paperback
ISBN: 1-932560-64-5 Hardcover
Printed in the United States of America by Llumina Press

Library of Congress Cataloging-in-Publication Data

Homer, A. R.
  The mirror of Diana : a novel of war and love / A.R. Homer.
     p. cm.
  ISBN 1-932560-64-5 (hardcover : alk. paper) -- ISBN 1-932560-63-7 (pbk. : alk. paper)
  1. World War, 1939-1945--Destruction and pillage--Fiction. 2. World War, 1939-1945--Italy--Fiction. 3. Germans--Italy--Fiction. 4. Ships, Ancient--Fiction. 5. Nemi (Italy)--Fiction. I. Title.
PS3608.O53M57 2004
813'.6--dc22
                                              2003027560

To all the treasures lost in war

And ere a man hath power to say, "Behold!"
The jaws of darkness do devour it up. . .

A Midsummer-Night's Dream
Act I, Scene i

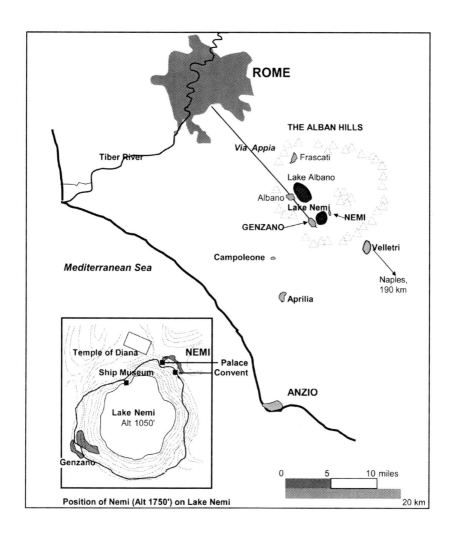

NEMI AND ENVIRONS

On the night of May 31st 1944, as the German army was retreating, two ancient ships housed in a museum by a lake south of Rome went up in flames. No one knows how. No one knows why.

Everything about these ships was remarkable. They were huge floating palaces, lavishly appointed for the Roman emperor Caligula. He took his court upon them to the lakeside temple of Diana, then already centuries old, ferrying them across Lake Nemi, which the ancients called *Speculum Dianae* (Diana's Mirror). When Caligula was murdered in 41 A.D., the ships were sunk in the lake to expunge his memory.

In 1928, after centuries of dreaming of the treasure at the bottom of the lake, Italian engineers began to recover the ships. A triumphal ceremony, Mussolini attending, was held in 1940 to celebrate the vessels' release from twenty centuries in a muddy tomb.

But in only four years they were gone again, this time for good. Perhaps this is the story of their final destruction.

CHAPTER 1

October 12th 1948

He stepped out of the car, lit a cigarette, and looked up at the Alban hills. They were little changed since the Roman legions came through on the nearby Via Appia, marching out the last few miles on their return to Rome from some imperial war; little changed since the German legions to which he had belonged but a few years ago had been here.

He ground out his cigarette and shook his head. He was lost. The forest was eternal, but everything else seemed different. Roads he was sure existed in '44 seemed to have vanished.

Perhaps he wasn't meant to go back, he thought; perhaps he was destined to live with the hellish images that pushed his sanity into a tight corner of his mind. But he had to go back. Would Rosanna be there? Instinctively, his hand went to the icon of Diana hanging at his neck, the icon she had given him.

And what of the others? Were four years long enough to bring the clouds of forgetfulness, to black out their memory of those days? He shook his head in doubt. And what if someone had found the hiding place?

He reached for his map. His finger traced the road north to Velletri, where the divisional headquarters had been, but the yellowed wartime map was indistinct. He always kept old things, long after their use had gone. It was the historian in him, clinging to the past, yet it was a past he wished forgotten.

He folded the map and put the car into gear. He wished he had never seen the town of Nemi and the ships of Caligula.

One hour later.

Velletri was unrecognizable compared with '44. The town was still littered with the detritus of war. Still rising above the piazza was the Torre del Trivio, the Romanesque campanile which had been the only building left standing when the remnants of his division had retreated from the town. A newly built bar occupied the corner of the piazza.

He parked the car behind the campanile as the bells chimed a lengthy noon. Young children played on the pavement; for them, the war was not even a memory. He walked around the piazza and went into the bar.

A pall of smoke hung throughout, rising from the half-dozen tables, as did the babble of Italian chatter to which his ear was rapidly becoming attuned. He responded to the bartender's look.

"Vino rosso, per favore. Mi sono perduto – dov' è Nemi?"

He spoke clearly, confidently. He had learned Italian while he was studying Ancient History in Berlin before the war; it had followed naturally from his Latin studies. Yet the bartender stiffened. Perhaps he had detected some hint of a German accent. The babble of the bar trailed away, and he heard a mutter of *'tedesco.'*

His confidence ebbed away and he looked at the floor, a little afraid. He needed to be careful. The war and the treachery were still seared into the minds of the men in the bar. Maybe some had relatives who had suffered at the hands of the S.S. These people would make no distinction between the ordinary serving soldier and the Nazis – they were all German to them. Perhaps some of the suspicious faces looking at him belonged to communists – Italy was awash with them – still harboring a grudge, still waiting for a chance to settle old scores.

"The way to Nemi is where it's always been – up the hill!"

The bar tittered briefly at the bartender's attempt at wit. The silence returned, and he felt a dozen pairs of eyes boring into the back of his head. The need to escape pressed him, but he decided to face it out and turned towards the tables.

"I am sorry. I mean no offence. Perhaps you will accept a drink as . . ."

he struggled with the words, partly from his own anxiety, partly from his wish to find the correct Italian phrase, ". . . as a token of new friendship."

Three of the crowd stood up and walked towards the door - younger men, who looked at him darkly, their eyes still fired with the illusion of some idealism, not yet dulled by the baleful light of the real world.

"The only good German is a dead German." he heard one mutter. Another looked over his shoulder as he went through the doorway. "A new friendship? With a fascist? *Il lupo perde il pelo, ma non il vizio.*" The young man spat onto the street as he walked away. The translation came immediately to the German: 'The wolf changes his skin, but not his evil.' As the young men departed, he looked around the bar, his head held high to disguise his anxiety. The silence again waited to be broken.

"And now it is our turn to be sorry."

The conciliatory voice came from a broad-shouldered man with graying hair and a moustache of the same color except for the tobacco stains. He wore some kind of uniform. The man rose, revealing himself to be short and stocky, and walked toward him.

"You must forgive them," he nodded toward the departing men. "They are young, and it takes time to learn the ways of the world."

The small man nodded to the bartender, who began to prepare the drinks, and the bar resumed its earlier animation as the glasses were passed around. Some glasses were raised to the German, though others looked away as they drank. The Italian pointed at his uniform with one hand, extending the other.

"Ich bin Antonio – ich bin der postmeister!"

For some reason, his new acquaintance talked to him in halting German, as if it were impossible for a *tedesco* to speak the most beautiful language in the world.

"Sono Klaus - Klaus Schmidt - Professore." He grasped the proffered hand and explained in fluent Italian to the postmaster that he was a Professor of Ancient History at Berlin University, and had come to see the antiquities of Rome. Although the postmaster was impressed with his grasp of Italian, Klaus knew that any conversation that followed would amount to no more than idle chatter. Food, wine, the weather and other wonders of Italy were discussed at length; but of the war, nothing. The war was a place where both of them had been and did not, in their conversation, wish to revisit.

Eventually, most of the Italians drifted away. It was time to return to work; they made their excuses and left. Even Antonio, who had displayed great kindness and courtesy, looked at his watch and took his leave.

"It will soon be two o'clock – I must go. You see, I am not only the postmaster – I was elected the mayor last year, which makes me very busy. I bring the news, and then have to sort things out when the news has arrived." He laughed. "It was good to meet you, Klaus."

"It was good to meet you, too, Antonio." Their hands met in a firm grip. The mayor turned to go, but he came back and tugged Klaus's sleeve. "Take care," he tapped the side of his nose, "and if you do meet with any trouble, do not hesitate to ask for my help."

Klaus nodded, and the broad shoulders of the Mayor disappeared through the bar door. He finished his drink and was about to leave, when he realized the bill had not been paid.

"*Il conto, per favore*," he called, wondering how much his generosity had cost him.

The bartender stopped collecting the glasses, returned to the bar, and produced a long scrap of paper from a drawer. He muttered over the addition, the pencil in his squat hand running over the figures. Eventually, he uttered a satisfied '*va bene*' and pushed the scrap across the counter. Klaus placed the bills on the battered wooden counter, ensuring there was enough for a sizable tip. The bartender counted the money deftly, smiling as he realized the tip. He leaned forward, conspiratorially, although they were the only two left in the bar.

"You have made some friends today, *signore*." His big hand swatted at a fly. "But you have also made a few enemies."

Klaus felt he did not need to be reminded of the menace of the three young men. He turned to go.

"*È curioso*," The bartender regained his attention. "I have not seen a *tedesco* for. . ." he looked at the ceiling as his memory flipped through time, ". . . for more than four years. And now, I meet two in the space of a week!"

Klaus's brow furrowed. "You saw another German?"

"*Sì*, another German. He did not speak Italian as you speak it. It took me some time to work out what he wanted."

Klaus was puzzled. Most Germans wouldn't risk coming to Italy. The memory of the war was too close, as his recent encounter had shown. Besides, times were still hard: not many could afford it – he had needed to secure a loan for his trip.

"What did he look like?"

The bartender looked up as he started to wipe the glasses. "He looked, as I can only say, like a German. You know, tall and blond."

"But not all Germans are tall and blond."

"But you are – and this one was." A shrug of the shoulders came with the reply.

Klaus knew that this line of questioning was going nowhere.

"What did he want?"

The bartender put down the glass and spread his hands along the bar.

"*È molto curioso* – the other German wanted exactly what you wanted!"

Klaus's brows furrowed.

"*Vino rosso* – and the way to Nemi!"

Klaus left the bar and walked across the piazza. The sun shone palely through streaky clouds, dappling the *campanile*. He stumbled over a cobblestone, and realized that the strained conviviality in the bar had caused him to drink too much. He paused, sat on a wall and looked out across the piazza, his mind swimming in memories.

When he had last been there, the buildings shook with the noise of the engines of war. Tanks, armored troop carriers, 88mm gun limbers, all roaring with their lust for destruction. The press of horses, the clamor of men, the futile urgency of war had filled the piazza. The men. So many young men, all caught up in the deathly maelstrom of war, not knowing when the grim reaper would tap on their shoulders as he came for his early harvest. Most, like himself, dimly aware that life should hold something other than the mad dance of fear and uncertainty, never knowing what tomorrow might bring. If there were a tomorrow.

He sighed. He should not have taken a sabbatical term to come back; he should have stayed in Berlin. The words of Heraclitus sprang to his mind: 'You cannot put the same foot in the same river twice; the only permanent thing in life is change.' Yet he always knew he would return to Nemi. He was driven, inexorably, back to the scene of his agony. He got up and began to walk across the piazza. History did not drive him back to Nemi; Rosanna did. Rosanna, her head thrown back with the loving laugh of life – she drove him. And the other Rosanna, bruised, agonized, her eyes widened with fear – she, too, drove him on.

His pace quickened as he walked in front of the church, as if he had been seized with the need to face his demons immediately. He would drive to Nemi at once. His mind was so preoccupied that he did not notice the symbol until he was about to get into his car. There was a swastika daubed on the hood.

Over five years earlier. August 3rd 1943. Rome

"She's not for you!" Gunther laughed as he caught Klaus looking at the pretty girl across the street.

"Besides," the *feldwebel* lowered his voice, "if you do get her, the Yanks and the Tommies will soon be here to take her from you!"

Gunther whistled at the girl, whose dress swirled as she turned to make an obscene gesture.

"With those legs and those manners, the Tommies can have her." Gunther returned the gesture. "Imagine taking her home to mother!"

Klaus laughed, but felt a long way from his mother. Her smiling face came to his mind, and her words of advice as he left Berlin after his last leave. 'Take care, remember to look smart, and keep out of trouble.' As if this hideous war were a fancy dress parade. She was like that: unwilling to grasp great events, she placed importance on the small things in life. He wondered what she was doing now. Probably preparing dinner for his father while he sat reading the paper and puffing his pipe. If he could get tobacco, that is. Things were getting tough in Berlin. Her last letter – it was the only one he had received in a month – told of the shortages and the unceasing air raids. "Mustn't grumble," she had ended, "when you consider what you and your soldier friends are facing." He felt a twinge of guilt. He hadn't seen any real action for three years. His parents were suffering hell, and he was on an afternoon stroll with Gunther in Rome, with the early August sun beating down.

"There'll be other fish to fry." Gunther gestured after the woman. "But I tell you these Italian women have all become stuck up. They're waiting for the Yanks with their nylons and newly-printed lira."

Klaus raised his index finger to his lips in an attempt to curb the *feldwebel's* indiscretion, but he knew it was a lost cause. Gunther spoke his mind without caring if a Gestapo agent were around the corner.

"You will get us into trouble." He leaned towards Gunther's ear. "Remember, there are no women in a Gestapo cell."

"Aw, captain, what's the point of going to war if you can't shag the women? Do you think I, *Feldwebel* Gunther Mattheus, am here for the greater glory of the German *Reich*? I am here to shag the women. The war will soon be over, the glorious *Reich* will disappear, and we shall all be dead because of those lunatics in the *Wilhelmstrasse*."

Klaus looked around him, thankful that no other German officer was within earshot.

"You really must watch what you say, Gunther."

He strode away, and Gunther jogged after him, their boots clipping on the Roman pavement as they strolled along. Klaus knew the *feldwebel* was a fool for speaking unguardedly, but there was more than a grain of truth in what he had said. Something was afoot. Only a month ago, they were on a cushy occupation duty in Southern France. Then the whole of the 715th Division had been uprooted at a moment's notice and raced down to Rome. Everyone thought it was in response to how badly things were going in Sicily, but rumors were rife that Mussolini had been arrested, and that the Italians were going to throw their lot in with the Allies. With the Russian front in retreat everywhere, '43 was turning out to be a bad year for Hitler. Maybe Gunther was right; maybe the war would soon be over, the madness would cease and he could go back to teaching in the university.

"Look, there goes another one with her nose in the air."

Gunther's usual preoccupation brought Klaus back to earth. But it wasn't just the women's response to Gunther's crude approaches; the whole attitude of the Italian people had changed since they had arrived a month ago. Nearly all the Italian soldiers averted their eyes; there was an unpleasant sullenness when dealing with shopkeepers and café owners; and in some areas he had heard of open hostility. The whole situation was simmering, and he wondered how long it would be before it boiled over. Perhaps he should take his chance to visit all the sites Rome had to offer before it was too late. At least the war had brought him here, to the place he had dreamed of when he was studying at the university.

"Come, Gunther." He placed his hand around the sergeant's shoulder. "By courtesy of our beloved *Fuehrer*, we have a free tour of the antiquities of Rome."

"You know what the *Fuehrer* can do with the antiquities. Antiquities are all dead stones; I want warm, living flesh. Gunther needs to dip his sausage."

Klaus laughed.

"Antiquities first." They strode out in the direction of the Palatine. "Sausage dip later."

An hour later.

"So how old is this thing?" Gunther craned his neck as he looked up at the arch.

"About one thousand seven hundred years." Klaus was pleased his friend was showing some interest in the Roman Forum, but he suspected that it was nothing more than the curiosity of boredom.

"It's known as the Arch of Septimius Severus – he's the emperor who built it." Klaus admired the four detached Corinthian columns standing before the façade to form a false portico, marveling at such an architectural heritage.

"Built it my arse!" The *feldwebel* had a way of destroying his musing. "It was built by his slaves. Emperors and *Fuehrers* don't do their own work – they have idiots like you and me when it comes to a question of getting hands dirty. Is all that up there about him?" He pointed up at the inscriptions at the top of the arch.

"Yes, and about his two sons Caracalla and Geta." Perhaps he could stimulate the philistine's interest. "Actually, Geta's name has been obliterated from the dedicatory text; Caracalla had him murdered to ensure his succession as Emperor."

"You mean he killed his own brother so he could become Emperor? That's worse than Hitler rubbing out all those brownshirts back in '34. What are all these people in chains?" He ran his hand along the base of a column.

"They're the prisoners of Severus from the Parthian war."

Gunther's eyes peered at him from under his bushy eyebrows.

"Murders, slaves, war and prisoners." He gave a sardonic chuckle. "Not much changed in seventeen hundred years, eh?"

Klaus averted his eyes, kicked aimlessly at some pebbles and walked away. Gunther, with only a modicum of basic education, had a way of deflating intellectual pretensions. The peasant farmer's son did not possess any qualifications, but he had an unerring knack of sweeping away bullshit and getting to the nub of any issue.

Klaus climbed on to the rostra, sat on its edge and tried to sense the sounds of history, the art of the orators who had declaimed from the platform. Perhaps Gunther would have been moved by such speeches. He shook his head; Gunther was moved only by the beat of the seasons, the love of the land, the sight of a beautiful woman, and, in his present circumstances, the need to survive. He looked across at the sergeant, who was idly walking around the columns. With his close-cropped head atop his broad-shouldered, immensely strong body, he created a sense of solidity, a permanence, insofar as any mortal of twenty-seven years can create such an impression.

Despite the objections of his fellow officers, Klaus held Gunther as his friend. Officers didn't usually mix with other ranks socially, but the two of them had become friends almost at first meeting. Perhaps it was because they were opposites, like black and white. The rarified intellectual air of Berlin University in which he normally moved would have had Gunther gasping for a breath of the peasant common sense on which his homespun philosophy was based. Despite coming from Bavaria, which had quickly become a bastion of Nazism, the sergeant was untainted with its ideology, for the simple reason that he thought its leaders were, as he said, 'a load of gangsters.'

Gunther had told him what trust he had was placed in the land, which rewarded his efforts without caviling or swindling. He would never have left his father's farm if it had not been for the platoon of men sent by Hitler's conscription units.

Besides, he owed Gunther a debt. Back in '40, in the latter stages of the campaign in France, he had overreached his company's position and had got caught in a murderous crossfire from the Tommy rearguard trying to hold up the advance on Dunkirk. Heedless of the danger – fear was a stranger to him – Gunther had maneuvered his machine gun unit behind the British position and got him out of a sticky situation.

Klaus had repaid the debt several times, but not with any great bravery. Gunther was always getting into scrapes when off duty. Like the time in the whorehouse in Aix-en-Provence, when he had threatened to cut the Madame into tiny pieces because she saved her best whores for the S.S. officers, whom, he assured her, 'could not satisfy one of his father's chickens.' Often it needed a box of chocolates here, a bottle of schnapps there to rescue Gunther from his own folly.

Yet Gunther, when on duty, always obeyed orders. It was the easy way, he would say: obey orders and you will survive. Thus the sergeant survived, and not only through Klaus's patronage. His prowess as a soldier, as a fighting man, made him an idol in the eyes of his platoon, and brought him grudging respect from the division's officers. If you were in a tight spot, Gunther was the man to have at your shoulder. He had brought his farmyard cunning to the battlefield, and it was better to go with his instincts than the rulebook. Above all was his instinct to survive; the sergeant joked that he had to survive because there were so many women to shag, but Klaus knew that all he wanted to do was to return to his farm.

He looked across at Gunther, who was cheerfully whistling as he urinated at the foot of a column. "Gunther – have you no respect?"

"Respect's not much use to you when you've been dead seventeen hundred years! Besides, the Russians will probably be pissing on the Brandenburg Gate in a couple of years. History has no respect."

He fastened his trousers and walked over to where Klaus was sitting. "So what's that particular piece of antiquity you've got your ass on?"

"This is the rostra, Gunther, from which great orators spoke to the senate and harangued the crowds – even Cicero stood here."

"So who was this great Cicero then? What did he do?"

"He was a lawyer, perhaps the finest in Rome." Klaus had a feeling he was following a peculiarly familiar path.

"So," Gunther continued with his inexorable logic of simplicity, "what happened to this great lawyer, then?"

"He was perceived as an enemy of the state. Mark Antony had him murdered, and his severed head and hands were displayed from this rostra."

Gunther gave one of his great belly laughs. "I'll say this for the Romans – they certainly knew how to deal with lawyers!"

Klaus could not help bursting into laughter. He jumped down from the rostra. "History lesson over." He slapped Gunther on the back.

"You mean I don't get to see the Vestal Virgins?" Gunther looked across at him mischievously. "Well, I'll have to see if I can get a sausage dip on the Via Veneto."

C H A P T E R 4

August 10th 1943. Nemi

"**L**ettera, lettera, Signor Giraldi, lettera."
The mail boy was shouting long before he reached the
door, jumping off his ramshackle bicycle, the prized mis-
sive held aloft.

"Coming, coming."

Paolo Giraldi pushed aside the photographs of the ships that he had
been studying and removed his pince-nez spectacles from his nose. He
chose not to hurry as he lifted himself from the battered wooden table
that served as his make-shift bench; it would not do for a whipper-
snapper of a post boy to see the Curator of the Museum of the Ships
rushing about. Still, he felt a little surge of excitement as he looked in
the mirror to adjust his tie. It was almost a miracle that any letter at all
got through these days. Only last week, the Allies had bombed Rome,
creating panic and disruption; the war was coming home. He had heard
that Mussolini had been arrested; everything was beginning to fall
apart.

"*Lettera, lettera.*" The shrill voice of the mail boy was insistent.

"Coming, coming."

His tone expressed annoyance at the youngster's impatience. He
shuffled through the kitchen, which was still heavy with the heat and
aroma of his wife's bread baking.

Perhaps the letter brought him good news; perhaps the Ministry had
decided…. The thought was soon shrugged from his mind. His sixty-
one years had taken a heavy toll on hope. Over the past few years, hope
had become a false friend.

The door latch clattered in his hand and the old wooden-slatted door
creaked open, letting in the late afternoon sun. He shielded his eyes, his
hand resting atop his eyebrows, for the sun was low, and the boy's silhouette was encased in the glare.

"It's from the Ministry, it's from the Ministry." The youth's spotty
face parted in a smile.

"Didn't your parents teach you not to stick your nose into other
people's business?"

He chided the youth, but the whole world could see with a glance at the envelope that it was, indeed, from the Ministry. The mail boy looked chastened, fiddling with the bell on his bicycle, but stood his ground, showing no inclination to remount his machine and cycle away.

"Well, what are you waiting for?" Paolo shouted at him. "Do you want me to read it to you? Why didn't you open it and read it out aloud on the Town Hall steps?"

He put the letter in his pocket casually, determined not to show the youth any sign of his anxiety regarding its contents. Appearances were important; the Museum Curator did not provide the mail boy with tittle-tattle to feed the town's gossip. The stupid gape on the boy's face eventually closed and, with a shrug of his shoulders, he scooted away on his bicycle.

Paolo climbed back up the steps to the house and closed the door. He took the envelope from his pocket, holding it gingerly, as if it would burst into flames at any moment. He stared at it; he was afraid to open it. Their answer would certainly be 'no,' he thought.

"That last chicken just will not lay." His wife slammed the back door behind her. "It's the pot for it!"

She wiped her hands on her dirty apron and rummaged in the cupboard for the old axe.

"Aren't you being a little hasty?" He put the letter down on the table, glad of any delay to prevent his opening it. "Perhaps it won't lay because it's not getting anything decent to eat."

"Well, at least *we'll* have something decent to eat." She pulled out the axe and began to slide a honing bar up and down the cutting edge. "Anyway, if we don't eat it now, it'll soon be nothing but a bag of bones. As we are." Her free hand tugged at her stained black dress, showing the loose inches of fabric that had once embraced a more ample body.

He looked down at the letter, ignoring her as she swung the axe through the air, practicing the coming execution of the hapless chicken. She raised the latch and turned around in the open doorway to continue her harangue.

"Damn this war. Damn Mussolini. He is the anti-Christ…. O, Mother of God…."

She was stopped by a loud thwack, a thwack like a tennis ball being smashed against a wall. He looked up with alarm as she stood transfixed for a moment, her eyes bulging. Her breath whistled in between her teeth.

"O, my God!" She cried out as she staggered and waddled like a duck across the floor to grip the edge of the table with her free hand.

"What's the matter?" Paolo directed the question to the reddening face that loomed above him.

"What's the matter? What's the matter?" She screamed at him. He retreated further into his chair as she fought to regain her dignity.

"I'll tell you what's the matter." She waved the axe under his nose, as her other hand went behind her, massaging her rump. "It's that Gianni. That Gianni Rossi and his damned slingshot." She put the axe down in order to cross herself for the blasphemy, but kept rubbing her backside with the other hand.

"Only ten years old, and already the devil incarnate!" She thumped the table to emphasize her point.

"No respect. That's the trouble with kids nowadays. No respect. What use has twenty years of Mussolini been? Still they have no respect. I'll kill the little *porco*."

She reached down for the axe, but stopped suddenly as she saw the envelope on the table.

"What's that?"

"Oh," he tried to keep a lack of concern in his voice, "it's a letter from the Ministry."

She suspended her murderous intent toward Gianni and the chicken. "What does it say? Is it about your salary?"

"I don't know," he looked down sheepishly, "I haven't opened it yet."

"Mother of God, you are an idiot. How can you know what it's about if you don't open it? Open it now!"

She made a move to grab at the letter, but he pre-empted her, lifting it slowly in his hands before running his index finger inside the seal. He reached inside and pulled the document out.

"What does it say? What does it say? Read it!" Her words came quickly, her hands clenched with impatience.

He pinched his glasses over his nose and slowly unfolded the letter. He looked across at his wife, cast his eyes down again and began to read aloud.

"The Minister thanks you for your letter. Although the Minister shares your concerns for the ancient ships...." His disappointment manifested itself as his voice trailed away.

"Stop mumbling, for God's sake! What does it say?"

He cleared his voice and started again.

"Although the Minister shares your concerns for the ancient ships, he sincerely regrets that the substantial resources required to move them to a safer place, if such exists, cannot at present be spared. The ships' artifacts have been moved to the museum in Rome for their protection, but, regarding the ships themselves, the Minister feels sure that you will understand that, with the present demands of the war, nothing can be done at this time."

He stopped. Although he had expected the outcome, the disappointment was still bitter. He removed his pince-nez and rubbed his eyes.

"Your salary, your salary," his wife screamed at him, "does it say anything about your salary? They haven't paid you anything for two months now!"

He shook his head, knowing it was prudent not to mention that he had not even asked about his unpaid salary.

"How on earth are we going to live? Don't they understand that we've nearly used up all our savings? It's all right for them, sitting on their fat bottoms in the Via Veneto, while we have to scrape a living…."

She stopped as she realized from his glazed look that her words were unheard.

"They will not move them." He mumbled distractedly. "What will become of the great ships? Rome was bombed again last week. One stray bomb and…."

He slumped down at the table, his head in his hands, shrinking into himself, as if his whole existence were threatened.

"The ships, the ships, that's all you think of." She thumped the table with both fists. "Just rotten pieces of wood that just sit there, and you think more of them than your own family. We cannot eat rotten pieces of wood, you know. Even if we could, I expect you wouldn't let us! What will become of the great ships, indeed? What will become of us and Rosanna? She's nineteen now, and not a suitor in sight. I'm not surprised with all the silly ideas you've put into her head."

Her words were wasted on him. He stared at the letter again, then rose from the table and began to put on his coat.

"Where do you think you're going?" She folded her arms, but he ignored the implied threat.

"To the museum to see if everything is alright."

"To the museum?" Her voice was heavy with sarcasm. "To that old concrete barn you call a museum? A museum that nobody visits?"

His need to escape her lashing tongue drove him to the door. *'La lingua non ha ossa, ma rompe il dorso,'* he thought. 'The tongue has no bones, but it can break a man's back.' She followed him to the door, shouting after him.

"Be off to your precious ships, then. And while you're there, see if there are any leftovers from one of Caligula's feasts!"

August 18th 1943. Afternoon. Velletri, south of Rome.

Klaus sighed, put down his book and swung his long legs off the bed. It was impossible to concentrate with all the noise going on downstairs. His stockinged feet padded over to his bedroom window and he looked down at the raucous throng of carousing soldiers on the pavement below. Most were barely older than youths, and made him, at twenty-nine, seem an old man.

It was their first leave for a month, and the news of the Allies' success in Sicily brought the war - and fear - nearer to them. Not many of them had seen battle action; the 715th had been formed as an occupation force back in '41, and most of the men in the street below had, until now, spent a pleasant war on their backsides guarding the inoffensive streets of Aix-en-Provence. Their wine-fuelled song reached a crescendo as they tried to deafen their minds to other sounds, the sounds of the first battle to come, the sound of a bullet whine as a harbinger of death.

Klaus still cursed them silently. Why didn't they take the drowning of their fears elsewhere? Didn't they know he needed his own escape? He had wanted to study his book, to learn more about the ancients, about the ships of Caligula, to seek his own refuge from the war.

The noise from below rose again to a discordant pitch, as the men sought to enjoy their respite. They had been stood down only that morning from a two-week long state of alert following the ousting of Mussolini: no one knew where the Italian government stood; if they decided to throw their hand in with the Allies, it would be necessary to be on guard. Division H.Q. had decided to give the men a break, but, in the future, no one was to venture out alone, and side-arms were to be carried at all times.

Perhaps the men did deserve their well-earned break, but he still wished they would go elsewhere. Despite the noise, he picked up the book again and attempted to read. It was nothing more than a tourist guide, not old, but already battered and dog-eared. He sat up on his bed and carefully turned to the index at the back. His eyes ran down the lists. 'Caligula: *navi, Lago di Nemi*, p95.' He read the Italian quickly, pausing only to delve into his small dictionary for some of the technical words.

"Lago di Nemi, about 5 ½ km in diameter and about 35 m deep, lies in an oval basin which is either a crateriform subsidence or a real crater. The water is beautifully clear and rarely ruffled by wind. The precipitous wooded slopes are over 150 m high. In ancient times it was called the Lacus Nemorensis, and sometimes the 'Mirror of Diana' from a temple and grove sacred to that goddess. Nemi is a small mediaeval town, with an ancient castle of the Colonna. The inn possesses a small verandah with a view of the lake, the castle of Genzano, of the extensive plain and the sea. Nemi is famous for its wild strawberries."

His eyes scanned down the page, looking for more information on the ships of Caligula.

"A little beyond Nemi, by the lakeside, is the recently-opened Museum of Roman Ships, which houses two ancient ships built by Caligula (Emperor A.D. 37-41) to convey his court across the lake for the festival of Diana. The ships were sunk at the time of Claudius to expunge the memory of the hated Caligula. After many attempts at recovery, the ships were removed from the lake in 1932 after almost two thousand years, and are now housed in the Museum."

He lowered the book, his eyes dreaming away in some long lost age. The continuing sounds of revelry came up from the piazza, disturbing him as his mind took position on the decks of the ships, the oarsmen straining, the prow furrowing through the placid waters of the lake. He held the dream as he realized that he had found the ancient ships that had intrigued him since his studies at the university.

He scanned the book urgently. For a tourist guide, it had little to recommend itself in maps. Nemi, he knew, must be close by. Although he had been occupied with the state of alert and the recent move of the division down from Rome, he was sure the town could not be far from Velletri.

The caterwauling from below was beginning to abate; although the sun still had more than an hour in the sky, there were orders from headquarters to close the tavern early to avoid incidents. He hoped there would be no problems; soldiers with war breathing down their necks and their bellies full of wine possessed little self control. Last week in Rome, several had staggered down the street firing their weapons into the air. Headquarters seemed to ignore the mayhem; they had little but contempt for the Italians, and felt no inclination to interfere with what was little short of a latter-day sack of Rome. He winced as he remembered that he had turned his back and walked away. There was nothing he could do.

The guilt, again, was easily discarded, like the book tossed onto the bed. He knew where he could get maps. He pulled on his leather boots, strapped on his sidearm and went out, easing his way through the thinning clutch of men.

Tomorrow, he would have to deal with the rosters and the follow-up supplies for the gun limbers that had to be transported down from Rome. The day after, he would visit Nemi and the ships. Maybe he could persuade Gunther to 'borrow' some transport from the supply pool. His boots clipped the pavement with the urgency of anticipation.

The same day. Late afternoon.

Rosanna was afraid. The three German soldiers stood leering at her. The tallest one was firmly gripping the handlebars of her bicycle. Beneath his cap, his shifty eyes leered at her. His breath reeked of wine and he was unsteady, but he did not relinquish his grip. Her fear was compounded by her inability to understand a word the soldiers were saying, although their actions needed no translation.

"Well, my pretty Italian whore, what nice tits you have."

Rosanna shook her head. She didn't understand. Her hands trembled with fear. Her mother had asked her to cycle down to her aunt in Velletri to beg half a dozen eggs. She stared at the *tedesco*; she was very frightened.

"Leave the Italian bitch alone, Fritz." The second German looked up from his haphazard urination into the ditch at the side of the road. "Can't you see she's only a kid—you like cradle-snatching?"

Rosanna averted her eyes from the disgusting scene, as the lurching German tried to control his flow without wetting his boots.

"I like young meat." The reeking breath wafted over her face again, causing her to gag. "What about you, Jurgen?"

The third German's response was to fall on his hands and knees and begin vomiting, a trail of viscous purple spittle dangling from his jowls as he threw up the excess of wine.

"Not up to it, Jurgen? Another case of brewer's droop?"

The first German guffawed at his own joke, and Rosanna tried to use the diversion to snatch the handlebars from his grip, but he held tight.

"Not so fast, my little Italian trollop. Don't you fancy a German boyfriend?"

Rosanna started to cry. She did not understand what he was saying, but she knew what he wanted. Ignoring her tears, the other soldier fastened his fly and lurched towards her.

"Say, Fritz, this one's got a rump made to fit the hands."

She let go of the handlebars and turned to run, but the German grabbed her wrist. She felt her arm seized inside the vice of his fist. She stumbled, half falling, but he dragged her back to her feet and swung her towards him.

"What's the matter – Germans not good enough for you?"

She began to pummel him with her free hand.

"I like a woman with a bit of spirit."

Fear drove her struggles, but his huge arms went around her, pinioning her arms until he held her two wrists behind her in one of his massive hands. His free hand began to maul at her left breast. She kicked at his shins, but her light shoes made no impression on his leather boots.

"*No, no, per favore….*" Her words came haltingly as she fought for her breath, the tears flowing down her cheeks. She thought of the shame, the look on her mother's face. Her feet continued to kick at her aggressor. She prayed to Diana, the goddess of women and virgins. Why had her goddess abandoned her?

He looked straight at her face, his ugly leer making clear his intentions. She began to scream, but her voice was stifled quickly as his free hand clamped over her mouth.

"Enough of these silly games." His hand pulled down on her imprisoned wrists, forcing her to her knees. As he descended with her, he forced his hips into her groin. He removed his hand from her mouth to free his belt. She screamed again, but he silenced her by lashing her across the face with the back of his hand. Her heart was pounding with fear; her struggles were not saving her.

He pushed his face alongside hers, his unshaven cheeks abrading her already-bruised skin. He mumbled something incomprehensible, and despair began to seize her. Her eyes vainly sought help from the other Germans, who stood watching with leering grins on their faces.

She shook her head, trying to escape his rough skin. Suddenly, her eyes fell on his ear. It was big, fleshy. Her teeth seized upon it, biting,

biting hard. The German screamed and began to lash blindly at her head, but she hung on, like a dog with a bone, until she could taste the blood that ran out of her lips and dribbled down over the bodice of her dress.

"*Mein Gott*, Jurgen - get her off me!" He struggled to his feet, lifting her with him. In panic, he lashed at her head, again and again, but still she would not let go, her jaws clamped to his ear. Before the others reached him, he was free of her. She fell at his feet, her chest heaving, her face and dress awash with his blood. She looked up at him with the look of a wounded tiger at bay; she spat out the mangled piece of his ear at his feet.

"You fucking bitch, you Italian whore, I'll show you!" He reached to his waist, undid the holster and pulled out his gun.

Rosanna knew she was going to die. She covered her eyes with her hands. The pistol shot startled the birds, sending them up from the field.

osanna fell forward, but she felt the road surface, and she could still hear the birds. Everything else was quiet as the echoes of the shot died away. She was still alive. Diana had saved her. She opened her eyes. The front wheel of her bicycle was gently spinning where it had fallen. The three Germans were looking back away from her along the road, her attacker holding his hand to the bloody remains of his ear.

Rosanna lifted her head, wiping the blood from her mouth with the back of her hand. There was another German, but he was different, wearing a peaked cap. The reflection of the late afternoon sun bounced off the visor, making Rosanna believe he was an angel sent by Diana. The pistol in his right hand was pointing to the sky. She did not understand what he said, but the other Germans looked stunned and frightened.

"You are lucky I did not shoot you." He strode slowly and deliberately towards the men, leveling his gun at the one clutching his ear.

"In fact, I might just do that." The would-be rapist cowered and began to whimper as the officer stood in front of him, towering over him.

"It was only a bit of fun…"

"Only a bit of fun? Only a bit of fun? And so is this only a bit of fun, you worthless scum!" The officer smashed the barrel of his pistol hard against the man's left cheek, drawing blood.

The man reeled back.

"Attention! Come to attention! All three of you!" He kicked at the one kneeling over a pool of his own vomit. "You, too, you miserable wretch!"

Rosanna got slowly to her feet, her hand held to the bruise on her cheek. She forced herself to look as the three soldiers staggered into a line. The tall officer continued to shout at them. Although she didn't understand his words, the look of fear on their faces caused her to hope that she was safe.

"So, this is the great German army." He placed the barrel of his pistol beneath a downcast chin and motioned it upwards. "Look at me when I am talking to you, *schweinhund!*"

"Never having fired a shot in battle, but good at getting drunk and raping young girls. To what unit do you belong?"

After a few moments without an answer, he brought the butt of his pistol down on the face of the soldier whose ear Rosanna had bitten off.

"I said 'What unit?'"

"774 *Infanterie*."

"Give me your pass books." They all dug into their breast pockets. He took the books and opened the one of the assailant.

"So, Corporal Fritz Scheer, it's a bit of fun to go around raping innocent young women?"

There was no answer.

"You disgust me, Scheer, you and these...." He spat out the word "...creatures. You are a disgrace to your uniform and a disgrace to your country."

He put the passbooks into his pocket.

"I shall speak to the Divisional Adjutant tonight, and you miserable scum will report to him tomorrow. We may be able to find somewhere for you to find out what war is like – maybe a transfer to the front in Sicily!"

The men blanched, and the youngest one began to vomit again.

"Now, get out of my sight. Report yourselves as under arrest."

They began to shuffle away.

"You, Scheer, you have forgotten something."

The soldier turned, bewildered.

The officer pointed his pistol to the ground.

"Take this with you. German soldiers do not leave refuse in the streets."

Scheer bent down, picked up his mangled severed ear and slouched away.

Rosanna saw all this, yet, in a sense, she did not see it, her mind trying to block out the horror of the trauma. She began shaking, the shock of her ordeal trying to free itself from her body. She spat, and spat again, trying to remove the foul taste of blood from her mouth. Above all, she felt an overwhelming need to bathe, to scourge her body, to wash the filth and smell of her attacker from her flesh.

She cowered as the officer began to walk towards her, looking fearfully at the pistol still in his hand. A look of comprehension came to his face.

"*Mi dispiace*." He replaced the weapon in its holster.

He came nearer, removing his peaked cap and tucking it under his arm. Rosanna stepped back, fear still controlling her reactions. He looked down at the roadway, as if he felt implicated in the attack.

"*Mi dispiace…*" He stumbled with his words. "*…È una cosa orribile, brutissima.*"

He was speaking Italian. Rosanna's senses were fighting to regain control. He raised his head to speak.

"Please forgive me. I do not wish to frighten you. Are you alright?"

She looked at him, just looked at him, her dazed stare answering his stupid question. He looked down, unable to meet her eyes.

"They will be punished, punished severely." He removed a hand-kerchief from his pocket and offered it to her with an unsure gesture.

Suddenly, she ran at him, screaming. "Damn you, damn you!" She leapt at him, and flailed his chest with her fists, before her hands came up and slapped his face.

"Damn you, damn all Germans, damn the war!" She shouted down into his chest.

She slapped him again, but he did not stir. He stood still, his hands at his side, not making any move to restrain her anger.

Suddenly she stopped. Her hands dropped to his shoulders, she fell against him, and her whole body shook with her sobs. She raised her head to look at him. His eyes were fixed on the hills, not looking at her. His face showed no emotion, but she saw tears in his eyes.

"I'm sorry." Her words came haltingly between her sobs. She felt his chest heave with a sigh. "Thank you for…."

He gently pulled her hands from his shoulders, stepped back and walked over to her fallen bicycle. He picked it up and wheeled it over to her.

"Here, you'll need this. Are you alright to ride it?"

She wiped her face on his handkerchief and nodded. He looked up at the sky.

"It's nearly sunset. You'd better go home quickly. Do you have far to go?"

She shook her head and mounted the bicycle.

"Try not to be out after dark. And take care."

She turned on the saddle of the bicycle and looked at him for several moments. "Thank you." Her voice was little more than a whisper. His arm came up to his cap as he saluted her in a formal way. She waved to him and began to cycle up the hill.

CHAPTER 7

The same day. Late evening.

"Ahi!"

Rosanna flinched as her mother dabbed at her face with a damp cloth. She drew her feet up under her onto the threadbare couch, hugging her knees as she tried to cope with the pain all over her body.

"There, there." Her mother simpered, dropping the cloth into an old enamel bowl, splashing its watery-red contents. She moved the small stool on which the oil lamp stood nearer to the couch to provide better light. Its flickering flame threw shadows of Rosanna's bruises across her face: a macabre dance of light, painting the wounded features of the young woman into a grotesque mask, as if the shadows were trying to cast the light of her youthful face into the darkness of age.

Rosanna did, indeed, feel older. Despite her escape, she felt abused, violated. She started to sob again, uncontrollably, until she was fighting for breath. Her mother's big arms came around her, like a hen's wings around its chick, trying to console her. She gently pulled Rosanna to her and cradled her head in her arms.

"*Bambina, bambina*, thank God you are safe."

The well-meaning words seemed futile, but Rosanna comforted herself in the warmth of her mother's bosom, her subconscious recapturing the age of innocence she had once spent there. Her mother held her, wishing that time could be unspun, before sighing with the acceptance of time's passing.

"You'll mend."

She stooped forward to kiss the tip of Rosanna's nose, her smile hiding her sad knowledge that there were things time did not heal.

"Maria, *mia cara*, perhaps a bowl of soup may offer Rosanna some comfort."

The voice came from behind a newspaper at the table, and suddenly the old woman was given a focus for her pent-up frustration, someone onto whom she could pass all her helplessness.

"A bowl of soup? Our daughter is attacked by..." Her eyes narrowed as she spat out her anger "...those animals, and all you can suggest is a bowl of soup! Why aren't you down at Velletri, lodging a complaint with the commanding officer?"

She had touched upon the raw nerve of his fear, of his lack of fiber, and he fell silent. Perhaps he should lodge a complaint, but what good would it do? There was every chance he'd get beaten up for his pains. He'd heard of others who had complained to the German army and…. The rationalization fell away; he did not complain because he was afraid.

His wife's fists pounded the table.

"No, you jellyfish, you won't complain. Your daughter is beaten black and blue, but you won't complain. But if anything ever happened to your precious ships, you'd be off to see Mussolini himself! Except he isn't around anymore."

Paolo said nothing, but he felt a great hurt. He put down his paper and looked across at Rosanna. The pain eased a little when she did not avert her eyes, but he did not detect any understanding in her look.

"These Germans are animals, bastards!" Maria's angry shout broke the uneasy silence. She looked across at her daughter.

"Did they…did they….?"

Her voice trailed away, her hands waving in the air to complete the question. Rosanna reached down and pulled out a bloodstained handkerchief. As she blew her nose to recover her composure, she realized it was the German's handkerchief, and she stuffed it back in the pocket of her dress.

"No, no, no! The goddess Diana saved me. Diana, she saved me!"

"Tsch!" Her mother's eyes rolled upwards in contempt. "You and your Diana!"

"It's true." Rosanna pouted. "Diana is the goddess of virgins - she protected me!"

"Where do you get all this nonsense? As if I didn't know." Her mother sighed, transferring her anger to the wet cloth in her hands, which she wrung until her knuckles whitened. She tipped the basin violently into the sink, the force of her anger causing the water to splash her apron.

"Why can't you be a good Catholic girl and go to mass like all the others?"

"And tell all my secrets to the meddlesome priest, like you and all those old biddies? At least my secrets are private between Diana and me."

Rosanna flounced off the couch, anxious to avoid another lecture from her mother. She turned as she reached the door to the stairs.

"I'm off to bed." Rosanna's voice was harsh, angry. "There is work to be done tomorrow. Someone has to bring some money into this house!"

She saw her father grimace. Cruelty had touched her that day and now she was passing it on. Her guilt drove her feet quickly up the stairs.

"It's all your fault." His wife turned onto him again. "You put all these silly ideas into her head – you've been giving her all those silly books on magic since she was a little child."

He decided against arguing that Frazer's classic on myth, *The Golden Bough,* and all the other books he had given their daughter were not silly; she would not understand. It would still be his fault. It was always his fault. The war, the privations, the whole wretched mess of existence were all his fault. If he had been a believer, he would have prayed for something to happen for which he could not be blamed.

"We should be thankful Rosanna is safe, whether it be by the blessing of Diana or of your Holy Virgin."

He picked up his pipe and sucked on it in vain. It was empty.

"You've always got an answer for everything."

She put two bowls of watery soup on the table. He could see from the tears welling in her eyes that the defense mechanism of her anger was beginning to fail her. He felt for her. He had loved her for almost thirty-five years. He had loved her as the young bride he had taken before the last war. He had loved her as she had waited so long to become a mother. And he loved her now, as a woman whom the world had aged prematurely.

"Oh, Paolo, Paolo, what has become of us?"

Her head dropped and he could see the graying hair of her bun beginning to shake with her sobs.

"The war, this damned war, it's destroying us all." Her words came slowly.

She looked up at him, her eyes reddened with fatigue and tears.

"Paolo, what happened to the good old days? What is to become of us?"

He reached out across the table and gently stroked the back of her hand. Everyone had good old days, he thought. Always a yesterday that intoxicated the mind like heady wine. Or a tomorrow, a tomorrow when the sun would shine and the war would be over. But the now, the here and now, the very present, was hell, caught between the pleasure of memory and the joy of promise. He continued to stroke her hand, wishing he could stroke away her anguish.

"Soon all will be well Maria." The false comfort came easily to his lips, but he sought some justification for hope.

"Think of it like the ships. Yes, think of it like the ships that cause you so much anger. They had their great days, days of majesty and wonderful splendor, their golden finery reflected in the lake, shining in the Mirror of Diana."

He rose and walked toward the fireplace, his eyes aglow with the images his mind conjured from two thousand years ago. Suddenly he turned and found himself back in the present: his wife's head was raised again, but she still shook with her sobbing.

"Then the ships fell into darkness, engulfed in the dark void of the lake, forgotten, abandoned."

He walked towards her. Her despairing look beseeched him, implored him to offer her hope. He picked up his chair, set it in front of her and sat down, his hands reaching out to grasp her upper arms. The helplessness in her eyes still reached for him; his heart ached with the pain of the unhappiness of the woman he loved.

"But now," his voice was soft, like the light from the lamp, "the ships live again. They have reached out across time, and are restored from the void. They live."

He ended on a triumphant note, but his inadequate explanation did not ease the ache in his heart. She threw herself into his arms and he felt the warm wetness of her tears on his cheek.

"It will be over soon, Paolo, won't it?"

The words were breathed into his ear, intermingled with the rhythm of her sobbing. He held her tightly, as if he could squeeze the fear and despair from her.

"*Sì*, Maria, *mia cara*, it will be over soon."

The untruth again came easily, but his smile hid his guilt.

"It will be over soon."

He repeated the lie, hoping the repetition would convince him as well. A year, five years, ten years, who knew when it would all end? She slowly loosened her embrace and looked up at him.

"And we can all get back to normal?" Her eyes begged him to say yes.

"*Sì*, Maria, we can all get back to normal."

He compounded the lie; he told her what she wanted to hear.

"Now, get up to bed." He gently patted her behind. "I've just got a few things to do and I'll join you."

He heard her footfall on the stairs and waited for the creak of their bed before he went to the table. His eyes looked at the papers before him, but the words were unseen, unread as his mind wandered. Back to normal, she had said. Things would never be normal again; the world they had shared was gone and would never come back. To think it would ever return was to chase a ghost, a specter.

From within him came a deep sigh, a sigh of a man unable to change the world in which he lived. He sought refuge from his anguish by rummaging in his desk for the last vestiges of his tobacco. He had intended to save it until after Sunday dinner, when Maria had promised them the last chicken, but he filled his pipe, tamped it down and applied a taper to the oil lamp. He sank into his favorite chair and wondered if his family, like the ships, would be given a second chance.

CHAPTER 8

The noise of the latch startled him and he turned to look over his shoulder. Rosanna was framed in the doorway; she had taken off her blood-spattered dress and stood there, fidgeting with her white shift, shuffling from one foot to the other. He waited for her to find the words she was seeking.

"Oh, *Papà, Papà!*" She rushed across the room and threw her arms around him with a ferocity that almost knocked him from his chair.

"I'm sorry, *Papà,* I'm so sorry."

She burst into tears and sobbed on his shoulder.

"There, there, *bambina mia.*"

He gently disentangled himself, motioning her to sit beside him.

"Sorry about what?"

"About talking about money coming into the house." Her words came in a torrent. "I know it's not your fault that you do not receive your salary. It was very cruel of me to talk about it. I know you've done everything for Mamma and me, and it was so unkind of me to suggest…oh, *Papà,* I love you so."

She broke down once more, throwing herself at him with a desperation born of her guilt, burying her face on his chest. He stroked her long black hair to calm her.

"You have no need for tears for that, *angioletto.* After what you went through today, it was understandable. Besides…."

He cupped her face in his hands and smiled.

"….as you love me, so I love you. And love means being able to put aside the faults of your loved ones. Of everyone you love."

He pointed to the ceiling and chuckled. Leaning forward, he kissed his daughter gently on her forehead, his eyes not betraying the anguish he felt at seeing her bruised face.

"And you must forgive me my faults, too, Rosanna."

He eased back into his chair as he drew deeply on the stem.

"*Papà,* you are so understanding. I am proud you are my father."

He stifled the swelling of his heart.

"But, Rosanna, how can you be proud of a coward? Your mother says I should report the attack on you to the German Commandant, but…" He shrugged his shoulders. "…what good would it do?"

"There is no need for you to make a complaint, *Papà*. The…" She checked herself; she would not swear. "…beasts have already been reported."

Satisfied vengeance flashed in her eyes.

"Do you mean to say that Diana has typed her complaint in triplicate and filed it with the commandant?"

He realized the foolishness of the joke as his daughter bridled.

"Do not make fun of Diana – she has been my savior!"

"Then in what form did Diana appear as your savior?"

The continuing irony in his voice did not goad her further. Instead, she looked sheepishly at her feet, as if frightened to reveal the source of her deliverance.

"It was another German soldier."

The answer was whispered, like a child confessing a sin.

"A German soldier?" His eyebrows lifted. "A German soldier saved you?"

"Yes, it was a German soldier." The pace of her voice increased. "He wore a big hat and had a gun and he beat the swine that attacked me and he gave me his handkerchief and he spoke Italian...and he was good."

His lips pursed as he tried to digest the disjointed explanation.

"An officer." The pipe waved in his hand. "And a good German. A *good* German?"

The continuing doubt lingered in his voice.

"Yes, he was good – and kind. After he had saved me, he looked at me…" Her eyes flickered as she sought the word. "…*con compassione, con pietà. E dolore.*"

He stood up and sucked on his pipe, searching for the right words to say.

"Not all Germans are bad, *bambina*, despite what your mother and old fool of a father might think. Not all people are bad – although in these days, you might have doubts. But in war, goodness and kindness are as rare as strawberries in the winter. Men are trained to kill, to be brutes to their fellow men, to be hell-bent on destruction. Today, you met an exception – a big exception to the rule. Your German officer could have just turned his back and walked away. Instead, he helped you."

He looked down and smiled at her.

"Without doubt, your Diana did indeed protect you today."

She smiled, pleased at his acceptance of her beliefs. He chucked her under her chin.

"Good – it's good to see you smile. There have been too many tears today."

He looked up at the clock.

"And now we must get off to bed. Tomorrow, you have work to do and I must go to check over the ships."

She knew his checking over the ships was little more than a daily ritual, but she kissed his cheek and hugged him.

"Goodnight, *Papà*." She turned in the doorway as she left. "And thank you."

He sucked on his pipe and was frustrated to find it had gone out. He touched the taper to the lamp once more and drew deeply. The smoke drifted through the air, wending its way to the ceiling in formless, meaningless patterns. The German who had saved Rosanna could find his goodness rewarded with death's bullet within a week.

His thoughts wandered on. It wasn't just the soldiers who slaughtered each other in their thousands every day – perhaps they were the lucky ones. The unlucky ones were those who were left, who had to try to heal the wounds, to try to recover a world which would never be again.

The smoke billowed around the pictures of the ships that stood above the hearth, and he realized why his life was so bound up with them. He needed them, these survivors of the millennia, just as his wife needed her Blessed Virgin, just as Rosanna needed her Diana. It was a grasping for something permanent, unchanging, that transcended time and the fragile, momentary impermanence of life.

He tapped out his pipe and snuffed the lamp. He would go down to the ships tomorrow. There was something he had to do.

CHAPTER 9

August 19ᵗʰ 1943. Early morning.

The heels of Klaus's boots clipped against the pavement as he crossed Piazza Garibaldi and headed for Colonel Guttman's headquarters, temporarily housed in a tent behind Velletri's Town Hall. The clip of his heels had always reassured him, but it was now an echo of his unease. He should not have reported the men, despite their despicable brutality. Headquarters took a dim view of such reports: there was a war to be fought, and there was no time for the niceties of protecting civilians. Besides, with the removal of Mussolini, most of the General Staff began to treat the Italians as enemies. But he was satisfied his actions had been correct; he would not have done otherwise. The memory of the young woman's face convinced him that he could have acted in no other way.

He looked at his watch and hoped the Colonel's early morning briefing would not take long. All his work was done, the supplies for his artillery unit had been cleared, and Gunther had promised to meet him at noon with some form of transport to get them to Nemi.

He strode across the piazza, seeking to avoid the few market stalls that appeared on some mornings, although there was little or nothing to sell. He tried to ignore the half-dozen or so old peasants who drifted around the stalls, but he was aware of their sullen looks. The clipping of his heels was an affront to them, an intrusion to the badinage of their market. Their voices became silent, and he felt that every Italian was looking at him as if he, personally, were responsible for the usurpation of their lives.

War is always personal, he thought. The hatred, the loathing, the fear demanded some living form on which it can focus, upon which it can wreak vengeance and exact retribution. He wanted to shout at their resentful faces that he didn't want to be there; that he wanted to be back in Berlin University teaching classics; that he wanted to leave them to their strawberries, their vegetables, and the slow, unhurried beat of their peasant lives. But he did not speak; neither did he look at them. In war, you did not speak what you thought; you did what you were told. It was easier that way.

He skirted the market, passing the Italian War Memorial at the back of the square. Its marble façade was faded with the grime of many years; through cracks in the slabs, grass and weeds thrust up in a sad bouquet of neglect. Klaus looked up at the names, etched forever in stone, but already forgotten and neglected by their compatriots. Less than thirty years on, and gone from memory. But wasn't that likely to be his fate, too? He shuddered, as if Time had run an icy finger down his spine.

His pace quickened as he tried to push the thoughts from his mind. He intended to survive the war; he had so much to do.

The guards on the gate at the back of the Town Hall looked at his pass and nodded him through. He pushed at the flap of the tent and walked in.

His fellow officers stood around in small groups, all involved in earnest discussion while they awaited the arrival of the colonel. The talk was of the war, and of nothing else. What had happened in Sicily? What had happened to Mussolini after his arrest? Would the Allies make a landing on the Italian mainland? All part of the mad mayhem of the war. Answers to the questions had already been decided in Berlin, London and Washington. The answers would be fed into the war machine that would impersonally decide his fate, and the fate of the others in the room. His mind shut out the words that cut through the pall of smoke rising from the animated groups; Klaus knew he should be interested, and it worried him that he was beginning to become detached, to think of things other than the war. A glance at his watch told him that Gunther would soon be arriving with the transport to Nemi, and he silently cursed the colonel for the delay.

At the cry of '*Achtung!*' the whole assembly snapped to attention, heels clicking in unison, as the colonel strode into the tent.

The commanding officer was unimpressive in appearance: short and stocky, he seemed to roll rather than march towards the small wooden platform erected at the front of the tent. Every time Klaus saw him, he felt he was more akin to an innkeeper than a professional soldier. His gruff, avuncular manner endeared him to his staff, but they were also aware that 'Uncle Hans' had an incisive military mind that did not suffer fools gladly.

"At ease, at ease, gentlemen, this is not the parade ground."

His hand waved to dismiss the formality and they all sat down.

"Well, I hope you are all enjoying Italy, because you're going to be here for some time!"

The officers laughed nervously. Klaus looked down at his cap.

"But I'm afraid that it isn't going to be like your vacation last year in France, telling the peasants not to be naughty boys in between your trips to the fleshpots of Aix-en-Provence. This time there's real work to do!" He picked up his pointer and walked towards the map that had been set up on the platform.

"Sicily…" The pointer slapped against the island "…was finally evacuated yesterday, our holding operation complete. We never meant it to be anything other than a sideshow."

The assembly remained quiet, attentive, but Klaus knew they had all heard of the casualties in Sicily. If that were a sideshow….

"When the Allies choose to enter the mainland…" He looked up as someone gave a soft, surprised whistle. "…and they will, gentlemen, they will..." He turned back to the map. "…our major defenses will be here…and here."

The assembly leaned forward to see him scratch a line across Italy south of Naples.

"Here, we shall build a defensive position across Italy, and ten kilometers behind that wall a stronger position, and behind that again a virtually impenetrable line. The Allies are going to get a bloody nose! And, with a little luck, we shall push them back into the sea."

The colonel turned, his grin full of confidence.

"Questions?"

"Shall we see action soon, sir?"

A young subaltern boldly leapt to his feet. Klaus looked across at the fresh face; it was always the young ones, the ones who had not seen a bullet fired in anger, who were keen to die. The colonel looked at the questioner dispassionately.

"As soon as you like, young man." An ironic smile broke on the colonel's face as he saw the questioner's face pale.

"Your request for a transfer to Russia will be treated favorably just as soon as it reaches my desk."

He guffawed, and the subaltern, chastened, sat down.

"Sir, what if the Allies break the line, or turn it with an amphibious landing?"

Klaus saw that some of the officers shuffled on their chairs, muttering to each other behind their hands as the question was asked.

"I see we have a tactical mastermind here today!"

The colonel smiled and continued confidently.

"For that unlikely event, a tactical reserve will be kept here, just south of Rome. In fact, we, the 715th, are to be part of that tactical reserve."

Klaus was sure he heard a collective sigh of relief; they were not going into the front line yet. Most of the officers had spent the last year on occupation duty in France and had become accustomed to its leisurely pace. All of them were prepared to do their duty, but no one was in a rush to see the sharp end of war.

"And if the Allies do penetrate, we can build other defensive lines, here, here – and here."

The colonel's pointer smacked against the map, south of Rome, then across the country at Florence, finally in the north at the valley of the River Po.

"Gentlemen, the terrain is ideally suited for defensive warfare. The enemy's bombers and *Jabos* will not be of much help to him. It could take years for the enemy to push us from Italy. In the meantime, hopefully Berlin will come up with some way to turn the tide in Russia. Every day we remain in Italy will suck in more and more of the Allies' resources. We shall defend Germany to the last hectare of Italian soil!"

The colonel's laughter was echoed by the assembly, but mainly out of relief that the war would, for the moment, remain distant, Klaus thought. The colonel held up his hand for silence.

"As no one has asked about Mussolini, you should know that he has been rescued from his Italian captors by our special parachutists and flown to the Wolf's Lair to see the *Fuehrer*!"

He continued through the low whistles of disbelief.

"What happens to Mussolini is, quite frankly, none of our concern. What does matter is which way the Italian government - and army - will jump. There's every indication that they have lost their stomach for war. It wouldn't surprise me if they threw in their lot with the Allies – and quite soon. In my opinion, I'd rather trust a pimp in the *Wilhelmstrasse*!"

Again, his raised hand stifled the laughter.

"It is also my opinion that, if their government has the effrontery to declare an armistice, the Italian army will disappear like ice cream on a summer's day. But we must be on our guard."

He emphasized his last words by punching his palm with his fist.

"From now on, you are to treat all Italians as potential enemies. You will continue to carry side arms at all times. There is to be no fraternization. That is all, gentlemen. Orders for next week's exercises will be issued later today."

The assembly snapped to attention as the colonel saluted and stepped down from the platform. Klaus looked anxiously at his watch. Gunther was not the most patient of men, and it was certain that his acquisition of transport was illicit and short-term. He shuffled quickly towards the aisle, only to find the colonel waiting for him.

"Ah, Schmidt!" The colonel's leathered face looked up at Klaus, smiling. The voice was lowered, but insistent.

"We need to talk, Schmidt. In my office. Now!"

The last word carried a menacing emphasis, and Klaus felt his heart sink.

CHAPTER 10

The same day. Early morning.

Paolo had never needed an alarm clock. Ever since he was a child, the pale fingers of dawn clawing at the night sky had always awakened him. He rubbed his eyes as the first light probed its insistent way through the shutters; he threw back the blanket and sent his feet fumbling for his slippers.

It had been so different then, he thought. Each day had brought new delights, even joy in mundane things. Getting the old horse from the stables, smelling the hay, the leather, the sweat as he slipped on her harness ready for the day's work.

He pinched between his eyes. He was getting old. Too many yesterdays were creeping into his mind lately. The shutter reluctantly rattled back with his push, letting in the growing light of the new day; he heard his wife stir from the bed. Maria had never been one for lingering between the sheets; often, she rose before him. There was always something for her to do and, if there wasn't, she soon found something. He stretched, turned to her and smiled.

"*Ti amo, tesoro mio.*"

His voice was low and sweet, but the words were earnestly said.

"You're a silly old fool."

She shook her head, but her dismissive voice was betrayed as she returned his smile, sharing again the emotions of the previous evening. His hug was accepted, but she put her fingers to her lips.

"It is better that Rosanna sleep." Her voice was a whisper.

He nodded. They pulled on their clothes and went downstairs, the creak of the old boards defying all their attempts to be silent. He raked the fire, found an ember, and threw on some dry twigs to rekindle it. The flames drew up and soon the old black kettle started to hum.

"Oh, if only we had some real coffee!"

Maria sniffed the air, as if she could conjure the smell of beans in her nostrils.

"Instead of this muck."

The spoons of chicory were dumped in the pot and she grabbed the kettle.

"At least we have your wonderful bread!" Paolo broke a crust off his wife's home-made loaf.

"That's the end of it – the flour's run out, and we couldn't afford any more if it were half the price."

He could sense that her earlier affection was beginning to evaporate like the morning mists of the lake, and he did not linger long over his breakfast, such as it was.

His thoughts were elsewhere. After the letter from the Ministry, he knew that the fate of the ships was almost entirely in the hands of Fortune. There was little he could do but hope stray bombs did not fall on the museum, but he had to make sure the museum was secure, to make sure the ships were not threatened by vandals or thieves. Heaven knew there were plenty about recently: chickens, ducks, even fields of strawberries disappeared into the night. He had thought of moving his bed into the museum, but the mere thought of broaching the subject with Maria had been enough to make him drop the idea.

These thoughts preoccupied him as he rummaged in the table drawer for his bicycle clips.

"I suppose you're off to those damned ships again, leaving me to try to conjure up something for supper tonight. There's only so much that can be done with cabbage, you know."

Paolo allowed himself an ironic smile. She was back to normal, he thought, her recent affection thrust aside by the demands of their meager daily life. He blew her a kiss, closed the door behind him and dropped the latch. The old bicycle came reluctantly from the tangle of rubbish in the shed. It was like him - old, rusty and creaking when in motion.

So we've both seen better days, he thought as he pulled down his cap and began to walk the machine down the steep path leading to the church. The sun was beginning to show above the hills behind him, trying to get a response from the walls of the church steeple, but the paint had long since flaked away, and the dull stone refused to join the sun in his morning's play. Paolo made a mental note to talk to the priest; somewhere in Nemi there had to be enough paint to make the steeple stop seeming as if it were cowering from the sun each morning.

"'*Giorno, Signor Giraldi!*"

His thoughts of church restoration were sent packing by the shrill voice that came from the church steps. He turned to see a dirty face beneath a mop of black hair that hadn't seen a pair of scissors in months.

"*Buon giorno, Gianni* – isn't it a little early for mischief?"

The small boy leapt up. Paolo could not fail to notice his spindly legs and long, skeletal arms as the lad bounced towards him like a living scarecrow. Barely ten, and already ravaged by the war. Signora Rossi was having difficulty in feeding her tribe of six on wartime rations.

"What d'ya mean, mischief?" Gianni's face looked up at him, his big eyes almost dwarfing the lantern of his face. "Besides, it was my brother."

"Mischief like shooting a slingshot at Signora Giraldi. Your brother is a good shot."

"He's nowhere near as good as me – he'd need a much bigger target than Signora Giraldi's backside…."

Gianni stopped and looked down at the oversize cap that he wrung in his hands as he realized how stupid he'd been.

"Maybe he got lucky, for once!"

Paolo smiled. He should have picked the rascal up by the ears and marched him home to his mother, but he admired the lad's resilience. As the curator of the museum, he should show such resilience by going to see the damn bureaucrats in Rome; as a father…he dismissed the troubling thoughts and mounted his bicycle.

"Your brother will be in serious trouble one day." His words were heavy with sarcasm to ensure the little reprobate got the message.

"Can I come with you to the ships today?" Gianni had clearly shrugged the message aside.

"Why do you want to come to see the ships?"

Paolo teased the boy. He knew that Signora Perona, who lived on the lakeside near the museum, had a soft spot for the little ruffian, and always gave him a piece of fish or anything else she could spare. His mother would beat him black and blue if she knew he had gone to the lakeside alone, so a visit to the ships with Signor Giraldi provided the perfect excuse. The prospect of a free tidbit was the only reason Gianni wanted to see the ships.

"I want to see the ships…because, well, because…" Paolo could almost see the lad's brain rattling for a reason. "Because they're big!'

The answer was shouted, in the child's simple belief that the volume would convince anyone that he spoke the truth.

"That's a good reason." Paolo humored the boy. "But you'll have to keep up with me."

He started the bicycle on a slow descent toward the *Corso Vittorio Emanuele.*

"That's easy!" Gianni jogged easily alongside the bicycle. "Besides, I'll run down the old path on the hill – I'll be there before you and your old bike get half-way!"

Paolo cursed inwardly. It was not only the bike that was old; his arms were old, his legs were old – to him, every part of his body seemed to creak and groan. Only ten years ago, he would have scorned the bicycle and chosen the path. It was not an easy route. The path dropped swiftly down the hill as it wove its tortuous way among the old oaks, its hidden stones waiting to trip the unwary. But he had always delighted in hearing the birds shrill at his approach, in seeing the summer sun force its way through the leaves to present a dancing mosaic at his feet. Now his body denied him such pleasures; every day, he needed all his strength to propel his bicycle along the upper path before turning down the gentle slope that passed by the side of the ruins of the temple of Diana.

Strange how the body betrays you as you get old, he thought, puffing at his exertions as he went through the arch and turned toward the old gate. He looked down at Gianni, trotting alongside him as if out for a stroll. He was like that once, bouncing along as if the world were a balloon. For some reason, he thought of a sculpture in the Capitoline Museum, a statue of a small boy putting on a mask of an old man. Gianni would pull on the mask one day. Paolo sighed, as if the weight of time were forcing the breath from his body.

"See you down at the museum, Signor Giraldi."

Gianni waved at him as they passed under the old gate. The young lad turned to begin the steep drop to the lakeside.

"Bet you a lira I'm there before you."

"Be off with you!"

Paolo began to push at the pedals. A museum curator should not bet, he thought. Particularly when he was bound to lose.

CHAPTER 11

The same day. 9a.m.

"There's no need for that, Klaus."

The colonel waved away the formal salute, his hand requesting Klaus to sit. As he did, Klaus looked across the folding field desk on which stood a family photograph; he thought of his own family and the legions of families that peered out from such pictures to German soldiers all over Europe. For how long would they have to trace their fingers over the cold images instead of embracing the living warmth?

"Klaus, why did you file the report?"

The colonel cut across his thoughts. Klaus looked up at the unsmiling face.

"Report?"

"*Verdamt*, Klaus, this report - the report about the attempted rape!"

Klaus stiffened at the sharpness in the colonel's voice as he tossed the file across the desk.

"Well, sir, I saw a soldier molesting a girl. He was threatening her with a gun and I intervened to stop him."

"Intervened?" The colonel rose quickly from his chair. "Intervened? You threatened to shoot the man, pistol-whipped him and kicked another *gefreiter*. Is that what you call 'intervention'?"

Klaus sat mutely through the angry explosion. His fears about submitting the report were being justified, but an inner voice insisted he had acted correctly.

"I thought it was my duty, my responsibility...."

The colonel held his palm up to stop his words.

"Do you know the impact of this report at Corps Headquarters?"

His finger tapped angrily on the offending file.

"Do you know what Colonel Schumann of the 774th said to me?"

Klaus tried to hide his feelings, keeping his face impassive as the commanding officer answered his own question.

"He asked how we were supposed to win the war if every German soldier who fooled around with an Italian tart was put on report. He asked if..." he looked pointedly at Klaus "...my artillery officer wouldn't be better employed with his gun battery instead of acting as an angel of mercy for Italian trollops!"

"But the young girl was about to be raped, sir. Should I have done nothing?"

The words came to his lips unbidden. Klaus knew he should keep his head down, stay quiet and let the whole affair blow over, yet he spoke despite himself.

The colonel sighed deeply and sat down, shaking his head.

"Klaus, modern warfare is not about shining knights rescuing damsels; as well you know, it is about killing and slaughter. Twenty thousand Germans are dying every month on the Russian front. As we speak, Rome is being plundered and sacked by our men, with the high command turning a blind eye. It is not pleasant, but that is war! I should have thought you would have known by now that the high-minded ideals that flourished in your university have no place here."

He smiled to break the tension, moving around the table to put his hand on Klaus's shoulder.

"Klaus, in war, men become animals. The veneer of civilization that usually masks our animal natures is shown to be paper-thin."

He returned to his chair, looking at Klaus in an attempt to judge his response.

"Klaus, you are the best artillery officer I have known. You must not be caught up in this sort of thing. Besides," his voice and face assumed an air of menace, "there are certain people who might view this report as..." Klaus saw him search deliberately for the right word, "...*ideologically* unsound."

He nodded to ensure Klaus grasped the meaning of the hidden threat.

After a few moments, the colonel picked up the file, weighing it.

"There are hundreds of such cases every day, and nobody gives a damn; thousands die every day, and nobody gives a damn. Why should you care, Klaus? Why not forget it? Just drop it."

The snap of Klaus's heels as he sprang to attention startled Klaus as much as it did the colonel.

"Sir, I insist the charge be placed on record. I intend to give evidence at the court martial."

Klaus regretted the words as soon as they had left his lips. Some hidden inner force seemed to drive him against his better judgment. Yet he knew the principle was right.

The colonel shook his head again, allowing his chin to drop to his chest.

"Very well, Klaus. I have done my best to protect your interests, and I promise you I shall continue to do so. But you must surely know that corps headquarters will put the file in some pigeon hole and forget it for as long as possible."

The colonel stood, replaced his cap and formally saluted.

"And I must tell you, Schmidt, that you are a *dumpkopf*. Get out!"

Klaus left the building in a daze, trying to come to terms with his emotions. His mother had always told him to keep out of trouble, and here he was walking into it. The colonel's question was burning into his mind. Why should he care? Why should he care? He found himself unable to answer the question. But he kept seeing the girl's face, and he knew that he did care, even if he did not know why.

"So there you are at last – I thought you had been summoned to Berlin and promoted to General!"

Gunther's mocking laugh halted his train of thought.

"Far from it, Gunther, far from it."

Gunther interpreted the subsequent silence as his friend's reluctance to explain further.

"Never mind, never mind – behold the transport I have obtained. It is, at least, fit for a General!"

The sergeant turned, theatrically, his arm outstretched like a master of ceremonies introducing a cabaret act. Klaus whistled as his eyes fell upon a DKW 350 motorbike complete with sidecar.

"How on earth did you get that? Did you steal it, Gunther?"

Gunther laughed at Klaus's reproachful look.

"Let's just say the sergeant at the supply depot is not a good card player!"

Gunther leapt astride the saddle, kick-started the engine into life and shouted to Klaus.

"Quickly, *Hauptman* - this lot has got to be back in the depot by to-night, and we've wasted enough time already. You may need these."

He tossed Klaus a pair of goggles. Klaus put them on, squeezed into the sidecar and pulled his cap down low. Gunther opened the throttle and the bike roared across the piazza toward the hill road to Nemi. As the wind plucked at his cheeks, Klaus pushed the memory of his meeting with the colonel to a harmless recess of his mind. He was going to see the ships of Caligula and the temple of Diana.

The same day. 10.30 a.m.

As Paolo expected, Gianni was waiting for him as he pedaled through the museum gates, a wide grin on his face and his hand outstretched for his prize. Paolo tossed him a coin and the young lad ran off towards Signora Perona's cottage by the lakeside to see what other prizes he could wheedle.

Paolo leaned his bicycle against the fence, looked up at the sun bouncing off the huge façade of the museum, and felt a surge of excitement as he pulled the keys from his pocket. He had always experienced the thrill, ever since he had been appointed curator. Probably even before, he thought - when he had been involved in the project to raise the ships from their centuries-old muddy tombs in the lake. He remembered how he had stood awestruck as first one, and then the other of the ships had emerged from the lake-bed after years of effort. He was little better than Gianni, he chuckled: like a little boy clinging to an old favored toy.

Paolo unlocked the door and walked through the vestibule to the grand hall. In the two cavernous wings, sitting on their trestles, were his 'babies' - the pride of Caligula's fleet. The smell of old wood excited him as he walked the 210 foot length of the first boat, gazing up at the deck level way above his head. The size had always overpowered him. It had taken seventeen hundred years before a bigger seafaring ship had been built; even Columbus's Santa Maria was only 120 feet long.

His mind pictured Caligula standing on the deck, attended by his court as the ship glided across Lake Nemi towards the Temple of Diana. As he circled the ship, moving alongside the port beam, Paolo wondered what tales the 2000-year-old timbers could tell if they could talk. That was the mystique, the magic of the ships. No one would ever be able to know the true purpose of the vessels. Paolo had always cursed the primitive attempts at salvage made in the previous century, which had served only to destroy the superstructures, rendering them into countless pieces of wood that ended up in local fireplaces.

But Paolo knew; history reached out across the centuries to fire his imagination. As he looked up at the magnificent prow towering above him, his imagination rebuilt the ship. Caligula stood at the rails on the bow, looking out over the night-stilled waters of the lake, shimmering with the lights of the ship's lanterns as they parted to allow the ship's passage to the Temple of Diana on the northern shore; the Emperor looked astern, beyond the walls of the ship's temple, to see the moon outshining the lanterns, its reflection bouncing off the mirror of the lake to bathe the hills with a ghostly hue. Paolo pushed his cheek against the wood, feeling the kiss of history on his face.

Suddenly, he moved back, looking around him to ensure that no one was watching him. If Gianni had seen him, there would be no end to the gossip in the village about how he had embraced the ship. He was becoming old and sentimental, he thought. Caligula probably did nothing more than come down to his ships on the weekend to escape the heat and stench of Rome, as a lot of latter-day Romans used to do before the war.

The war. The present tore his fingers from the chalice of the past. Damn the war. The war was ruining everything. The bureaucrats in Rome were too busy saving themselves to give a thought to saving the ships. The ships had been useful to them, and to Mussolini, as a tool to bolster their foolish dreams of building another empire. Paolo groaned, more in self-disgust than in his hatred of the politicians.

He had supported Mussolini in the early days, back when it looked as if he was restoring some pride to Italy. He looked across at the doors of the museum and remembered how he had seen Il Duce perform the opening ceremony, drums beating and flags waving. It had been so good, then, before the war. Now the war engulfed everything, Mussolini was gone, and those bastards on the *Quirinale* sat on their backsides and did nothing.

Paolo was angry and frustrated. He patted his pockets and became angrier as he realized he had no tobacco to console him. The bureaucrats had been quick to move the artifacts from the boats at the start of the war. The beautiful bronze head of Medusa, the beam end covers of wolves and lions, the sculpted marble capitals, the mosaic floor panels that had felt the tread of an emperor, all the things that had given life to the ships' timbers were now lying in the dusty storerooms of the *Museo Nazionale Romano*. Heaven only knew when they would see the light of day again, Paolo thought; for all the good the priceless relics did lying hidden in the dark cellars of the museum, they might as well have remained at the bottom of the lake.

His instinctive search for tobacco caused him to search his pockets again, only to produce the letter from the Ministry. He read it again, and crumpled the paper in his hand. They were too busy saving their necks to do anything to protect the ships, content that they had all the treasures under lock and key. So they thought. A wry grin came to his lips. So they thought.

He walked back to the museum door, turned the key to secure it, and peered through the window. It was unlikely that anyone was about, but he didn't want any surprises. Satisfied, he turned and walked between the ships towards the storeroom at the rear of the museum. The hulks of the great ships looked down on him like giant sentinels, as if they were guarding his secret. The door opened at his push, revealing a small room littered with the odds-and-ends of the museum. Brooms and buckets stood idly in a corner, unused since the museum was officially closed; cardboard boxes, full of old newspaper cuttings of the heydays, were stacked against the far wall; and a makeshift bookcase held books unread for years. Paolo ignored the damp, moldy odor of decay and neglect, his eyes fixing on the old piece of canvas lying in a corner under the workbench.

He looked out again into the museum hall; he knew no one was there, but caution forced him to check. Returning to the corner of the room, he reached under the workbench, his hands tugging at the canvas. The cloth fell to the floor, revealing an old seaman's chest. Paolo's breathing quickened as he dragged the chest out into the middle of the storeroom floor. He paused, looking down at the chest, its dull wood bruised with time. It was his secret.

Somehow it had missed the audit done by the officials of the *Museo Nazionale* when they had moved the artifacts; he had discovered it himself but six months ago when he had decided to clear out an old outhouse.

The original lock had been broken, the wood splintered around the flange, but Paolo had replaced it with a stout padlock. He stooped down, inserted the key and eased the lid open. At the top of the chest, immediately below the lid, was a three-inch deep tray; in each of the compartments of the tray were ornaments – rings, brooches, chains and pins. Paolo had not needed to consult any textbooks to know their origin: Roman, and from the ships.

Paolo had quickly realized that he had found plunder, treasures that had been stolen from the ships. Plunder had been almost a way of life for the previous expeditions that had scoured the ships' wrecks at the bottom of the lake. Men more interested in profit than history, like Borghi, who had salted away as many relics as he had sold to the government fifty years ago. Paolo winced as he thought of the figurehead of the sun god, Helios, which had decorated the prow of the first ship and which had disappeared without trace to swell some private collection, along with so many other treasures.

That the contents of the chest were part of such plunder, Paolo knew without doubt. Perhaps the chest had been hidden away for later collection, then moved by a later expedition, thus confounding the thief; perhaps death had claimed the scoundrel, leaving the treasure to the winds of chance that had blown it into Paolo's path.

Although the small array of treasure on the tray was an archeologist's dream, Paolo knew he had found something else that by far surpassed it. He lifted the tray from the chest and delved into the inner compartment. There was a slight tremor in his hands as he lifted a small metal case from the chest and laid it on the workbench. He opened the case and lifted the felt sack within. With great care, he unfolded the cloth until the light glinted off the treasure within. It was a mirror, a lady's hand mirror of pure silver. Flawless and unmarked, it looked as if it had been made yesterday instead of twenty centuries before. It was The Mirror of Diana.

Paolo scarcely dared to breathe as he freed the mirror from the cloth. The handle, some six inches long, was fluted in perfect symmetry, as was the supporting arc above it. He gripped it gently, wondering what imperial Roman hand had held it before. Whose face had beheld its reflection in its flat, polished surface? Maybe Drusilla, Caligula's sister, had preened herself, her face smiling within the confines of the mirror. Perhaps the face of the emperor's wife, Caesonia, had looked out from the surface.

No matter whose visage, it had been better-looking than the leathery, lined face that grimaced back at him now.

He gently turned the mirror over. The rim was about nine inches across, and the precious metal had been exquisitely sculpted. A master's hand had crafted the scene from the myth of Diana and Acteon. Paolo knew the story well. Acteon, out hunting, had had the misfortune to come across Diana in her bath. Diana adored Acteon, but knew that for a mortal to see a goddess unclothed bore the punishment of death. Thus was Diana obliged to turn her beloved Acteon into a stag, to be savaged and killed by his own hounds.

The scene on the mirror portrayed the precise moment of the transformation. Acteon, while still in human form, had the vaguest image of a stag appearing behind his head; his dogs, not recognizing their master, were beginning to attack him. Diana, eyes cast down, stood in anguished remorse, sorely regretting her choice of duty over love.

Paolo marveled at the masterpiece. He let his fingers lightly trace the outlines of the relief, then hastily withdrew them, as if their touch was an act of sacrilege. The mirror, to him, was a sacred object fraught with significance. It not only embodied the myth of Diana, it embodied the eternal human conflict – of mind versus heart, of need versus want, of duty versus love. Since the birth of the gods it was ever thus. And how much more so now, at this time of war.

Enough of these daydreams, Paolo thought. A glance at his pocket watch endorsed his stomach's reminder that it was lunchtime. He carefully stowed the treasure back into the chest, which he eased into its hiding place under the canvas. He walked back between the ships, let himself out, and locked the museum behind him.

As he delved into the basket of his bicycle for his lunch, Paolo grappled with his feelings of guilt. Of course, he should have reported his find to the authorities in Rome. Keeping the mirror hidden made him no better than the thief who had first plundered it. He had, in fact, written a letter but, for some reason he could not fathom, the envelope still lay in his drawer.

He pulled open the cloth to reveal a meager lunch: a little bread, a morsel of cheese and two red apples shining from his wife's polishing. A further dig into the basket produced a bottle of wine, which he hoped would provide some comfort for the paucity of the meal. He walked towards the shore of the lake. The sun had climbed high in the sky, the mist was gone, and the birds bobbed like corks as a gentle breeze caressed the water. An old tree trunk provided a rest for his back as he sat down and began to devour the bread and cheese. The bureaucrats in Rome did not deserve to have the mirror, he thought. Besides, there was every chance it would never be seen again; stories of the Germans plundering great works of art were widespread. His rationalization was encouraged by the wine, its taste sharpened by the apples, yet bringing a mellow warmth to his stomach. He adjusted his cap to provide some shade from the noonday sun, and drew deeply on the bottle. He would return the treasure after the war; yes, when things were back to normal, he would take the mirror to Rome.

His head nodded, and his half-hooded eyes looked out across the lake towards Genzano, where the jetty for the ancient ships had been built. One ship was at its moorings, the golden pillars of its temple adding an extra luster to the sun. Coming towards him, its prow softly parting the waters, the second ship gleamed with the opulence of Rome. The bronze heads of the beasts dedicated to Diana stood out from the beam ends. The emperor stood, amidships, his hand resting on the bronze rail. Paolo tried to focus on the figure standing by the prow. Her white gown was teased by the breeze, and she was admiring her long black hair in a mirror. It was Diana's Mirror! She turned her face, and he saw that it was Rosanna!

"Signor Giraldi, Signor Giraldi!" The ships vanished as the voice of Gianni shattered his reverie.

"The Germans are coming! The Germans are coming!"

CHAPTER 13

The same day. 11.30 a.m. Nemi

Klaus eased himself out of the sidecar and rubbed his backside. "It's certainly an invigorating way to travel!" He pushed his goggles up onto the front of his cap as Gunther killed the motorcycle engine.

"I'm sorry, but Field Marshal Kettering's staff car wasn't available."

The sergeant's humor was lost on Klaus as he massaged the use back into his legs.

"Do you think the machine will be safe here, boss?"

Klaus followed Gunther's eyes as he looked up at the building behind him and read the Latin inscription above the portico.

"Gunther, it's a convent," he said, wearily, "full of nuns."

"But they're Italian nuns, aren't they? Besides, I knew a nun once who…"

"Enough!"

There was a sharpness in his voice that made Gunther fall silent as they walked to the wall on the west side of the convent. Beyond the wall was a belvedere that overlooked the convent garden and, beyond it, the lake. The silence persisted as they looked down the wooded escarpment falling sharply down to the water, where the late morning sun played amongst the gentle ripples. Both men remained quiet as their eyes feasted on the beautiful view.

"What's up?" Gunther broke the silence.

"What's up?"

"Well, boss, I know you can be a bit of a stuffed shirt at times, but today you've been very touchy."

"I'm sorry, Gunther, I should not take it out on you, but," Klaus turned and leaned back against the wall, "things have happened."

He told Gunther about the girl, his report and his meeting with the colonel. He spoke dispassionately, as if he were not talking about himself. He did not turn his eyes from the lake until he was finished. Gunther lit a cigarette and looked at him with mild astonishment.

"*Mein Gott!* Why on earth do you want to land yourself in a heap of shit like that?"

"You think I should not have done as I did, Gunther?"

"Yes. No. Oh, shit." Gunther struggled for his words. "Don't get me wrong. I don't have any truck with the rape thing - Gunther prefers to charm the panties off his women - but to make a *report*? Weren't you just happy enough to beat the bastards up?"

"So you agree with the colonel, then?"

"You bet your sweet ass I do! Do you know what could happen if some jumped-up Nazi got wind of it? Worse still, the Gestapo?"

The sergeant drew his finger across his throat before he spoke on.

"Klaus, the powers-that-be think that the dagoes are little better than animals. All the German army - myself included - thinks they're a bunch of cowardly shits. And you dare to file a report against the soldiers of the Third Reich," his voice became heavy with sarcasm, "against the master race in defense of *untermenschen*?" He smiled wryly at his own irony. "Can't you see that's how it will be interpreted?"

Klaus knew Gunther had a point: that was exactly how it would be interpreted.

"So you don't think I have a duty to press the case?"

"Duty? Duty?" Gunther's eyebrows lifted above his wide-open eyes. "My friend, you do not seem to know there's a war going on. You saved her from the so-called fate worse than death, didn't you? What more do you want? A medal?"

Although he did not reply, Klaus shook his head as his dilemma tormented him. He turned, glancing down at the oak-strewn slopes as they tumbled to the lake's edge far below, trying to find an answer. His friend's advice was sound. He would withdraw the report as soon as they returned. But he still felt uneasy; it was as if some force had possessed him and was driving him against his own interests. For some reason, the image of the young woman invaded his mind, her eyes fixing him with an entreating look.

Gunther flicked his cigarette end over the wall as they turned to cross the small piazza in front of the convent and made their way toward the town.

"What was she like?"

Gunther's question caught him unaware, as if the sergeant could read his mind. He feigned indifference.

"What was who like?"

"The woman, for God's sake, Klaus. You're supposed to be a Professor and one of the best artillery officers in the *Wehrmacht*, but sometimes you can't seem to understand elementary German. God help us when the Allies arrive! Well, what was she like?"

"I don't remember." Klaus lied. He remembered all too well. "She was young and innocent."

"Outside of my field of research, then." The sergeant guffawed at his own joke, and Klaus could not repress a smile.

They turned to walk along what passed for the main street of the town, a cobbled road overhung with old buildings which had seen better days. The houses on the west side of the street cast the shadow of the sun, enfolding the street in its shade. To their right, the houses beyond the street littered the climbing hill, wash hanging to dry from almost every window.

"This lot don't look young and innocent," Gunther nodded towards a clutch of old women gossiping at the side of the street, "but old crones are also outside of my field of research."

He laughed again, and his laugh caught the attention of one of the old women. She looked at them, squinting against the sun until her eyes discerned their uniforms. She crossed herself, then babbled something behind her hand to the other women. Their chatter ceased as six pairs of eyes fixed on the German soldiers. A brief moment passed before they all hurried away, scurrying for their doorsteps.

"Looks like we're not welcome, boss." Gunther grinned wryly. "Perhaps they were expecting the pope." He nodded toward the other side of the street. "Now, that looks more interesting."

His eyes fastened onto a young woman who emerged from a doorway by the side of the church. She glanced at them briefly from under her headscarf, her brown eyes full of fear, then scampered across the road to scoop up a small child who had been playing in a puddle by the side of the road. Without a backward glance, she disappeared back into the house, her offspring tucked under her arm. Gunther shrugged his shoulders.

"You know, boss, Italy is beginning to lose its attraction for me. Please arrange for my transfer back to Bavaria."

"Perhaps if you forgot about the women, you might find other things to interest you."

"Are there other things?"

Klaus shook his head at his friend's single train of thought.

"Well, there are Caligula's ships and the Temple of Diana, which is what *I* have come to see." He looked at his watch. "And if we don't find them soon, we'll have to get the motorcycle back to your friend."

"Who are we going to ask where they are?"

Gunther waved a dismissive hand in the direction of the street. Klaus realized he was right. The street was deserted; the only sound came from a bar, where the door was being hastily shut and locked. As this sound died away, a silence descended on the village; there was no noise, and the only movement came from an emaciated dog that eyed them before skulking away. It was the silence of fear and hatred, Klaus knew, and from behind that silence, a hundred pairs of unseen eyes were watching their every move.

"God, I'm hungry." Gunther looked at his watch.

Klaus wasn't sure whether Gunther was reacting to the silence or his hunger, but they continued walking along the street. The sergeant showed no unease, but he developed his theme.

"I've got some sausage and pumpernickel under the seat in the sidecar. Why don't we call it a day and try again when we're next off duty?"

The deserted street was about to convince Klaus of his friend's argument when an old man staggered across the piazza at the end of the street. He was clearly drunk. His rheumy eyes were sunk deep into his gaunt face, which was preceded by a bulbous red nose. His dirty trousers were tied at the waist by string, and from his undersized jacket projected long, bony hands, one of which clutched an old canvas bag. He lurched across the piazza, heedless of their presence.

"We'll not get much out of him."

Gunther half-turned to walk away, but stopped as the old man put down the bag and began to dig into it, almost falling on his face as he did so. The sergeant started, reaching behind him for his Schmeisser, but Klaus stopped him as the old man's hand re-emerged with nothing more dangerous than a newly opened bottle of red wine. He raised the bottle to his lips, staggering backwards as he drank deeply; with some difficulty, he pressed the cork back into the neck of the bottle, which he stuffed back in the sack.

Gunther spat on the ground.

"Come on, let's get out of here."

The old man heard him and peered at their uniforms with his

hooded eyes. Suddenly, he marched towards them, goose stepping, although he almost fell over with every step. The foul odor of wine and garlic hit them as he lifted his arm and gave a mocking Nazi salute.

"He's full of piss, let's go." Gunther tugged at his officer's sleeve.

"Heil Hitler and all the other mother-fucking German sons of bitches."

"What did he say?" Gunther looked bemused, unable to understand the babble of Italian.

Klaus said nothing, but he leaned over the old man, grasping him by the shoulders. He spoke slowly and in perfect Italian.

"And what if these mother-fucking German sons of bitches asked you the way to the ship museum?"

The drunken eyes opened wide, and the bravado collapsed into fear. The head of the man shook in disbelief at hearing his own tongue, and then his whole body began to shake.

"*Mi dispiace, mi dispiace*. I am sorry. I am a drunken old fool."

His body convulsed with fear and self-pity, and he would have fallen had not Klaus held him up. Klaus continued to instill the fear of God into the wretch.

"Well, drunken old fool, do you know what the penalty is for insulting our Fuehrer and the soldiers of the Third Reich?"

The man was a gibbering wreck of fear; tears filled his eyes. Klaus shook him by the shoulders.

"Listen, you foolish sot. We shall take no further action in this matter providing you tell us where we can find the museum of the ships."

The eyes looked back at Klaus, unbelieving, as the old man jumped at the chance of escape. His words, though slurred, came quickly.

"*Sì, sì, il museo delle navi. È làggiù*. It's down there."

His hand waved loosely toward the wall overlooking the steep descent to the lake. Klaus thrust him forward, half carrying him to the wall.

Gunther hurried after them, trying to fathom his officer's actions.

"Hey boss, I don't care what he said – he's just a drunken old fool. There's no need to throw him down there."

At the edge of the wall Klaus steadied the old man, whose gnarled hand pointed down to a huge building far below at the edge of the lake. Klaus thought the building looked like an aircraft hangar.

"Sir, that's the museum, there, sir – but it's best to take the road through Genzano, sir."

His other hand waved unsteadily to the town perched on the western hillside, its red roofs clinging to the opposite rim of the crater. Klaus could just pick out the road that ran from the town down to the museum, carving its way through the trees. He released his grip on the old man, who dropped into an abject sniveling heap at his feet, babbling incoherently.

"Come, Gunther, we're finished here."

He motioned to the sergeant to follow him. They strode back down the street, past the prying eyes, and returned to the motorcycle. Klaus gave Gunther the directions, but the sergeant could not suppress his curiosity.

"What did he say? What did he say?"

Klaus squeezed himself into the sidecar, adjusting his goggles.

"He told me the truth, Gunther."

"Truth? What truth?"

"You know – *in vino veritas*. He said you were a son-of-a-bitch.'

Klaus's laugh was drowned by the roar of the engine.

"The bastard. You should have shoved him down the hill."

CHAPTER 14

The same day. 12.30 p.m.

Paolo shook himself out of his reverie and looked towards where Gianni was pointing. *Tedeschi!* The motorcycle sidecar bore the black and white cross of the German army. A squat, barrel-chested soldier sat astride the machine, while beside him, climbing out of the sidecar, a tall man lifted his goggles onto the front of his high-peaked cap. An officer.

Paolo's first thought was for the Mirror of Diana; these Germans had come to plunder it. He had heard several stories from Rome of how many of the great works of art had been loaded onto trucks and sent off to Germany. He began to run toward the museum, or at least move as fast as his legs would carry him. He cursed his old legs, and he cursed himself for having dozed in the sun. In his panic, he gestured Gianni to follow him.

"*Buon giorno!*"

The surprise of being greeted in Italian caused him to stop and look behind him. The officer was only ten meters away. Paolo realized that he did not have time enough to do anything; besides, the thought crossed his mind that the mirror was safe enough in its hiding place, and his actions so far would only create suspicion.

"*Buon giorno.*" The officer stood before him, removing his gloves. Paolo saw he held a small book. "Do you know who is in charge of the museum?"

"I am the curator," Paolo began, unable to prevent a stammer in his voice, "*ma, ma è chiuso, è chiuso, il museo è chiuso.* I have all the relevant papers from the Ministry in Rome…"

The officer laughed, causing Paolo further alarm. Perhaps his papers would offer him no protection; maybe the German would just tear them up.

"You do not understand, Signor Curator." The German maintained a broad smile on his face. "This is not an inspection. I do not wish to see your papers. I have come to see the Ships of Caligula!"

Paolo was perplexed and stood dumbfounded. Why would a German come to see the ships? What were they to him? And why was it that this German officer's speaking Italian caused him unease?

"You do have the Ships of Caligula here?"

"*Si, ma il museo è chiuso.*" Paolo prevaricated. "It has been closed since the start of the war."

"But you are the curator? Surely you have the keys?"

Paolo saw that the officer was smiling but, despite his insistence, he saw no reason why he should help the German. What right had he to come trampling over Italian monuments that had been created while the Germans still lived in caves? Besides, there were bound to be prying eyes looking down from the walls of the town high above him; if word got back to his wife that he had played host to a German, there would be hell to pay.

"But there are regulations." He shrugged his shoulders and spread out his hands to feign helplessness, hoping the keys in the pocket of his pants did not jangle and betray him. "The Ministry will have to be informed – there are forms to be completed."

The officer sighed heavily and shook his head. Paolo started as the German's hand went to his breast pocket, but he produced only a silver cigarette case. He took out a cigarette and began tapping it on the case.

"I understand that there are procedures. Of course, I could go back to my headquarters and return with all the necessary papers…."

Paolo's eyes caught a movement behind the officer's head. "Gianni, Gianni!" The other German was tossing Gianni into the air, catching him under the armpits and then repeating the process. Gianni shrieked, and Paolo felt his breath catch in his throat. But Gianni's cries were of delight, not fear. The officer looked behind him to see the cause of Paolo's concern and returned his gaze to the curator, a wistful smile on his face.

"That is my sergeant, Gunther. He probably has the strength to crush an Allied soldier's skull with his bare hands, but he's quite harmless otherwise. And he loves children. However, if it bothers you…."

He shouted at the sergeant, reverting to his own tongue.

"Gunther, you're frightening the natives. Put the boy down."

"But he was enjoying it, boss. And I don't need to know the lingo to realize that the little beggar was after our pumpernickel; he just pointed to his mouth and his stomach. No wonder, he's as thin as a rail - all bones." The boy shouted something at the sergeant. "What does '*ancora*' mean, boss?"

"It means he wants you to do it again."

Paolo had stood anxious and bemused during this exchange, and the officer turned to him to explain.

"A hungry child has no country and doesn't understand 'isms.' I know things are difficult, but can't you feed your children?"

Paolo looked down at the path to avoid the German's eye.

"We manage. It has been difficult lately."

The officer looked out toward the lake, the reflection of the town high above on the hillside rippling across the water.

"It is sad. It is the war."

There was an uneasy silence; Paolo felt that the German was embarrassed, as if he felt responsible for Gianni's hunger. He continued to tap his cigarette absent-mindedly on his case.

"I'm sorry – would you like a cigarette?"

He offered the silver case. Paolo felt the temptation of mortal man. He knew he should refuse; it would be the first step along the path of compromise. He looked at the cigarette. It was one of those fat ones, gorged with tobacco, which hadn't been seen for a long time. He knew he must refuse, but he could see that he could fill his pipe if he broke the cigarette down. This was how a man sold his soul to the devil, he thought, as his fingers reached out for the case.

"I'll take one for later, if you don't mind."

"Not at all." The German nodded as he clipped the case shut and returned it to his pocket. "Now, about the ships…." He let the word hang in the air.

Paolo realized that the price of the cigarette was being demanded. "*Non è possibile*. It is necessary to provide the paperwork…."

The officer said nothing, but fixed him with a look that asked how many cigarettes he wanted. Did this German really think he would accept a bribe? Didn't he understand that the cigarette had been accepted as a gift?

Paolo saw her first. She was walking along the path to the museum, her arm in an elegant arc cradling the basket full of flowers she had plucked from the fields. Her free arm rose aloft in a greeting. As she came nearer to them, Paolo tried to signal her to go away, amazed she could not see the German.

His gestures alerted the officer, who turned to see Rosanna approaching. She took another step, then stopped, her eyes widening, her mouth opening in shock. Paolo looked at the German, who stood stock still, as if he were unable to believe his eyes.

Paolo cursed himself for his own stupidity. Could it be – surely not?

Of course, the German officer who spoke Italian! He was the man who had rescued his daughter!

"I'm sorry, I did not realize...."

Paolo knew his words were unheard. The officer was staring at Rosanna as if he had seen an apparition. Paolo gently tugged on his sleeve, and leapt back when the German turned sharply towards him.

"I'm sorry, I didn't know you were the one responsible for saving Rosanna...."

His voice trailed away as the German's incredulous eyes turned from Rosanna and fastened on him.

"You know this woman?" His uniformed arm pointed in Rosanna's direction.

"*Sì*, she is my daughter. My wife and I cannot thank you enough...."

Paolo suddenly knew how he could thank the German. He moved towards him, his voice dropping to a conspiratorial whisper.

"Can you come back Saturday? Early in the morning?" He looked up at the town ramparts as if the very walls were striving to hear what he said. "And bring some paperwork – it doesn't matter what, as long as it's got an official stamp."

Without waiting for an answer, he grabbed his bicycle.

"Gianni, Gianni, come quickly." He beckoned to the lad, who had insinuated himself into the sidecar seat of the motorcycle. Gianni jumped out, laughing and pumping himself up like a peacock as he received a mock salute from the sergeant.

Paolo collected his bicycle and put on his clips. "You, too, Rosanna, we must be off back home now."

Her white dress flowed with the rhythm of her walk as she moved toward the German. "I'll follow in a few minutes, *Papà*. I need to say a few words to...."

"Klaus. My name is Klaus." He stiffened to attention, inclining his head in a formal greeting.

Paolo hesitated and considered arguing with his daughter, but thought better of it; after the events of yesterday, she was surely in safe hands. Nevertheless, he checked that the museum door was locked.

"Very well, but no more than five minutes. And remember," he looked upwards at the town, "that the walls have eyes."

As her father disappeared along the path with Gianni trotting at his side, Rosanna spoke in little more than a whisper. "I want to thank you for rescuing me yesterday."

Klaus felt awkward. His hands fidgeted with his cap and he looked down at his boots. He began to feel guilty over his decision to withdraw his report when he returned to Velletri.

"It was nothing," he mumbled as he reached in his uniform for another cigarette. "Are you alright?"

She pulled back her long hair from her face, revealing the bruise on her left cheek. Klaus winced.

"Mamma told me I'd mend." She let her hair fall back over her cheek. "Besides, if it hadn't been for you, it would have been much worse."

She put down the basket of flowers she had gathered, the pink cyclamen blooms catching the afternoon sun. Klaus watched her as she perched herself on the low wall in front of the museum. Her eyes were elsewhere, looking out at the ripples playing on the surface of the lake. She did not speak, and Klaus wondered where her thoughts had taken her. A gust of wind came off the lake, catching her dress, shaping it against her body, pressing the fabric against the contours of her thighs.

Klaus cursed himself for the sexual feelings that came upon him. He looked away to try to hide the red face of his guilt. To save her from rape had already caused him so much trouble; now he himself felt attracted to her and he knew no good could come of it. He looked at her again; her brown eyes were still wistfully gazing over the water. She was nineteen, he guessed, a full decade younger than himself. Little more than a child. She had an unworldliness about her, an untouchable, indefinable quality that made him feel guilty about his physical reaction.

"Of course, you were destined to save me - made to save me by Diana."

Her words, breaking the long silence, caught him unawares, but they mercifully broke into his troubled thoughts.

"Diana? Which Diana?"

"By the goddess Diana, of course!" She sounded annoyed at his ignorance.

"Ah, that Diana!" He laughed at her naïveté as he eased himself down beside her on the wall; perhaps he could tell his commandant that it was the goddess who had made him submit the report. He laughed again as he pictured the commandant's face.

"Don't laugh. It was Diana who sent you. You know nothing of Diana!"

She pouted, and he noticed that the dimple on her chin appeared to smile, and he wondered why he thought such things. He pushed the distraction aside and sifted through his memory, searching for the right period in his classical studies. He decided to tease her.

"Which Diana sent me? Was it Diana the huntress, Diana the goddess of the moon, or Diana the protector of women?"

"You know about Diana?"

Her eyes were wide with amazement and her mouth fell open.

"I have read about her." He rested his cap on his knee and assumed a nonchalant air.

"But how can you know?" She waved her hands in exasperation that someone could know of her goddess. "You're a…you're a…."

"*Tedesco?* Do you think Germans cannot read?"

"I'm sorry, it's just that…."

She flushed and looked down. Klaus felt guilty again.

"No, it is I who should be sorry. I shouldn't have said that. You see, I studied classical history when I was at the university. I know of the cult of Diana and of Caligula's visits to her temple, which is why I know of your father's ships."

He looked at her and saw she held her head high on her swan-like neck.

"You really do know about Diana!"

"Yes, but I would like to know more. I understand there is an ancient shrine to Diana near the museum that has survived the centuries. Would you show it to me?"

He regretted the request as soon as the words left his lips. He knew he should walk away and disappear into the war.

"*Sì, sì*, it is not far." Klaus saw how enthusiastic she was now, happy that someone shared her interests. She became radiant in her excitement.

 He knew he had to go; Gunther was signaling him, raising his arm and pointing to his watch.

"Look, I'm coming back on Saturday, if I can. Tell your father I'll be here at half past seven in the morning. Perhaps after then...."

He left it open-ended. Perhaps he would withdraw the report, he would not come back, and that would be an end to the matter. He waved an acknowledgement to Gunther.

"Now, you must go home. Your father will be waiting."

He wanted to offer his hand, but instead saluted her.

"Yes, I must be away. And thank you again, Klaus."

She twisted her tongue around the unfamiliar vowels of his name, and, as she turned to go, he sensed the fragrance of her hair.

"Oh, and which manifestation of the goddess was it?"

She blushed and lowered her eyes.

"You know very well which Diana it was."

For a few moments, he watched as she walked away, then he strode back towards Gunther and the motorcycle. He turned to look at her again, and was surprised to see that she, too, had turned. She smiled, waved and was gone.

"Well, you made an impression there, boss. And what a stunner!"

Klaus ignored his sergeant and climbed into the sidecar. Gunther shrugged his shoulders and kick-started the engine.

"What was the boy's name, boss?"

"Gianni." Klaus replied automatically, his thoughts elsewhere.

"That's a nice name, even if it is Italian. He's full of fun. Such a nice kid. Yes, a nice kid."

"Gunther, we need to wangle some leave, and you need to play cards with the depot quartermaster again. We're coming back again. On Saturday. Now I'm hungry. Where's that sausage?"

"It's wrapped up in some paper on the floor of the sidecar." Klaus felt under his feet in vain.

"There's nothing here, Gunther!"

"He stole it. The little bastard. He stole it."

Klaus laughed as Gunther opened the throttle, the rear wheel spinning in the dust as they sped away.

CHAPTER 16

The same day. Late evening

"You're going to show the ships to a German?"

Maria chopped the onion with greater vigor than usual.

Paolo had known there would be trouble. He lifted the newspaper in front of him as if it would offer him some protection. He knew he shouldn't have told her, but she'd have probably found out from some nosey gossip, and that would have been worse. He cringed behind the paper.

"You look after those ships more than you do your own family. You won't let anyone from the village see them – not that they would want to, anyway – and now you open the doors of your precious museum – to a German!"

He remained silent; silence, he had discovered, was sometimes the best method of defense. The chopped onion sizzled as she tossed it into the pan. He savored the aroma as it drifted across the kitchen, and it reminded him of other days. Better days. When things had been normal. When he would come home at the end of the day with hope in his heart, and she would greet him with a smile, their dinner bubbling in the pot. When things had been normal. He smiled to himself ironically as he realized he was using his wife's expression. Things would never be normal again.

"Well, it was the German officer who saved Rosanna," he offered lamely, "I thought we might owe him something."

"But he is still a German." She put down the spoon that had been stirring the onions and wiped her hands nervously on her apron. "Isn't it collaboration? What will the neighbors think?"

To hell with the neighbors, he thought, but he did not give utterance to the thought.

"No one will see – he's agreed to come early Saturday morning."

"Someone will see."

Maria added the onions to the pot that simmered with the measly carcass of their last chicken. What if that someone was that old busybody Grazia Gismondi, she thought? She could picture the old crow looking down her long nose at her during mass, and then tittle-tattling with the other women on the church steps afterwards.

"Think of the shame!" She clattered the plates and cutlery onto the table.

Paolo did not think of the shame. He could think of little else but the aroma of the chicken and onions. Maria began tossing some greens she had picked from the field in oil and vinegar.

"Where's Rosanna? She's late, and it's nearly dinner time."

He withdrew behind the newspaper again, wondering what would happen if his wife knew that he had left Rosanna alone with the officer. The thought of the consequences cemented his decision to say nothing.

"At least she's not involved. It's bad enough for you to go bowing and scraping to the Germans, but for her to be involved…" She paused in her stirring of the pot. "Mother of God, think of the scandal!"

"You worry too much about what other people think." Paolo's words were accompanied by a sigh of resignation as he buried himself deeper into the newspaper.

"It's alright for you – you live in a dream world with your blasted ships. And you've taught Rosanna to be the same. Neither of you goes to mass, but *I* have to hold my head up in church."

The rattle of the door latch stopped her tirade. Paolo looked up over the paper as Rosanna entered. He was not a believer in God, but at that moment he was praying fervently that his daughter would say nothing about their encounter with the German.

"There you are, at last." Maria looked from her daughter to the old clock standing on the mantelpiece. "Where have you been?"

Rosanna seemed not to hear her mother; her thoughts were else-where, hiding behind her smile.

"You see?" Maria turned to her husband. "Living in a dream world, just like I said!"

"At least I managed to dream up some cyclamen." Rosanna put the basket on the table, the neatly arranged blooms spilling over the side. "Perhaps they might get a few coins in Genzano market."

Maria looked chastened. "I'm sorry, *bambina*, I didn't mean to shout at you, but after what those Germans did…"

Her maternal instinct overcame her anger as she brushed her daughter's hair back.

"How are your bruises?"

Paolo rustled the paper and began praying again.

"It's alright, mamma, they don't hurt anymore. I was saying to…"

"Heavens above, that chicken smells delicious. I'm starving!" Paolo interrupted hastily.

He stood up quickly, folded the paper and walked over to the stove, his nose hovering above the pot. He had meant his action as a diversion, but he, himself, was diverted by the wonderful aroma pervading the room.

"Chicken?" Rosanna's eyes widened. "We have chicken tonight? We haven't had chicken for months!"

"Well, if you can call it chicken." Maria busied herself ladling the stew from the pot. "If I hadn't killed it this morning, it would have probably died from starvation anyway."

"But it looks superb – you have worked wonders with it, *mia cara!*"

Paolo felt the demanding gnawing in his stomach; he salivated in anticipation.

"And I, too, have a surprise!" He went out of the back door, rummaged in the shed and returned holding a bottle aloft.

"It's a Frascati."

He gripped the bottle tightly as the corkscrew dug deeply into the cork. Maria smiled and brought down three glasses from the china closet.

"I've been saving it for a special occasion."

Paolo poured the wine, and they all gathered around the table, enjoying the pleasant sound as the bottle yielded its contents.

"I suppose the last of the chickens is a special occasion! Here's to it!" Paolo raised his glass.

His wife and daughter sipped at their glasses, while he took a full draught, savoring the wine as it washed against his tongue. He seized a piece of Maria's newly baked bread and dipped it into the gravy, allowing its rich flavor to mix with the aftertaste of the wine before picking up his fork to attack the stew.

"*Mia cara*, you cook divinely – it is superb!"

They ate in silence, as if words would spoil the feast. Paolo wondered when they would next eat such a meal again, and prayed that Rosanna would not mention the German officer in front of Maria. He hoped the German officer would not show up on Saturday. That would solve all problems. Perhaps Rosanna had forgotten all about him.

"Mamma, that was delicious." Rosanna used the last crust of bread to mop up the remains of the stew. "Now I am happy, but tired. Please excuse me, but it has been a busy day." She hugged her mother and moved around the table to plant a kiss on her father's forehead. She turned as she opened the door to the stairs. "Don't forget about Saturday, papa." She smiled and closed the door behind her.

No wonder he didn't believe in God. He moved to his armchair and took refuge again behind his newspaper.

"What's all that about Saturday?"

He heard the rattle of the plates as she cleared the table. He ruffled the paper and pretended not to hear her, hoping the problem would go away.

"She's not going to be with you when you see that German, is she? Mother of God...."

He peered over the paper as he sought a believable lie.

"Good Heavens, no. Rosanna and I are going to look at another site beyond the temple. She thinks she's found something. We'll do it in the afternoon, long after the German has gone."

"More of your nonsense. Why don't you try to give that girl a proper education? No wonder all the young men give her a wide berth. Half the time she's not in this world. Like you!"

At that moment, Paolo felt very much of the world, and he didn't like it. Although his wife had been diverted, he now had to tell Rosanna to compound the lie. Perhaps he shouldn't go on Saturday morning. But, if he didn't go, the officer would surely seek him out; the thought of Maria's answering the German's knock at the door did not amuse him. Then there was Rosanna; she would go, anyway, and it would be better for him to be there. Of course, he could forbid Rosanna to go, but that would make her only more determined. And, from what he had seen of how the officer had looked at Rosanna, he would probably come looking for her, too.

It was a mess, all caused by his wanting to show a little gratitude to someone who had helped his daughter. In the future, he'd stay quiet and keep his nose clean, like everybody else.

Yet – what was his name? – Klaus, yes, Klaus seemed a decent man, and, in protecting Rosanna, he'd done something he didn't have to do; he could have turned and walked away. Yes, he was a decent man. For a German. But Maria was right on that point – hanging around with a German would not go down well with the rest of the town.

His inability to find an answer to his problem frustrated him, and brought on an irresistible urge for a smoke. He patted his pocket and was seeking his pipe when he remembered that he had used the last of his tobacco the night before. Nothing was going his way. He was about to curse when his fingers, searching for his pipe, felt something else in his pocket. It was the cigarette. He pulled it out; it was long and fat, bursting with tobacco. In moments, the cigarette was crushed, the tobacco tamped into the bowl of his pipe and a taper applied.

He drew deeply, exhaled with a long, satisfied sigh and drew again. The tobacco had an unusual aroma, but it was rich and strong. So engrossed was he in his pleasure that he had not noticed Maria looking at him.

"Where did you get that sort of tobacco?" She laid aside her drying cloth.

Her question caught him unawares, with his lungs full of smoke, and a bout of coughing overcame him. Before he could recover, she answered her own question.

"You got it from the German, didn't you? You'll be making a pact with the devil next. No good can come of this, mark my words."

As she put away the plates in the cupboard, he saw the flames from the fire catch the anxiety on her face. A beseeching look replaced the anger that had been in her eyes.

"Please be careful, Paolo. For my sake and for Rosanna's sake, if for nothing else."

She made her way to the stairs, leaving him to ponder her words as the last cloud of smoke rose from his pipe.

CHAPTER 17

Saturday August 21st 1943. 5.00 a.m.

K laus checked his uniform in the mirror and looked out of the window of his room overlooking the piazza in Velletri. It was first light, with the dawn beginning to sidle into the sky. He went down the stairs of the inn quietly, closed the door and waited in the deserted street. He looked at his watch. He wanted to be in Nemi early. Where was Gunther? The piazza was quiet; only a few birds heralded the first glimpse of a new day. The silence was shattered by the rattle of hooves on the cobbles, accompanied by a succession of profanities from the horse's rider.

"Whoa, you damn beast, stop!" The horse appeared with Gunther sawing the reins as he struggled to bring the animal to a halt.

"Sorry, boss, I can't make it." Gunther whispered as he dismounted, although he had made enough noise to wake the laziest dog in Velletri. "Couldn't get any leave – my unit is rostered for guard duty today."

The disappointment showed in Klaus's face, and Gunther looked surprised.

"Why the sad face, boss? *You* can go!"

"What about transport, Gunther? How am I going to get there?"

The sergeant's face grimaced in bemusement.

"Transport? This is the transport!" He pushed the reins into Klaus's hands.

"A horse? What happened to the motorcycle?"

"Even with my luck, I can't win at cards every time. Mount up. Didn't they teach you to ride at artillery school?"

"I could ride before I went to the university, but this one looks a bit frisky!"

Klaus pointed to the flecks of sweat on the horse's flanks.

"It's just an old mare. She doesn't like having to start work so early in the morning. You've just got to treat her like all females – show her who is boss!"

Klaus stuffed the parcel of food he had prepared into the saddlebag and motioned for Gunther to offer his hand for a leg-up. As he hit the saddle, the horse reared, and he eased his weight forward to bring her under control. Gunther slapped his cap against the horse's rump, and Klaus felt her take up the bit before moving into a trot.

"Bring her back before sunset," Gunther shouted after him, "alive, if possible, or I won't have my stake for the next game!"

It took an hour to reach the outskirts of Genzano, and Klaus was beginning to wish that he had not come. He was hot and sweaty, although the sun had only just cleared the horizon behind him. The horse beneath him lurched from side to side, refusing to slow to a walk, tossing its head against the bridle, as it had all the way from Velletri. It had been a difficult ride, and Klaus yearned for the relative comfort of Gunther's sidecar.

Genzano was still and deserted. The uneven rattle of the hooves on the cobbles echoed back from the walls on either side of the street. The animal just would not maintain an even pace. At the crossroads, two guards saluted him; he could see that they were trying vainly to stifle their laughter at his ungainly progress. He pulled to the right and the horse shied away from him before reluctantly turning. He dismounted, and the mare immediately took up a leisurely walk as he led her by the reins.

Perhaps she was telling him not to go on, he thought. Yet he was going to see the ships of Caligula; thus he rationalized his actions, but knew at once that it was not the real reason why he had taken such pains. What was it about her that drew him? Her hair? The dimple on her chin? Or her naïveté, the mystery of her innocence? Or was it the feel of her body against him when she had pounded him with her fists?

He stopped, and the mare stopped, too, awaiting his decision. The road leading down to the lake came upon them. Perhaps the curator of the museum wouldn't turn up. The thought reinforced itself as Klaus remounted; if the curator didn't show, he would go back.

The mare shied again, as if in protest at his decision, but he urged her forward down the road to the lake.

The same day. 7.45 a.m.

" *W*underbar!*"* Klaus lapsed into his native tongue at his first sight of the ships in the museum.

"Simply magnificent!" His neck arched back as he looked up while he walked slowly alongside the first of the vessels.

"Imagine this great ship on the beautiful lake – what a sight! Signor Giraldi, did Caligula have these huge ships built simply to enable him to worship at the Temple of Diana?"

Paolo was pleased that the German saw the same dream as he did. He had hoped that he would not show up, and had been somewhat frightened when he had emerged on his horse along the Via Virbia. But he had been overwhelmed by his sheer enthusiasm, and by his grasp of historical detail. He felt at ease with the German

"Well, he certainly wasn't going to sail them to Gaul – there's no outlet from the lake!"

They both laughed, but there was a nervous edge to their laughter as they sought to avoid their differences and seek the common ground they shared.

"It was this ship that Caligula actually used for his own personal floating palace. The other – the second – was a floating temple." Paolo led Klaus across to the other side of the museum where the sister ship stood towering above them, and the German stood in awe.

"Well, Signor Giraldi, we have something for which to remember Caligula, other than his record of cruelty and depravity."

Klaus ducked under the trestles to obtain a better look at the hull.

"But it wasn't his insane cruelty that brought him to a sticky end - it was more his worship of Diana, as you probably know, Signor Giraldi. The senate didn't like how he loved all things Egyptian, how he wanted to integrate Isis in the form of Diana into the Roman pantheon. And, of course," he waved his arm in the direction of the ships, "he was costly!"

He came out from under the hull and looked along the length of the ship.

"What a remarkable feat of engineering – and nineteen hundred years old!"

"*Sì, Sì, Signor Capitano*. But the second ship was retrieved from the bottom of the lake only twelve years ago."

"Please call me Klaus." The German looked at Paolo and smiled.

"Come, follow me, Klaus." There was a slight hesitation before Paolo used the German's name for the first time, and the Italian felt he had crossed a bridge. "There's a better view from the gallery."

Klaus followed as they climbed the spiral staircase to the balcony.

"How were the ships sunk, Paolo?"

The old man turned as they reached the top of the staircase.

"It's not really known." He waved his arms as he sought to explain. "They could have sunk in a storm."

They walked across to a window overlooking the lake, sitting serenely in the morning sun that glimmered on the tranquil surface. Klaus felt far removed from the war that had been his life for the past four years.

"Do not be fooled by that view – that's how the old artists painted it." Paolo waved his hands again. "It's usually quiet like that, but, at times of bad weather, the crater around the lake can whip up the wind and the water into a maelstrom."

"But it's unlikely the ships went to the bottom that way." Paolo led Klaus across to the edge of the balcony. "It's more likely they were deliberately sunk – maybe by Claudius, who knows? – to try to expunge Caligula from history."

Paolo grasped the handrail of the balcony, inviting Klaus to look down on the ships.

"Whatever, he certainly ensured that his ships had everything – baths, a temple, a triclinium, not to mention the opulent imperial quarters. Sadly, all the superstructure was lost in excavations in the last century, but it is estimated that, all in all, this ship supported some six hundred tons."

Klaus looked at the huge wooden beams and tried to picture the vessels as Paolo had described them, to hold in his mind's eye their splendid majestic passage across the lake.

"Both ships are so big!"

"Yes, Klaus, it took seventeen hundred years until any vessel approaching their size was built – Columbus's ships were pigmies in comparison! And, speaking of the Romans' knowledge, I had forgotten to show you something."

Paolo beckoned to Klaus; they descended the stairs and walked across the concourse of the museum.

"Of course, all the treasures that were movable – the bronze wolf head beam-end covers, the guardrails in the form of herms, the marbles and mosaics of many colors – all were spirited away to the *Museo Nazionale* in Rome at the start of the war. But there was this treasure left."

Paolo pointed to a huge anchor; mounted on a stand; it rose above them, almost eighteen feet in length

"Of course, much of it has been reconstructed, but the significant thing is that it was equipped with a movable stock."

Klaus's brow furrowed and Paolo immediately answered his unasked question.

"In 1850, the British Admiralty claimed to have invented the movable stock, and fitted all their ships with this so-called new device – a device which the Romans had perfected eighteen centuries before!"

"So, about ten years ago, we sent a copy of the original anchor to London."

An impish grin came to Paolo's face.

"Of course, embarrassing the mighty British empire was the farthest thing from our minds…." Paolo's wry grin turned into a laugh.

They sat down on the recessed steps by the side of the second ship. Klaus gazed upward at the vessel.

"Paolo, the technical aspects of these ancient ships are marvelous, but it must have been an equally magnificent engineering feat to bring them up from the bottom of the lake."

The old man smiled as he shook his head.

"Ah, you see, we didn't bring them up from the bottom of the lake."

His smile broadened as Klaus's eyebrows lifted in bewilderment.

"We lowered the level of the lake to the ships! To get this one, the second ship," he pointed to the vessel before them, "we had to lower the level sixty feet!"

Klaus's face still held its look of incredulity.

"But, Paolo, that would mean moving millions of liters of water, and you've said there is no natural outlet to the lake."

The smug look on Paolo's face told Klaus that the old man was enjoying dragging out his story.

"Ah, but you do not know about the drainage tunnel. Come, I'll show you."

Paolo made his way back across the lobby to the entrance doors of the museum. As Klaus followed, he noticed that the sun had climbed above the rim of the crater encompassing the lake; the beams bounced off the mirror of the water, and the light dazzled them as it came through the windows. Paolo threw open the door and pointed to the trees on the western side of the lake.

"It's there – the entrance to the tunnel is there! It runs for over a kilometer before coming out beyond the crater."

Klaus shaded his eyes against the light, yet he could see little but a mass of late summer foliage that swayed in the light wind caressing the wall of the crater.

"But, Paolo, even the greatest mining engineers in Europe would have needed years to have built a tunnel so long, and to be able to carry so much water!"

"But we didn't build the tunnel."

Paolo smiled wryly, obviously savoring his air of mystery; Klaus wondered how much longer the Italian would continue to talk in riddles.

"The tunnel had already been built. Probably by the Etruscans – in the fifth century before Christ – before the Romans! What do you think of that?"

He finished on a triumphal note, waving his arms in the air. Klaus looked wistfully across the lake before turning to give his answer.

"Ships, anchors, tunnels – I think we have much to learn from the ancients."

"But we have learned nothing! We still make war, everywhere there is destruction, fear, and hunger."

Both men were silent for a while. Klaus's eyes took in the beauty of the lake and of the reflection of the wooded slopes hazily painting its surface like a watercolor. The old man was right, he thought. The serenity he saw was but a small oasis in a wilderness of war and violence. Little had changed since the Romans, except that man had perfected more powerful engines of destruction; he had improved the efficiency of death-dealing machines.

Paolo was the first to break the uneasy silence, to try to steer their talk to more mundane matters.

"Speaking of hunger, I have a little chicken broth if you have not eaten. I lit the stove before you arrived, so it will not take long to warm up."

The suggestion prompted Klaus's stomach to remind him that he hadn't eaten any breakfast.

"Now that's a good idea! I've brought some ham and bread myself."

He bounded across to his horse, which shied at first until it knew that Klaus was not going to mount. As the mare steadied, Klaus pulled his package from the saddlebag.

Paolo held the door open as Klaus returned to the museum.

"The stove is in the office at the back of the building. I'll soon set things up. There's a little coffee we can share, but there's not much."

"Let's to it!" Paolo felt the friendly arm of the German around his shoulder, and he was not quite sure it was a friendship he wished to embrace.

CHAPTER 19

The room was still heavy with the aromas of chicken and coffee, intermingled with the mustiness of neglect. After an hour spent discussing the origins and fates of the ships, Klaus had taken a small pad from his pocket and was busy sketching.

"I hope you don't mind. It's a thing of mine. I'm not very good, but I try to capture the things I value."

"Not at all." Paolo was in his element; not for three years had anyone visited the museum, let alone sketched the great barges and asked him searching questions about their recovery from the lake. He sat perched on a high stool by the side of the workbench, declaiming to the attentive German as if he were delivering a lecture at the Archaeological Society.

Klaus had removed the tunic of his uniform, and sat on an old chair, relaxed; he put down his pencil and clasped his hands behind his neck.

"Your knowledge of ancient history is remarkable, Paolo."

"And so is yours, Klaus!"

"But mine is intellectual, detached, while yours is of the heart, involved. You really can see those ships, can't you?"

"Yes, but so can you. I've seen the look in your eyes."

Klaus knew Paolo was right. He half-closed his eyes, and he could see the ships, emerging from the mists of the lake, the gold of the temple catching the newly-freed sun, the oars paddling the water with a slow rhythm, the insistent rhythm of history and time.

"But of what use is history?" Paolo dispelled his reverie, and Klaus looked up at the Italian, whose face had assumed a despondent, resigned look. "As I said before, history has taught us nothing."

"Perhaps it has taught us nothing. But has not history brought us together, at least? Two men who were born a thousand miles apart, united by these antiquities?" Klaus leaned his head backward in the direction of the ships.

"United by these ships, perhaps. But brought together by war."

Paolo looked at Klaus, and then let his eyes drop to the floor. "And the war can part us tomorrow. Today's friends, tomorrow's...."

He stopped, the implication obvious in his voice. "With Mussolini ousted, the government doesn't know which way to jump. They could throw in their lot with the Allies. Who knows?"

Klaus remained silent for a moment, then slapped his thigh and stood up.

"Heavens, Paolo, you are too serious. Let's enjoy today, sharing these wonders!" His hand waved behind him to the ships that lay beyond the room. "Look, see what I have brought!"

Paolo's eyebrows lifted as Klaus reached into his bag and brought out five packs of cigarettes, which he laid on the workbench. The old man stiffened.

"There is no payment needed. I gave my word that you could see the ships. That is enough."

"Don't be silly, Paolo. It's not a payment – it's a gift!"

The Italian hesitated, then reached down and lifted one of the cigarette packs, thrusting it under his nose. The temptation of the aroma broke his resistance.

"Thank you, Klaus." Paolo opened the packet. "But I prefer a pipe." He reached into his pocket and pulled out the battered wooden bowl. "Do you mind if I…" He rubbed his hands together, to indicate how he wanted to break down the cigarette before he pushed the tobacco into the bowl of the pipe.

"Not at all." Klaus was already drawing deeply on his own cigarette. "Next time, I'll try to bring pipe tobacco."

Paolo looked up from the palms that were crushing the tobacco. "Do you think there should be a next time?" He hesitated, as if unwilling to offend his generous guest. "If anyone found out, do you know what they would think about me in Nemi?"

Klaus's selfish pleasure vanished into contrition.

"I'm sorry, I hadn't thought about that."

"Perhaps you don't know how these people feel." Paolo struggled to explain. "There is already some talk among the hotheads of Genzano about reprisals against collaborators. It's not just me, I have to think about my wife." He looked down, picking at some imaginary speck on his pants.

"And then there's Rosanna. She is so precious to me."

Klaus looked about him, avoiding Paolo's eyes, seeking some reason to justify himself.

"I do have the official papers you asked for, giving me permission to visit the museum!" His hand reached toward the pocket of his tunic draped on the back of the chair. "Won't that help, Paolo?"

The curator got down from his stool. The shaking of his head and the shrugging of his shoulders showed his confusion.

"Perhaps, who knows? But I would prefer it if you did not see Rosanna again, Klaus. Genzano is full of communist sympathizers, and who knows what could happen to her…."

He stopped suddenly, knowing he had said more than he should; his concern for Rosanna had overcome his prudence. His loose talk about communist sympathizers could lead to searches and arrests. He was surprised at the German's reaction.

"But she said she would meet me after you had shown me the ships. Do you want me to walk past her?"

Paolo realized that his guest was thinking more of Rosanna than of the politics of war. He thanked Heaven that his indiscretion had been ignored, but now he knew that he had a different problem.

"No, of course not. But I must ask you, Klaus, never to see her again. It is for her own good. You do understand, don't you?"

"But of course. I promise." Klaus smiled and reached behind the chair to pick up his tunic. "But I hope I can visit you again. I've so many more questions about these great ships. Promise, please."

Klaus saw the nod of acceptance as Paolo picked up the cigarettes and ushered him towards the door of the museum. He wondered if the old man would keep his promise. Of his own, he had already begun to doubt.

CHAPTER 20

He saw her, as he and Paolo approached the window set in the museum's door. She was standing by the side of the horse he had ridden from Velletri, gently patting its neck, the imprint of her hand gleaming on the animal's coat. Klaus could almost smell her innocence in the breeze that came in from the lake, bouncing off the small waves lapping the shore. Perhaps her innocence did radiate from her touch, he thought. The old mare, so fractious during his ride that he had thought he had mounted the spawn of the devil, now stood placidly like an old sheep, her head lowered to receive Rosanna's ministrations.

As he waited for Paolo to retrieve the keys from his coat, Klaus noticed once more her long fingers as they tweaked the horse's ears. Every aspect of her was long and slender, Klaus thought. Her neck held her head high, emphasizing her strong jaw line and high cheekbones. The horse raised its head at the sound of the key in the lock, and Klaus noticed Rosanna's tensed calves as she stood a little on tiptoe to whisper laughingly into the mare's ear. He bit his lip and remembered his promise.

She turned to them, smiling, as they emerged from the museum, and Klaus saw how she smiled not just with her mouth, but with her eyes, with her whole face, even with her dimple. Her long fingers lifted from the horse's flanks and waved to them.

"Ah, *Papà,* there you are at last! You must have been talking for hours."

Paolo stuffed the keys into his pocket and leant towards Klaus's ear.

"Remember your promise – and remember what I told you about the danger. Her safety is in your hands!"

He bent down to put on his bicycle clips as Rosanna approached.

"What did you say, *Papà?*"

"I said you must be back home soon."

The old man set his bicycle in motion and settled in the seat.

"And I mean soon."

His final shout died away as the bicycle turned the bend in the road leading away from the museum back up the hill to Nemi.

There was an awkward silence as the two stood looking at each other on the steps of the museum. Only the raucous cry of a gull, wheeling above the lake, disturbed the murmuring of the leaves in the breeze.

"Well, my brave soldier, do you want to see the Temple ruins or not?"

Klaus looked at her. Her arched eyebrows and wry smile were mocking him, and he realized he was standing like a tongue-tied youth, wringing the band of his cap between his hands. She turned away and he began to follow.

"You'd better bring your horse." She looked back at him, her arm waving gracefully in the direction of the mare.

"Do you wish to ride?" He hoped to redeem himself with his gallantry as he quickly untethered the mare.

"Of course not!" She threw her head back and laughed, as if he were being incredibly stupid. "But she's a fine animal, and you wouldn't want her to end up in somebody's pot, would you? Besides, it's a long walk back to Velletri!"

She laughed again as she set out along the path. He cursed himself for his own stupidity and pulled the reluctant horse behind him as he caught her up. He felt he must have seemed like an ignorant oaf in her eyes.

"I suppose my father bored you to tears with his stories of the ships?"

"No, no, I found it very interesting. He is very knowledgeable about the vessels." Klaus found himself talking quickly and uttering banalities, betraying his anxiety.

"They are his life's passion – he was involved from the start of the project. When I was five, he carried me on his shoulders down to the lake to see the first ship emerge from the water. I can remember there was a lot of cheering." She smiled at the memory, and then turned her head to Klaus. "Why are you interested in the ships?"

"I told you that I studied Ancient History when I was at the University. I have always been interested in all things to do with the Roman Empire." He stopped walking and halted the horse as Rosanna stooped to pick some wild pink cyclamen that grew at the path's edge. "Where did you learn about the myths of Diana?"

"I'm not sure it is all myth." There was a coyness in her voice, and Klaus was not sure whether she was being serious or teasing him. She pushed the flowers into the neckline of her dress as she led him along the road.

"My father taught me, of course, but I learned much by myself!" She deliberately held her head high to emphasize an independence of spirit; Klaus caught the accompanying flash in her eyes. "I would have liked to have gone to university, but the war...."

She turned and looked at the lake, but Klaus could tell that she was seeing another world, a world that had been denied her by the advent of war.

"I'm sure you have learned more from your father than any university could teach you." He felt he had said the wrong thing. It wasn't the learning that she had missed; it was the opportunity that had been denied her.

"Your father is a wonderful man and he cares much for you." Klaus felt the need to be honest with her, to avoid any deception. "He is concerned lest you be seen with me because of, you know...." His arm waved in a futile gesture before pointing to his uniform.

She stopped and gave him a wan smile.

"Because of those young hotheads in Genzano? They don't frighten me. Besides, Diana will protect me."

Klaus was startled by her naïveté. Perhaps she actually believed in the fairy tales.

"Anyway, I owe you something from the other day." Her eyes were lowered, and he felt embarrassed, saying nothing. "No one will see us where we are going."

She realized she could be misunderstood and bit her lip.

"It's alright, I understand." He hastened to reassure her. "But you must be careful – I have promised your father."

The concern on her face lasted but a moment and was replaced quickly by a smile.

"Of course, you know it's probably bad luck bringing a horse into the Temple of Diana."

She looked straight ahead, avoiding his eyes, but there was a hint of calculated disdain in her voice. She had recovered her composure, and he felt sure she was still making fun of him.

"Bad luck?"

"Yes, you know the story of Hippolytus?"

"Of course, of course!" Klaus pulled on the reins of the reluctant horse, thinking how stupid he must have seemed to her.

"Saving himself for his beloved Diana, he refused to be seduced by Phaedra and escaped from her, fleeing in his chariot."

Klaus saw Rosanna turn off the road and followed her along a meandering path that was hemmed in with oak trees, with scarcely enough room for the horse.

He searched his mind for the ancient legend. "In revenge, Phaedra asked Neptune to call up a monster. Hippolytus's horses were terrified, and he was dragged to his death."

His breath came fast as he tried to keep up with her fleet-footed movement along the path rising away from the shore of the lake.

"Is that why it's unlucky to bring a horse into the temple?" The old mare snorted, and pulled at the bridle again, as if she did not wish to be caught up in the old tale.

Rosanna turned and smiled when she saw his struggle with the horse.

"'Here Hippolytus lies, who by the reins of his steeds was rent in pieces; hence no horses enter that grove.'" She orated the quotation, slowly, deliberately. "That's what Ovid says about it."

The afternoon sun was fighting its way through the huge canopy of the oak trees, the light and shadows playing across her face.

"We're almost there." She looked back at him as he coaxed and cajoled the horse along the ever-narrowing path between the trees.

Klaus could see that the glade was about to come to an end. The boughs of the trees on either side came together to form an arch, through which the sunlight shafted down. As they moved into the open space bordered by the trees, Klaus was relieved that the mare appeared less fractious, although there was still sweaty foam on her quarters.

"Is this it?" Klaus looked about him at the open ground. At the far end of the glade was a high wall lined in mosaics that still bore color. There were a few broken columns, but otherwise little evidence of a vast temple. It was just a clearing in the trees, littered with a few rocks, some bracken, and a few errant saplings.

"No, this is merely the site." Rosanna spoke as if to a child. "See what I found over here." She led him to a barren spot, brushed aside some stones and lifted a piece of canvas to reveal a rich mosaic. "But most of the temple is down there!" She pointed to the earth beneath her feet. "It is covered by the debris of the centuries."

Her hand waved toward the trees and the orchards that enclosed the clearing.

"The site stretches over there. Have you ever seen the Parthenon? The Temple of Diana was twice as big as that!" She tossed her head to emphasize her point.

A perplexed look came to Klaus's face as he tethered the horse to a branch.

"But it can't all be buried. I'm sure I read that antiquities had been recovered from the Temple of Diana."

"You mean stolen!" Rosanna shouted the accusation. One of Klaus's eyebrows rose to ask for an explanation.

"You may be pleased to know it was an English aristocrat who stole them." Rosanna gave him a half-smile. "At the end of the last century, he excavated many artifacts – bowls, oil lamps, brooches, rings and pendants among many others – and carried them off to England."

"Was nothing left here?"

"Yes. There are a few pieces that were taken by the government - they're in a museum in Rome."

"But we had our own thieves here in Italy." She pointed up to the rim of the crater five hundred feet above them, where the Palazzo Ruspoli sat, its mediaeval tower casting its dominant shadow over the town of Nemi.

"Prince Orsini lived there, and owned this land, so he decided to throw out the Englishman and steal the treasures himself. Many things, including beautiful statues of Diana. He sold them to rich foreigners."

Klaus detected a sense of outrage in Rosanna's voice, almost as if the treasures had belonged to her. She dropped to her knees, her jaw set with a determined look.

"But the greatest treasures of Diana are still here."

She symbolically scooped up a handful of earth and let it trickle through her fingers. Klaus offered his hand to help her up, and was surprised at the strength of her grip. She released his hand and swept the dust from her dress with her palms.

"All this is very important to you, isn't it?" His voice was gentle, but her eyes flashed with indignation as she turned to him.

"Diana is important to all women! She protects them!"

She breathed deeply in an endeavor to control her emotions.

"I am sorry. I'm too emotional. But can't you feel her presence?"

Klaus wanted to tell her that he felt the presence of someone sweet and lovely; of innocence with black hair in a white dress, but he bit his lip and looked sheepishly down at his feet. Before he could offer an answer, she picked up her theme again.

"Do you know that the women of Rome came by the thousands to seek Diana's help? At dusk, on Diana's day, they came down that road, the Via Virbia…" she pointed to the road Klaus had ridden down to the lake's edge, "…all carrying torches and votive gifts to ask for her blessing."

Klaus was aware that her eyes were looking at the lake, but not seeing it. They were seeing the rippling lights of the torches playing over the faces of women dead centuries ago, yet still living in her. Faces of hope. The consuming look of innocent hope on her face shamed him, forcing aside the corruption of the world he inhabited, and denying the contagion of the war. He turned away from her and gazed up at the mountain that towered over the lake.

Rosanna returned from her tryst with the past and followed his eyes.

"That's Mount Cavo – the Romans knew it as Mons Albanus."

"You mean that's the mountain that was the seat of the gods, the home of Jupiter the thunderer?"

Rosanna was clearly impressed.

"You do know your classical history, don't you? Look, can you see the crevice which tradition says was the throne of Zeus?"

She came close to him so he could look along her outstretched arm. He felt her shoulder press in under his arm, and their faces were but a few inches apart. He nodded automatically as he turned to look at her, their eyes meeting for a prolonged moment. She held his look before lowering her eyes and moving away.

"Do you think we should go soon?" There was a hint of reluctance in his voice. "I promised your father I would make sure you were home early."

He thought of his other promise to Paolo. Never to see her again. She pulled a flower from the bunch of cyclamen she had tucked into her bodice and raised it to her nose. She looked up at him and smiled. He felt an ache gnawing at his heart.

They began their way back through the forest, and the horse at once became fractious again, whinnying as she twisted her head from side to side. Klaus pulled on the reins and she followed reluctantly.

Ducking through the branches, Rosanna led the way. The fingers of the afternoon sun, fighting their way through the canopy of the forest, reached down to touch her gently, as she moved from their light to the shade and then back into their caress.

"The forest always enchants me, Klaus!" He felt a quickening as she used his name for the first time. "Let us stay for a moment to enjoy it. We still have time." Her eyes pleaded with him.

"There is nothing I would enjoy more..." he paused, knowing that he sounded stiff and formal "...Rosanna – may I call you Rosanna?"

"*Perchè no?*" Her head was thrown back and she laughed, almost musically. "It's my name!"

Klaus loose-tethered the mare on a branch as Rosanna found a spot at the foot of a tree, her back arched against the gnarled trunk of the old oak. She closed her eyes and inhaled deeply, her nostrils flared.

"The smell of the forest is intoxicating!"

Klaus sensed the aroma of the carpet of pine needles scattered over the warm, moist loam, but he was distracted by the shaft of sun shimmering through the leaves, playing over her dress. He sought escape by looking up into the top reaches of the tree behind her.

"That's a very old oak – look at its girth." He looked around him. "What a dense forest this is!"

She opened her eyes and tilted her head to look up at him. "There were many more trees – a lot were cut down to enable the ships to be lifted from the lake. They stretched all around the water's edge."

He decided to tease her.

"And there was a King of the Forest, no doubt?" He smiled. "A *Rex Nemorensis*?"

She leapt up excitedly, like a child discovering a long-lost toy. "You know about the King of the Forest?"

He tried to look nonchalant as his mind raced once more through the recollections of his studies before the war.

"It is an old tale, passed down through the ages. In Germany, the legend is called '*Der Vildeman.*' Even today, someone dresses up in green and carries an uprooted tree at the spring festival. In Thuringia, he is called the *Strohbar* – the straw man – while in south-west Germany, the *Hisgier* battles winter's evil spirits, and in Hesse, the *Maimann* defeats winter." Klaus smiled smugly.

"No, no," she became agitated, "they are all only symbols of renewal, the triumph of Spring over Winter. The King of the Forest was special – he was Diana's protector!"

"He paid a heavy price to be her protector," he laughed. "The legend has it that the King of the Forest was always a runaway slave, and that he was slain by another slave who came to usurp him when he grew old. And so it went on. Each usurper would seek to break off the Golden Bough in order to kill the reigning king. Not much of a job – he had to have eyes in the back of his head, dare not sleep, and was doomed anyway. Not very good career prospects!"

She looked at him intently, ignoring his laughter.

"You know about the Golden Bough? Have you read the book? It's my favorite!"

He saw that her eyes shone with the fire of her enthusiasm, and he knew that he wanted to be burned, to be consumed by that fire. The renewed whinnying of the restless horse irritated him as it cut across his thoughts.

"Of course. Frazer's work is the bible of legend and mythology."

"What you say about the King of the Forest has another interpretation – the first king was Hippolytus, in the form of Virbius." He tried to listen attentively as she stood before him, her gesticulating arms helping her words as she developed her theme. "Of course, you are right about the ritual of renewal – Virbius means, as you know, 'twice born' and…" She stopped suddenly, a scream coming from her throat. "LOOK OUT!"

Her warning came too late for him. He heard the frightened horse's cry and felt a thud in the middle of his back. The blow of the hoof threw him forward, his flailing arms enveloping Rosanna as they fell to the ground together. For a prolonged moment he felt the softness of her body and saw her lips but inches from him. The blow had not hurt him, but he felt paralyzed, incapable of movement. The lips moved.

"Are you alright?" Her eyes searched his with some anxiety.

"Yes."

"Then perhaps you could get up so I can move?" She gave a wry smile and arched her eyebrows. Klaus realized he was not acting in a gentlemanly way and struggled quickly to his feet, blushing.

"I'm so sorry." He stammered. "Are you – are you hurt?"

He extended his hands to help her up. As she came to her feet, he was sure her hands lingered in his for a moment.

"I'm fine. I think we should attend to your horse – she was probably frightened by a rabbit or something."

Klaus followed her as she hurried down the path, but their haste was unnecessary. The mare had overcome her fright and, although her tail switched and she fretted, she had stopped running. Rosanna approached her without any fear, her hand soon stroking the nuzzle, comforting the animal, as Klaus secured the reins.

"I think we should get her out of the forest quickly. Besides," Klaus glanced at his watch, "I have to get back to Velletri before it gets dark."

Rosanna led the way back along the path, the light dim under the arch of intertwined branches over their heads; the forest floor cracked to their footfalls as they made their way to the open light at the end of the glade.

"Perhaps you are my King of the Forest!"

Rosanna smiled coyly at him as they emerged onto the road. And you are my Diana, Klaus thought, but did not speak. He knew the moment of parting was upon them; his mind sought ways to postpone it, but he knew he must keep his promise to her father.

"When shall we meet again, Klaus?" In her innocence, she was making it more difficult for him. "We have so much to talk about."

"I don't know – we are very busy with battle exercises." He swung himself up into the saddle and looked down at her, his mind seeking to hold forever the image of her face.

"I could cycle down to Velletri." Yes, he thought, please cycle to me tomorrow as quickly as you can, but these were not the words that came from his lips.

"No, that would be unwise, given what happened." He felt he could surely see disappointment on her face. "Besides, my division will be on the move soon." Lie was following lie, and he was powerless to stop it. He brought the reins through to his left hand and was about to spur the animal when he saw her hand raised toward him.

"It was very nice talking to you, Klaus." He reached out to her hand and was surprised that she grasped his tightly. "*Buona fortuna!*"

Their hands slipped apart, and he saluted her as he goaded the mare to the trot. Some thirty meters along the road, he turned to see her still looking at him. He waved, then stabbed his spurs into the horse's flanks, and became angry with himself for imposing his frustration on his steed.

By the time he reached the outskirts of Velletri an hour later, Klaus knew what he wanted to do. All through his journey, his mind had been preoccupied with the vision of her, of her naïve charm and infectious enthusiasm. He would see her father and ask him to release him from his promise. But then there was the rationality that knocked on the side door of his mind, telling him that it was all futile, that no good could come of it. The battle was still raging in his mind as he turned the mare down the street off the piazza. Gunther was anxiously waiting outside the taverna where he was billeted. As Klaus approached, the sergeant leapt up and hastened towards him.

"Thank God you're back, boss!"

"What's the problem, Gunther?" Klaus dismounted and threw the reins over the pommel. "I'm not late."

Gunther clutched at his sleeve. "There have been new orders. We're to strengthen the line down south in case the Allies land. The division is to move out."

"Where?" Klaus's memories of the past day were already disappearing.

"To Naples. The day after tomorrow."

Two days later.

Klaus had decided to withdraw the report. He was leaving for the front; his world was changing. The chances of his seeing the girl again were remote in the extreme. He felt his heart sink at the thought and his pencil doodled absent-mindedly on the order sheet in front of him as the memory of her walking with him through the woods drifted through his mind.

The pencil was suddenly slammed to the desk. He had to be realistic. The war was moving on, and it was taking him with it. It was no time to be acting like a moonstruck youngster. He pulled the Transportation Order across the desk and began the mental checklist to ensure his artillery unit was ready for the move south to Naples.

He had spent all morning at the army camp outside the town, checking over the four eighty-eights that were his charge. He'd inspected the guns with his lieutenants, pored over the maintenance reports and ensured that the stock of ammunition was both sufficient and safe. His attention to detail was admired by his officers and men, and they followed his example; in exercises, they had obtained the reputation of the most efficient battery in the corps. Klaus was insistent that his unit would prove their reputation on the field of battle that lay ahead.

The colonel had informed them that the change of plan was not a panic reaction but, with the Allies' landing imminent, the High Command had decided that it was necessary to make the defensive wall south of Naples as strong as possible. The whole of the 715th was to be committed. Klaus shuffled his papers into a neat pile and shook his head. Although he was sure of his troops' ability, he was not confident of the outcome. He remembered the colonel drawing his series of defensive lines across the backbone of Italy, each line retreating farther north. Wars are not won with defensive lines, he thought; the initiative now lay with the Allies, and for the first time, he began to think that it was unlikely that the war could be won.

He put such depressing thoughts aside as he stuffed the papers in his officer's attaché case and left his billet. He strode down the road that fell steeply from the *campanile*, wending its way down between the old shops to the piazza in front of the war memorial.

A wall of noise greeted him as he entered the piazza. Marching feet tramped on the street as formations gathered to wait for their transport; the exhaust fumes of trucks filled the air, their acrid smell making Klaus cough. A mounted troop went by at the trot, hooves clattering on the cobbles. Everywhere a cacophony of sound: engines roaring, orders shouted, men cursing, as the engine of war began to sense its power.

Klaus made his way through the throng, leaping out of the way of an armored troop carrier as he crossed the piazza. It was imperative that his guns be limbered up to their trucks. Gunther would have made sure that the infantry support unit was prepared....

The planning in his mind stopped. She was there, in front of the war memorial, her hands clutching her bicycle as her eyes scanned the press of men scurrying in the piazza. God, Klaus thought, she was looking for him! He pulled his cap down over his forehead, hoping she would not see him. Anger swept through him. She was mad, insane. Didn't she know the risk she was running? What if the *schweinhunden* whom he had put on report saw her?

"Klaus, Klaus!"

She had seen him. He tried to ignore her voice, stooping over, hoping he could reach the *Kommandutur* and escape.

"Klaus!"

Several heads turned. There was no escape. He had to stop her calling his name. He marched towards her, and the smile on her face vanished as he grabbed her roughly by the arm, pulling her and her bicycle away to the edge of the piazza.

"Don't you know you're causing an obstruction?"

He spoke to her in German, and she looked at him incredulously, shaking her head. He leaned closer to her, her fragrance full in his nostrils as he changed to her native tongue, whispering urgently in her ear.

"What are you doing here, Rosanna? Don't you understand the danger?"

"Don't handle me like that!"

She pulled her arm free, her eyes flashing reproachfully at him.

"I'm sorry, but don't you realize the risks?" He looked anxiously about him, and was relieved to see that everyone was busily engrossed in preparing for the division's departure. "Why have you come here?"

She leaned the bicycle against the wall, her chest still heaving as she recovered, rubbing her arm where he had grabbed her.

"I wanted to give you something before you leave."

"How did you know I was going to leave?"

"There was talk all over Genzano market this morning." She looked around her cautiously, now aware of the possible danger. "The soldiers there are leaving, too. *Papà* said that he heard that the Allies are about to land down south."

He saw the colonel emerge from the *Kommandatur* and look about the piazza as he waited for his staff car.

"Look, I must go now. Go home as quickly as you can."

She reached into the pocket of her dress, her hand emerging with a handkerchief tightly wrapped around a small object.

"I found it at the temple. It will protect you."

She moved to his side, so that she could press her gift into his hand unnoticed. She smiled at him wanly for a moment, then turned and was gone, scooting away on her bicycle. Klaus watched her until she slipped onto the bicycle seat and pedaled out of sight. She did not look back.

CHAPTER 23

Five months later. January 16th 1944.

Gunther watched the arc of the cigarette as he flicked it into the gathering dusk. His jowls were darkened by a three-day stubble, and weariness drained his body. For three weeks they had moved the guns from hilltop to hilltop. The temptation to prop himself against a gun wheel and go to sleep was strong, but the captain needed to know the news.

He picked his way through the gun emplacement. The barrels of the four eighty-eights pointed menacingly through their camouflage shrouds at the clouds scudding across the already-darkening January sky. The guns were silent now, but they had spent most of the day belching destruction on the enemy lines approaching Cassino. He lit another cigarette, cupping his hand against the wind, the light from the match finding the hollows in his stubbled, gaunt face.

He permitted himself a smile as he drew deeply on the cigarette. For four months the Allies had pushed against the Gustav line, but they had been held at bay and had been given a bloody nose. Gunther had regretted leaving behind the whorehouses when they abandoned Naples, but he had to admit that old man Kesselring knew his stuff. The Field Marshal had said the line was impregnable, and the Allies were going nowhere fast.

The men who were servicing the guns looked up at him, briefly, as they dragged up more shells for the next barrage. He didn't like to be the bearer of bad news, but he had heard something on the grapevine that could spell big trouble for the boss. The whine of an enemy fighter-bomber made him and the rest of the gun crews look anxiously upward, but the aircraft banked and wheeled away, obviously with other prey to find.

Damn *Jabos*!" He muttered under his breath. The Yankee fighter-bombers had found them out two weeks ago, and the unit had only just received the replacement for the guns that had been smashed up.

How he hated Italy. The dark scudding clouds denied the sun as the winter day approached its end. In Bavaria, it would be cold, too, but it would boast the warmth of home and the pleasures of his father's farm.

He could see the flames leaping up from the crackling wood fire in the hearth, but the persistent cold wind sweeping down the hillside robbed Gunther of his nostalgic vision. He turned up the collar of his greatcoat and stamped his feet. "Damn Italy!" He cursed to no one in particular. "And damn the war!" The mud clung to his boots as he made his way along the path to the camouflaged tent that served as the battery headquarters.

Klaus rubbed his eyes, fighting off the demands of sleep. The battery had moved its position twelve times in the past month, always trying to elude the enemy fighter-bombers that swept up from the south, seeking them out.

He threw his mud-bespattered tunic onto the cot bed in the corner of the tent, resisting the strong temptation to place himself beside it. There was still work to do, to analyze the observation spotter's report, to check ammunition supplies, and to work out the co-ordinates for the next day's dawn bombardment.

He lit the lamp on the folding table that served as a desk, taking care that the shade guided all the light downward; even with all the foliage and the camouflage net on the roof of the tent, he didn't want to give any clue to the American *Jabos* that sometimes flew dusk patrols looking for artillery emplacements. His fingers began to trace across the map grid as he read the spotter's report identifying possible targets.

He found the fingers of his left hand toying with the talisman hanging from his neck, and his train of thought changed. From the map emerged her face with those brown eyes looking at him confidently but softly, with a hint of concern. Her long, dark hair framed her face, gently enfolding her smile and the dimple beneath it, which also smiled. The vision of the two of them gazing down on the lake of Nemi filled his eyes, and he remembered the momentary feel of her body beneath him. He sighed, trying to force his attention back to the map, to the war, but his fingers persisted with the talisman.

Klaus hadn't really thought of her gift as a lucky omen. He had taken the small two-inch long icon of Diana and attached it to his dog tag chain, more as a token of remembrance, to recall the brief time they had spent together, than as a lucky charm. But perhaps there was something lucky about it after all. Rosanna had said it would protect him, and he thought of what had happened two weeks ago.

Two Allied planes had swooped down on the battery, catching them unawares as they moved along the road. A burst of fire from the first had swept the truck in which he was traveling; he had turned to speak to the driver and saw his head was missing. The truck had fallen into the ditch at the side of the road, and he remembered pulling himself up through the broken window to escape the flames. As he had jumped down onto the road, the second plane had made its run, and he had watched in horror as its bomb detached itself from the fuselage and made its way down. He had been transfixed as the tiny speck grew larger; somehow, he had felt it was destined to hit him, but it had fallen about a hundred meters short, exploding as it hit one of his guns. There had been a whine of shrapnel, and he had felt a tug at his shoulder. He looked down to see his epaulet had been torn off by the metal; the shoulder of his tunic had been ripped apart, but he had been unharmed.

Perhaps Rosanna had been right. A foot to the right, and the shrapnel would have torn off his head. Perhaps the icon of Diana did protect him. What else had she said? That the icon would bring him back to her. Was fate playing with him? He walked over to the cot and fished an envelope from the breast pocket of his tunic.

The envelope turned in his hand as he toyed with it before pulling out the enclosed document and unfolding it on the table. It was a furlough, a ten-day furlough, complete with all passes and transport authorization to Berlin, beginning on Saturday.

Soon, he would escape the war for ten whole days. Away from the smell of death and sweat, away from the fear and the grinding hopelessness of existence at the front. For some reason, he thought of the bath in his parents' home, and he smiled. A bath! He could wallow in the bath, smoking a fine cigar as he washed the grime of war from his body. Suddenly, he looked down at the photo of his mother on the table, and the smile left his face. Her last letter – his father rarely wrote – told of the never-ending air raids, of the bombs that had claimed their friends' houses and lives.

He tapped the furlough nervously. Perhaps the bath was no more; perhaps the house was no more, his parents…. He should go to see them, before the war consigned them – or him – to oblivion. But his fingers caressed the icon again and he tried to deny the first touches of a feeling of guilt.

The scrape of the camouflage tree branches dispelled his thoughts as Gunther's cheerless face came through the flap of the tent. The scant light from the lamp gave an almost skeletal look to the face of the sergeant, who saluted perfunctorily.

"Your face tells me we're on the move again." Klaus knew that Gunther's grapevine gave him most news before the actual orders filtered down. His wave dismissed the formalities, and Gunther took off his helmet before lighting a cigarette and sitting on the rickety cot.

"No, it's just the war – I'm totally pissed off with the war." Gunther sighed as he tossed his helmet onto the bed.

"What I wouldn't give now for a stein of beer served by some Bavarian barmaid with big tits and thighs like a heifer! And then a roll in the hay...." His voice trailed off as his imagination outran his tongue.

Klaus smiled, more in relief that his guns did not have to move that night than at the sergeant's crude humor.

"What would you give for that, my friend?" He chuckled slyly as he tossed the furlough envelope to Gunther.

"You lucky bastard!" Gunther spat on the floor as his eyes saw the heading of the document. "You fucking lucky bastard! How did you fix that?"

"I told Colonel Guttman that I hadn't had any leave for twelve months, and that I wished to see my parents. I'd hoped to get it for Christmas or the New Year. Late January is not the best time to visit Berlin," his face adopted a wry grin, "but it's better than a kick in the balls."

"You bet it's better than a fucking kick in the balls!" Gunther exploded, his face reddening with rage. "I've had no leave for twelve months, but I'm stuck here to fight this fucking war single-handed while the officer corps swans off to Berlin and those bastards in the *Wilhelmstrasse* swig champagne and roll with their whores on silk sheets...."

The sergeant's invective suddenly stopped. He stiffened and began to pore over the furlough. "You sure that this is signed by the Colonel?"

Klaus walked across and pointed to the bottom of the document. "There is the signature of the old man himself. He signed it three days ago."

Gunther's eyes looked searchingly at Klaus.

"Then you haven't heard?"

Klaus's brow furrowed.

"Heard what, Gunther?"

"The old man's gone – left this morning."

"Gone?"

Gunther stood up, his eyes looking at the muddy floor.

"He's been posted to the Russian front. The official story is that his experience is needed to stem the Russian offensive." Gunther sniffed and drew his sleeve across his nose.

"And?" Klaus looked searchingly at the sergeant.

"The grapevine says he's upset the powers-that-be. Some Nazi bigwig has been sticking his nose in."

Klaus's mind raced. Was it something to do with his report about the rape? Why hadn't he withdrawn it when he had had the chance?

"So, if I was you, I'd use that furlough while you've got a chance." Gunther coughed and spat again as he reached for his helmet. "Seems like his replacement is a bastard of the first order, if you can believe the word going round. They say he was on the Russian front, clearing out partisans. Dirty work. Not the sort of officer to get on the wrong side of."

Gunther put on his helmet and moved toward the entrance to the tent.

"Apparently, the new colonel has asked to see you specifically – you'll soon get the official invitation." Gunther chuckled ironically at his euphemism. He flicked the rim of his helmet as he lifted the tent flap.

"One moment, Gunther."

The sergeant stood at the tent entrance, holding the flap aloft, as Klaus scribbled on a piece of paper.

"I want you to get me as much of this stuff as you can by Saturday – no questions asked."

He pushed the list at Gunther, who scanned it quickly.

"That's easier said than done – I'll do my best."

Gunther's expression told that he knew why Klaus wanted the stuff.

"Look out for yourself, boss." The flap fell and Klaus was left alone.

Klaus's fingers nervously plucked at his talisman. He lifted the photograph of his mother and placed it face down on the table.

CHAPTER 24

The next day. January 17th 1944.

Klaus felt uncomfortable. He nervously tugged at his gloves as he strode through the gates of the town hall that served as the new headquarters. Gunther had been right, as ever. Colonel Guttman had been transferred to the Russian front, ostensibly to plug some gap in the command structure, and Klaus had been summoned by his replacement, who was, by all accounts, a nasty piece of work. He hoped it had nothing to do with his report.

He almost forgot to return the sentry's salute as he entered the building; his mind was so preoccupied with the coming encounter. Who was this new commanding officer? His hand reached for the order in his tunic pocket. Dressler. He had never heard the name, but Gunther had told him the word was out that he was a bastard, and Gunther's grapevine always knew these things.

Klaus removed his gloves as he entered the antechamber and gave his name to the adjutant. If it was about the report, he could be in big trouble. The adjutant gave him a glacial look, asked him to sit and wait, and disappeared through the high vaulted doors of what was clearly the new colonel's office. The tent and informality that had been the trademark of Colonel Guttman were clearly not suitable to the new man's style. Dressler obviously had a sense of his own importance, given that he had commandeered the huge council chamber as his headquarters.

His hand brushed at a speck on the sleeve of his tunic. He should have withdrawn his report long ago. Everyone – Gunther, Colonel Guttman, even his own rational thoughts – had advised him to do so; Gunther had almost pleaded with him. But he had not. He stood up in his anxiety, walked a few aimless paces and returned to his chair. He didn't know why he hadn't – he had only to go to the *kommandatur* office and sign a piece of paper. It was as if some inner voice kept telling him to keep going, to insist on pursuing the charges. Maybe Rosanna was right in her naïveté, maybe the goddess Diana was at work. He sat down again, surprised with himself that he gave any credence to her childlike beliefs.

But he thought of her and saw her, her lithe figure leading him through the oak trees to the Temple of Diana at the lakeside. He saw the beam of her smile, captured by the sun filtering through the trees, an innocent smile that gave him respite in his war-weary world. He looked down at his hands, the hands which she had held and, at the memory, a smile came to his own lips.

"Perhaps you could share the joke, *Hauptman*? I am in need of some amusement."

Klaus jumped as the shock of the voice scattered his daydream. He looked up at the tall, spare figure framed in the doorway to the chamber. His mouth fell open as he recognized the black uniform contrasted by the red and white swastika armband. *Schutzstafeln!* Dressler was SS!

The shock momentarily paralyzed Klaus. The pale blue eyes beneath the Spartan crop of blond hair seemed to fix him, like a rabbit before a ferret. The fine-lipped mouth beneath the eyes twitched at the edges and the eyebrows lifted slightly. Klaus realized he was still sitting. As his suspended reflexes returned, he leapt to his feet, his heels clicking as he reached for the peak of his cap in salute.

Dressler smiled mockingly. "I can see the army has not taught you to salute properly, *Hauptman*." The black uniform stiffened to attention, the arm raised rigidly with outstretched palm. "*Heil Hitler!*"

The blue eyes flicked over Klaus as he remained at attention.

"You do not return my salute, Schmidt?"

The question was softly spoken, but the tone only added to the menace in the voice.

"*Heil Hitler!*" Klaus returned the Nazi salute.

"Better." Dressler's voice was still low and soft, but he eased his head back and looked patronizingly down his nose at Klaus.

"And now, *Hauptman* Schmidt, we have much to discuss."

Dressler's extended arm lowered as it pointed an invitation through the large door, like some black vulture arrogantly inviting his prey to dinner. Klaus followed the black uniform as it moved with confident assurance around the large ornately-carved desk. Dressler turned and stood in front of a blazing wood fire burning in the hearth below a huge mirror that reached almost to the high vaulted ceiling. Klaus sat on the chair in front of the desk. Dressler turned to him with a look of mock surprise.

"I cannot remember asking you to sit, *Hauptman*."

Klaus leaped to attention. He knew Dressler's sort. Probably a clerk before the Nazis arrived, a ticket inspector or bank teller who took shit every day, some non-descript going nowhere. The Nazis thrived on such people and their impotence. Almost overnight, they were big-shots in uniform with the power of life-or-death over their erstwhile betters, a power they exercised with pleasure.

"Forgive me, Schmidt," he motioned Klaus to the chair, "I am forgetting my manners." His arm reached for a decanter on the table beside the desk.

"You will take a drink? I understand that Berlin University professors have a penchant for cognac."

Klaus shook his head, his fears mounting. Dressler had clearly done some research on him.

"A pity – it is, in fact, the finest Napoleon cognac." He poured a generous measure into a brandy goblet. "I have it shipped in from France." He swirled the amber liquid in the glass before raising it to his lips. The blond head went back as he rolled the drink around his tongue before swallowing.

"Ah! The pleasures of the conquerors!"

He toyed with the glass, turning it in his long fingers before setting it down.

"Aren't you proud to belong to the master race, Schmidt?"

Klaus felt Dressler's eyes were piercing him, probing for weakness.

"Of course." He replied automatically, sensing that Dressler believed his own propaganda.

Dressler flicked open the folder on his desk and shuffled through the papers.

"I see, *Hauptman*, that you are a fine artillery officer – in fact, according to Colonel Guttman, one of the best."

"Colonel Guttman was – I mean, is – a highly professional officer. His report of me is very generous."

"Well, he is now applying his professionalism on the Russian Front. I trust he will not extend his generosity to the communists!"

Dressler's hollow laugh rang back off the paneled walls, but he suddenly stopped and looked at Klaus coldly.

"But, behind Guttman's assessment of a fine artillery officer, I find this."

He held a piece of paper at arm's length as if it were repellant.

Klaus started. It was his report. Why hadn't he withdrawn it?

"Really, Schmidt, you said a moment ago that you were proud to be a member of the master race," he threw the paper on the desk, stabbing it with his finger, "yet here you defend *untermenschen*?" The last word was shouted with disgust.

"You do not understand, sir...."

"I understand perfectly, Schmidt." Dressler's fingers punched at the report with every word. "You chose to defend the so-called honor," his fist thumped upon the desk, "of an Italian whore!"

Klaus's knuckles whitened, but he said nothing.

"It is you who does not understand, Schmidt – these Italians are nothing – gypsies, dagoes, harborers of Jews."

"But weren't they our allies?" Klaus immediately regretted the rhetorical question as Dressler's face reddened with rage.

"And see how they rewarded our Fuehrer's friendship – with treachery! At the first crack of gunfire, the cowardly scum run with their tails between their legs into the arms of the mongrel Americans. Even though the Fuehrer has reinstated Mussolini in the north, I doubt that puffed-up overblown dago can do anything. The Italians are rotten to the core. *Untermenschen!*"

He slammed his empty glass down on the desk in his temper. Klaus felt fear seize his tongue. Dressler walked toward the grand fireplace at the end of the room, breathing deeply as he sought to control his rage. After a few moments, he turned and spoke in a more reasoned tone.

"Schmidt, you must push from your mind all these poisonous thoughts of liberalism."

The last word was sneered from the side of his mouth.

"Liberalism, pity, compassion are our enemies, as much as the Allies are. We are at war, Schmidt, and we are at war for the mastery of the world. For this prize, we have neither morals nor ethics, except those that bring us victory. We must do anything in order to win the struggle."

He refilled his glass and sat down.

"Or perhaps you would prefer the Jews and the communists to strut around in Berlin, as they used to before the Fuehrer cleared them out?"

Klaus shook his head perfunctorily, but wondered at the prospect of Dressler and his ilk ruling the world. Over the past few months, his own world, the world he thought he inhabited, was unraveling, beginning to fall apart. Dressler continued to fix him with his eyes.

"You see, Schmidt, we – the National Socialists, the Third Reich – must show no mercy if we are to win this war."

He picked up a pencil and tapped it repeatedly on the desk.

"For example, when I was on the Russian front, a German officer was shot by a communist partisan. What action do you think I took?"

He leaned forward across the desk. Klaus was mesmerized by the incessant tapping of the pencil.

"I take it, Schmidt, from your silence, that you would have been paralyzed into inaction."

Dressler expressed his disgust by tossing the pencil aside. He stood up, walked around to the front of the desk and eased his frame against it, looking down at Klaus.

"Well, let me tell you what a National Socialist officer does in such situations."

The arm of the black tunic reached behind him and opened a silver cigarette box.

"I suppose one shouldn't smoke French cigarettes," he smiled as he lifted his lighter, "but they are the very best."

He inhaled deeply, and then slowly blew out the smoke.

"I had a dozen of those foul Russian peasants rounded up at random and had them shot like the dogs they were."

He spoke in a matter-of-fact way, as if he were describing a soccer match. Klaus sensed Dressler was waiting for his reaction, but he sat immobile, forcing himself to fix his eyes on the supercilious gaze.

"Of course, I issued a proclamation that there would be no further shootings if the culprit was turned in."

He flicked his ash into an ashtray.

"No one came forward – sometimes there is a false sense of loyalty, even with *untermenschen*."

Dressler laughed and Klaus shuddered involuntarily, as if the laughter was shaking his bones. The brandy glass went again to Dressler's lips.

"So I had another dozen rounded up and had them shot, too."

He walked behind Klaus's chair, holding his glass to the light.

"This is excellent cognac."

Klaus kept his head rigidly forward, staring at the empty chair.

"Eventually, the message got through. The next day, some pathetic youth was handed over. Do you know, Schmidt, the creature pissed himself when he was brought before me?"

The black uniform moved into Klaus's line of vision as Dressler stubbed out his cigarette.

"To be honest, I wasn't sure he was guilty – perhaps he was some sacrificial lamb offered up by the spineless Russian peasants. But I had him shot, anyway." Dressler put down the brandy glass. "Publicly."

Klaus detected no trace of emotion in the voice as Dressler returned to his seat, leaned back and placed his black leather boots onto the edge of the desk.

"You must learn these lessons, Schmidt! If somebody is doing something you do not like, you smash them in the face," he emphasized his point by repeatedly smacking his fist into the palm of his hand, "time and time again, until they stop. This maxim must be applied to all the enemies of the Third Reich – the Jews, the communists, the Americans, everyone!"

He smiled and pulled his legs down from the desk.

"And thus endeth the first lesson, Schmidt." Dressler chuckled at his sacrilege and Klaus sprang to attention, clicked his heels and saluted, eager to escape.

"Apart from one thing." The long fingers retrieved Klaus's report and held it up.

"You have withdrawn this report." His fist clenched around the paper, screwing it up before tossing it onto the fire. "I have filed it where it belongs. Dismissed!"

Klaus seethed, but said nothing. He wanted to protest, but he realized the futility. Who would take his word against a high-ranking Nazi officer? And Dressler could make his life hell. He found himself walking to the door, demoralized, doubting himself, his beliefs, his courage.

As he reached the door, Dressler's voice followed him.

"I see you are going on leave."

Klaus half-turned in the doorway; the bastard was going to rescind his furlough.

"Enjoy it. Give my respects to your parents. And to Berlin."

Klaus closed the door, relieved as it shut out the sound of Dressler's voice from his ears. But it did not silence the inner voice that gnawed away at his soul.

The next day. January 18th 1944

"**P**apà, Papà, see what I found yesterday!"
Rosanna bounced excitedly into the parlor, where her mother and father were picking at their meager breakfast. She made her way to the table, opening her hand to reveal a tiny statuette, barely two inches long.

"Amazing!" Paolo put down his coffee cup to take the treasure gently from her palm while his other hand fished in his breast pocket for his glasses.

"It's a votive offering for Diana. Possibly first century B.C." He whistled softly in astonishment. "Have you tried to classify it?"

Rosanna nodded eagerly as her father turned the piece in his hand.

"Yes, I searched through the reference book in bed last night after I came back from the temple site. I found it close by where I found the other.…"

"You were out far too late last night."

Her mother's reproachful voice cut across Rosanna's excitement.

"The curfew had long since passed. You will find yourself in serious trouble one day!"

Rosanna's smile fell from her face. Paolo put down the idol and took refuge behind his paper from the coming storm.

"I'm nearly twenty, and quite capable of looking after myself!"

Rosanna snapped the words at her mother, whose countenance hardened as her growing rage drew breath.

"You ungrateful daughter!" She rose from her chair, waving an admonishing finger under Rosanna's nose. "Don't you care about our feelings?" Her fingers now drummed angrily on the table. "Don't you know there's a war going on?"

"I didn't ask for the war – wasn't it older people who are supposed to know better who caused the war?" Her voice was heavy with sarcasm.

"Rosanna, stop it. Your mother is right." Paolo lowered his paper, his voice gentle but firm.

Rosanna looked at him with surprise and gave him a pained look.

"I would expect you to understand, *Papà*."

The tears welled in her eyes as she grabbed the icon off the table and made toward the door. Her hurried footfall on the stairs was followed by the resounding slamming of her bedroom door.

Paolo removed his glasses and wearily pinched the bridge of his nose.

"Maria, surely you understand that she is young."

"I do understand, Paolo." There was a hint of tears in her eyes. "But I want her to have the chance to grow old!"

She brushed her hand across her eyes as she cleared the table, the plates clattering as she gathered them.

"You heard what happened to that young lad from Anzio – he was shot for breaking the curfew." Her voice broke to a sob. "I don't want that happening to Rosanna."

"But he was trying to steal from the German depot, Maria."

He knew it was a lame excuse.

"These Germans are capable of anything, Paolo." She looked at him, her eyes pleading. "She is all we have, *mio caro*, she is all we have."

Paolo embraced her, holding her hard to him, as if he were trying to squeeze hope back into her sobbing body.

"I will talk to her, Maria."

She snuffled as she freed herself from his grasp, wiping her nose on her apron.

"Well, I can't hang around here blubbering all day."

She blew her nose once more and finished washing the dishes in the sink.

"I'm off to see if I can find anything for supper tonight." She reached for her shawl from the peg by the hearth and wrapped it snugly around her neck. "It's unlikely, but maybe I can persuade that old rogue Colella to part with one of his scrawny chickens for a reasonable price."

She pulled the shawl around her as she opened the door, allowing the cold January air to swirl around her legs. She turned, fixing her husband with her eyes.

"Please talk to her, Paolo – she'll listen to you."

He nodded and smiled at her. The latch dropped, and she was gone.

Paolo pondered what to do, and decided against going to Rosanna's room; she would come to him in her own time, when her anger had abated. He settled in his chair to wait, and patted his pocket for the tobacco that he knew was not there. He hadn't had a decent smoke since....

His mind began to form a picture of Klaus. What had become of him? Not a bad man for a German. Saved Rosanna. Knew a lot about the ships. And had some of the finest tobacco. His pipe went to his mouth by habit, and, although it hadn't seen tobacco for two months, he sucked vigorously on it. Probably dead by now. He'd heard that the Germans were losing a lot of men, even though they were holding the Allies at Cassino. There was only a handful left in Genzano, as many had been sent south as replacements to plug the gaps. Yes, probably dead. Pity, he thought, as he took the pipe from his mouth and shook his head. Damned war.

The sound of movement upstairs stirred him from his thoughts, and he shuffled across the floor to the hearth, grabbing a log to throw onto the ailing fire. God, it was cold, even for January. Thank heaven there was no shortage of logs, even though it was almost impossible to get anything else; there was enough wood in the forest if the war lasted a hundred years, which he hoped to God it would not.

Sparks flew up the chimney to welcome the new log, and the flames began to lick around it greedily. Paolo rubbed his hands, and then, as was his habit, turned to appreciate the warmth on his backside. There were some pleasures not to be denied a man, he thought, and this was one. The footsteps above paced back and forth but showed no sign of coming downstairs. There was another pleasure; he walked around the table and delved into the bottom cupboards of the huge armoire that stood against the wall.

He grabbed the old gramophone lurking at the back of the cupboard, pulled it out and lifted it onto the table. It had been a wedding present from his parents. He brushed the dust away with the sleeve of his coat, opened it, and tested the needle. As he felt its prick, he remembered what he and Maria had enjoyed during their brief honeymoon in Rome, and returned to the cupboard to find the old records. There weren't many, and soon his fingers found the music he loved. Puccini's *Crisantemi.* Baskets of chrysanthemums had filled the church for their wedding so many years ago and the music was always their favorite. As he wound the handle of the gramophone, and slid the record with the evocative music onto the turntable, he heard Rosanna's footsteps on the stairs.

Her eyes were downcast as she came into the parlor, seeking to avoid his. She moved to the table and sat, her fingers toying with the treasure she had found. Paolo said nothing, enjoying the music that came from the gramophone as he tenderly conducted an imaginary orchestra in front of the fire. She smiled, and they listened together in silence until the clockwork motor wound down, and the music ground to a halt. Paolo folded the arm back into its rest position.

"You see, *Papà*, I was right." Her finger stabbed at the reference book. "The icon is from the first century B.C."

"Rosanna, you must not stay out after curfew."

She looked up at him, realizing that her diversion had not worked.

"But I am always careful, *Papà*."

"It does not matter whether you are careful or not – haven't you learned your lesson from what happened in Velletri?"

Rosanna looked down at the floor, her lips pouting a little as she knew she had no answer to give. Paolo believed he had made his point and broke the silence with a friendly grin as he picked up the icon.

"First century B.C., eh? That's quite a find!"

"Not only that, *Papà*," Rosanna spoke quickly, excitedly, "it's exactly like one I found some weeks ago!"

"You have a matching pair of these treasures?" Paolo looked at his daughter incredulously. "They must be worth a small fortune – where's the other one?"

He had said the wrong thing. Rosanna was not interested in the monetary value. But she said nothing, withdrawing into silence as she took the icon from his hand.

"You have got the other one, *mia cara*?"

"No, *Papà*." Her voice became emotionally charged. "I gave it to Klaus."

Paolo sat down, momentarily stunned. There had been no mention of the German since the day his unit moved out over four months ago and the old man had thought his daughter had forgotten all about Klaus's visit to the ships and the temple. The look on her face told him that there was still fond remembrance, possibly more.

"He will come back to us, *Papà*." The tone of her voice told him that she was not merely trying to convince herself, but was drawing on

something deeper, perhaps an article of faith that had become a touch-
stone of her existence.

Her eyes fixed upon him. "Diana will work through the icon to
bring him back. And now that I have the twin icon," she held up the
image triumphantly, "he must come back!"

Paolo pondered what he had to say. She reminded him of himself
when he was young; he, too, had been able to withdraw into a world of
his own, a world safe and secure with its skin of certitude that seemed
eternal until the claws of time scraped away at its mortality. Even now,
the ships offered him a temporary re-entry into that world.

"Rosanna," his voice was gentle, but earnest, "you must prepare
yourself for the fact that he may never come back."

"No, no!" She threw her head down onto her arms, her body sobbing.

Paolo blamed himself. He should have taken time to teach her the
ways of the world, but her innocence had shone brightly throughout all
her growing years, and he had foolishly fought to preserve that innocence. Perhaps he had done it selfishly, to remind him of a time long
since lost.

"War is a vicious monster, Rosanna." There was nothing he could
do to mitigate the knife thrusts of his words. "It can tear asunder people
who have been together for years, let alone for a few hours. It is an in-
strument of hate, bringing death and destruction to everyone." He
watched, saying nothing as her body continued to sob. After a few
minutes she suddenly stopped crying and got up from the chair. Her
eyes spoke of the hurt within her, but she looked at him defiantly.

"But war can also bring love, *Papà*." He dwelt on this paradox, but
said nothing, affording her more time to rebuild her defenses. "He will
come back, *Papà*, Diana will bring him back."

There it was again – that statement of blind faith, the impenetrable
wall that his words simply bounced off. His efforts had failed, and it
would be left to another to bring the real world crashing in on her
dreams. Perhaps in a year's time, when Klaus had not returned. For
now, he felt the need to console her, to offer her some recompense for
the hurt he had caused. His mind sought for the gift, and it came to him.

"Rosanna, can you come to the museum tomorrow – say about mid-
morning? I have something to show you."

She started to ask the obvious question, but he waved his index finger at her.

"No, it's a secret until tomorrow. Will you be there?"

She beamed her innocent smile and nodded. Paolo felt warm inside and returned her smile. He was going to show her the secret in the old chest. He was going to show her the Mirror of Diana.

The next day. January 19th 1944. 4.30 a.m.

K laus looked through the windscreen at the road ahead, barely visible in the narrow shaft from the hooded headlights picking out the edge of the road. The driver was huddled over the wheel, making his way carefully through the darkness, his eyes not moving from the road.

"We only make this supply run at night, nowadays." The driver spoke from the corner of his mouth. "Any movement during daylight, and the American *Jabos* come down, shooting at anything in sight." He emphasized his point by making a swooping movement with his hand and clicking his tongue against the roof of his mouth to imitate cannon fire.

"You're lucky to get a lift." He glanced at his watch. "Should be in Rome about seven – just after first light."

Klaus decided not to talk of the way his artillery unit had been shot up twice in the last month; no doubt his own men would prefer to be driving trucks.

"So you've got a furlough back home?" The truck driver shifted gear. "I'd give my right arm to get a trip back home. Ah, Helga…" he gave a sigh as he vanished into his reverie.

Klaus turned up his greatcoat collar. The cold night air blew in through the door, which had long since lost its window. He didn't feel like small talk, but he thought it wise to humor the driver.

"It's only for ten days. By the time I get to Berlin, it will be time to come back."

"One day in bed with Helga would be enough for me. You married?"

"No. I'm going to see my parents." Klaus saw the young driver shake his head as he flicked his cigarette out of the truck.

"What a waste of a pass!" How are you going to get to Berlin?"

"With a bit of luck, I'll get one of the military trains out of Rome."

Perhaps he should go to Berlin after all. He had written a long letter to his mother, telling her it was impossible to get away from the front. It was a lie. He stamped his feet against the cold. Much of his life was becoming a lie. His duties were performed mechanically, like a robot; he had lost the belief in the possibility of victory.

Worse, he had lost belief in himself. He hadn't had the guts to stand up to Dressler. Now he was lying to his mother. Was he really doing that for a young woman whom fate had briefly tossed across his path? Would he rather see her than his mother? He closed his eyes, trying to shut out his thoughts.

It was six in the morning when the driver nudged him awake. There was a trace of pre-dawn light in the sky, reaching from behind the mountains in the east, as the driver pulled over at Velletri to refuel.

"Any chance of a coffee?" The driver handed his papers to the guard who inspected them.

"We have some of that *ersatz* crap."

The driver looked across at Klaus.

"Won't be a minute. Need to take a leak. Want some coffee?"

Klaus smiled wryly and shook his head. Drinking *ersatz* coffee was like drinking something dredged up from the bottom of the river Tiber.

The engine died as the driver turned the key and jumped down from the cab, leaving Klaus to ponder the images that continued to visit him: Paolo, his mother and father, Rosanna - all ran amok through his mind. Maybe he should go back to Berlin. Choices, choices. He wished he were back in the university, where the ability to make decisions was nothing more than a philosophical discussion.

He lit a cigarette and kicked the two bags beneath the seat. In one were the provisions that Gunther had begged, borrowed, or, more likely, stolen from the Quartermaster: cheese, tobacco and – heaven knew how he had got them– a dozen plump sausages. In the other were some old civilian clothes that he had bought with a bribe of a carton of cigarettes to the old Italian who worked in the officers' mess: jacket, pants, an old shirt, and one of those big caps so favored by the Italians. He hoped the stuff was big enough to fit him.

The sun was lifting itself over the peaks of the Alban Mountains as the truck lurched its way through the outskirts of Genzano, but it was still cold, the mist hanging in the air. The sentry at the checkpoint waved the truck down. Klaus shuffled forward.

"Ok, I'm getting out here." His hands reached for his bags as the truck pulled over.

"I thought you wanted to go to Rome?" The driver's face was full of questions.

"I've an old friend stationed here." Klaus tossed his bags from the truck and jumped down. "I want to see him first. He'll run me into Rome later." He threw a packet of cigarettes to the driver.

"Papers please, *Hauptman*." The guard looked at his epaulette, saw the rank and saluted.

Klaus thrust the documents into the soldier's hand. "I'm going to see an old friend stationed at Nemi before I go on to Berlin."

"Very good, *Hauptman*." The guard returned the pass and saluted again. "But you may find your friend has gone. Most of the units have been moved up to the front." He threw a thumb over his shoulder, pointing south. "We are barely more than company strength here in Genzano. Everything is needed for the front."

"I'll take my chances." Klaus picked up his bags and began to walk along the main road.

He remembered the road well from his visit months ago, but wished he had the horse again, despite its fractious spirit. The bags were heavy, and he was sweating by the time he reached the crossing in the town center. No one was about, as the curfew had still some minutes to run. He hoped the clip of his heels on the cobbles would not draw noses to windowpanes.

He turned right off the main road and walked up the hill until he found the path leading down to the lake. That, too, was deserted. After a few minutes of struggling with the bags, he paused, laying them on the ground. The trees, devoid of leaves in their winter slumber, afforded him through their unclad branches a view of the lake, although the early morning mist hung over it like a ghost reluctant to leave the night, despite the sun's promptings.

Klaus lit a cigarette and watched its smoke intertwine with the mist. Why was he here and not on a train to Berlin? It wasn't her, he assured himself, despite the pang he felt as her face momentarily appeared between him and the lake; maybe it was the ships – yes, that was it, the ships, the pull of immortal history. He flicked the cigarette away and shook his head. The human mind had such a power for self-deception, he thought. How to avoid the truth, postpone decisions.

He walked a little more before he spotted a small clearing behind the trees edging the pavement. Slowly and carefully, he looked around him to make sure no one was watching him before he hauled the bags into the clearing and began to take off his uniform.

CHAPTER 27

The same day. 8.30 a.m.

There were too many of them already. Paolo got off his bike and eyed the scruffily-dressed vagrant sitting on the low wall in front of the museum. The refugees were everywhere. It wasn't their fault: they had fled from the relentless tide of war that was slowly but inexorably inching its way north. The Germans had become brutal since the declaration of war, and these southerners had suffered badly. Even though the privations had affected those living in the countryside around Rome, the refugees from the south had nothing left; they were sullen, bitter and without any hope. The abrasion of war had scraped away the thin veneer of civilization. Some were living in the caves and grottos at the edge of the lake, and the townspeople had been alarmed at the tales told and retold in the streets and the church. Extra locks had been fitted and he himself checked out the museum more often. He knew they should be offered the milk of human kindness, but there was little to spare. What would happen to him, Maria and Rosanna when the war, the fighting war, reached them?

Paolo had few charitable thoughts as he reached down, pulled off his bicycle clips and walked towards the shabby bundle of clothes sitting upon the wall. Being in the caves was one thing, but here was one right in front of the museum.

"Be off with you," his hand flapped dismissively, "there's nothing here for…"

He stopped suddenly as the old hat turned toward him, revealing the handsome young face that sat beneath it. His neck craned forward.

"Is it you? Klaus?"

Paolo was not sure. He remembered a younger face. The skin looked sallow and the lines around the eyes and mouth were etched deeper. The eyes seemed to be set deeper, too, looking out from above dark patches of fatigue. The face smiled, a hand came up to remove the peasant cap, revealing the short blond hair and dispelling any doubt.

"Yes, it's me, Paolo." The old clothes walked toward Paolo, a hand extending from the sleeve.

For some unknown reason, the thoughts of Rosanna and her icons came to Paolo's mind, and the distraction made him stand, his mouth agape, looking at Klaus's outstretched hand. He grasped it warmly.

"What on earth are you doing here, Klaus?" His eyes flicked upward to look at the wall of the town, checking for prying eyes.

"I've got a furlough, so I thought I'd come to see you and the ships again."

The German broke the eye contact by looking past Paolo to the museum, as if searching for something. Paolo knew at once that Klaus had not come back to see him and the ships; or, if he had, it was merely an excuse. He had come to see Rosanna. Paolo felt anxious.

"But where's your uniform?"

Paolo's eyes ran up and down the shoddy clothes tightly squeezed around Klaus's large frame.

"I've packed it away – I thought it would avoid misunderstanding."

A cold gust blew in from the lake and Klaus shuddered.

"You must be freezing." Paolo pulled the museum keys from his pocket. "Come with me – I'll soon have the stove going."

Klaus picked up his bags and followed Paolo into the museum, looking up at the great ships as they made their way through the hall to the room at the back.

"The ships are still safe, I see. Aren't you ever worried about air raids and bombs?"

Paolo pushed an old paper and some dry tinder wood into the stove.

"I'm always worried about bomb attacks." He stood up as the flames took hold in the stove. "But we haven't seen much of the Allied planes."

"I can tell you I have seen plenty." Klaus dropped his bags. "Enough for a lifetime."

The room began to get warmer, the crackle of the burning wood and the heavy smell of the smoke bringing some comfort to the two men. Paolo turned to warm his backside.

"Excuse me while I warm up my brains!" His laugh echoed back off the bleak concrete walls. "I would offer you some coffee, Klaus, but…" he shrugged his shoulders, his arms half raised, palms uppermost.

"I have some here!" Klaus's hands delved into one of his bags. He opened the packet and handed it to Paolo, whose eyes bulged incredulously.

"Mother of God!" The Italian thrust his nose into the open packet

and inhaled deeply. "Even the smell is delicious. We haven't seen anything like this for months."

"It's yours," Klaus smiled, "so long as I can have a cup."

A coffee pot was produced from nowhere, the water was soon boil-
ing on the stove, and both men sat quietly for a moment, savoring the
flavor of the coffee. Paolo looked across at Klaus and chuckled as he
eyed the motley collection of old clothes.

"You know, you could pass for a southerner – but you need a sullen
look on your face."

His brief smile faded as he put down his cup and fixed Klaus's
eyes; there was an awkward silence as he sought for his words.

"Klaus, your return here is most difficult for me." He stood up and
shuffled uncomfortably, unable to press his argument. "How long is
your furlough? Where are you going to stay?"

He knew he was avoiding the issue, raising foolish logistical points
to mask his real concern. His anxiety drove his hands to pat his pockets,
a force of habit as he searched for his pipe, but he had only an empty
bowl to suck upon.

His thoughts were sent into more turmoil as Klaus reached again
into his bag and pulled out a packet of tobacco. Paolo hesitated. He
should say no, refuse to have any obligations, but his hand reached out
for the packet.

"It's only for ten days." Klaus lit up a cigarette. Paolo broke the
seal and buried his nose in the packet. Coffee and tobacco. Nectar and
ambrosia. He filled his bowl quickly, tamping the tobacco down before
pushing a piece of paper into the stove.

"Perhaps I could stay here?" Klaus waved his arm about the clut-
tered room. "I need only a few blankets."

Paolo sucked his pipe and drew on it deeply, holding the smoke in
his lungs. It was a preposterous idea, but what could he do? He knew
the emotions that were driving Klaus; he remembered when he had
been a young man, and had set his heart on Maria. Even if he refused,
he knew Klaus would find a way, any way, of meeting Rosanna and the
problem then would be worse. He puffed on the pipe again and sipped
his coffee.

"I could even do a few odd jobs – tidying up, cleaning out. You
could say you hired me."

Paolo knew he could no longer skirt the problem that worried him.

He lifted himself from his chair and stood facing Klaus, forcing himself to look him in the eye.

"Klaus, you do respect Rosanna, don't you?"

He saw Klaus's face stiffen as the impact of the question struck him.

"But of course." There was a slight stammer in the voice and the face wore a hint of affront.

Paolo broke off from the eye contact and sucked earnestly on his pipe.

"Good. You know why I ask you?" It was more a statement than a question and Klaus remained silent.

"I could ask you to honor your promise not to see her – and I know you would – but my age makes me a little wise in the ways of the world." He tapped the side of his nose. "Once Rosanna finds out you're here…." He stopped as he caught the look on Klaus's face. He had probably said too much already.

"She is very young, Klaus." His pipe was going out and he began to grind some more tobacco between the palms of his hands. "Young people are very headstrong. The war has perhaps made you older than your years." He tapped nervously on the tobacco as he refilled his pipe, awkwardly searching for his words. "But you are still young."

Klaus stiffened. "I assure you that I am a man of honor, Signor Giraldi."

Paolo brushed aside the rigid formality.

"I have no doubt of that, Klaus, after what you did to save her." He leaned forward and his voice became gentle, but firm, as a father speaking to his son. "But I know, Klaus," he pointed his pipe at Klaus to emphasize his point, "that you didn't come back merely to see the ships."

Klaus's attempted protest was waved aside.

"Yes, I know you appreciate history, and you find the ships interesting – from an academic point of view. But you don't love them," he brought up his hand and jabbed his heart with his thumb, "here, as I love them."

Klaus looked down, shame-faced, as Paolo's eyes watered.

"But, much as I love the ships, I don't love them as much as I love Rosanna." His voice caught on his daughter's name. He returned to his stool, shaking his head as he struggled with his emotions. The smoke rose as he drew on his pipe; Klaus remained silent as the old man breathed deeply, composing himself.

"Klaus, I know I can't stop you from seeing Rosanna, even if I wanted to, but I beg you to take care. There is so much evil in the world today, and the war has created people who would sell their souls for…" he turned his pipe in his hand and smiled wryly "…a pipeful of tobacco."

"It was not meant as a bribe – it's a gift!" Klaus's voice was sharp and he immediately wished he had not spoken. But his own emotions were in turmoil and he thought about leaving at that moment, before he saw Rosanna. Perhaps Paolo was right. It could only lead to trouble.

"Of course, of course." Paolo went over to Klaus and clasped him on both arms in reassurance. "Are all Germans so formal? You must relax, Klaus."

"I'm sorry. I could blame the war, but …" Klaus left the sentence hanging for a moment. "But we Germans also know how to enjoy ourselves! I have also brought some wine. And some sausages! Perhaps we can have a feast tonight."

Paolo's eyebrows raised and he realized he was salivating at the prospect of such food. With great difficulty, he thrust the vision of the sausages aside.

"All in good time, Klaus, but first we must make sure we get your story right if you're going to stay here for a few days. First, your name."

He turned his back to the stove and rubbed his backside.

"Carlo – yes, that's it – we must call you Carlo!" Paolo laughed. "You see how quickly my brain works when it is warm." He turned again to warm his hands. "Now we must find somehow to make you different from those peasants who live in the caves over there." He waved his hand toward the north shore of the lake below Nemi.

"You have refugees here already?" Klaus looked surprised. "Perhaps I can be a refugee?"

"Too many – but they're all poor, and don't go wandering the countryside with tobacco, wine and sausages! And they don't speak with your upper crust accent!"

"Perhaps I could be a refugee professor from Naples, escaping…" a smile crossed Klaus's lips "…the Germans."

Paolo drew on his pipe, nodding. "It just might work. But stay here.

Carry on with the drawing you started last time, anything, but don't go wandering off into the town, and don't speak unless you're spoken to."

The knock on the glass of the museum door startled them. Paolo motioned Klaus into the shadows, his voice dropping to a whisper.

"Stay here. I'll see who it is."

Klaus listened to Paolo's footfall as he crossed the concourse and heard the key turn in the lock.

"*Papà*, here I am. What is the secret you have to show me?"

It was her voice. The painful joy Klaus had felt on that day in Velletri when she had pressed the icon into his hand returned. His hand moved to the token around his neck. He could not resist leaving the office and looking down the concourse between the great ships towards the door beyond the entrance vestibule.

He saw only her silhouette; the winter sun had shaken off the shackles of the mist and was beaming down from behind her as it fought to climb in the sky above the southern rim of the crater of the lake. The low rays bounced off the surface of the lake, enveloping her in an aura that danced around her, the light shimmering around her form.

Klaus stood transfixed, overwhelmed by the image that hung in the air for a brief moment. Suddenly, she saw him and her voice rang out.

"Klaus! Klaus! You have come back. Praise be to Diana!"

CHAPTER 28

Rosanna emerged from the aura of the sun, her soft shoes walking quickly towards Klaus. As she neared, she remembered her father's presence, and stopped a few feet away from him, reining in her happiness. Her head turned towards her father, shuffling his way across the concourse behind her.

"You see, *Papà*, I told you Klaus would come back." She turned to Klaus. "But where is your uniform, Klaus?"

"His name is Carlo." Her father saw the puzzlement on her face. "We'll explain everything later. Now, come, I have something to show you."

He beckoned them through the door of the museum and looked to ensure no one was about before carefully locking it behind him.

"Follow me." Paolo led them to the storeroom at the back of the museum and dragged the chest from its hiding place. He paused for a moment, as if he were about to change his mind, then opened the chest and pulled out the mirror. He offered it to Rosanna.

"It's wonderful, *Papà!*" She turned it in her hand. "I have never seen anything so beautiful."

She held the mirror at an angle, so that she could see Klaus's face. He saw her face framed in the shiny surface and looked for long moments into her eyes until she smiled. He reached out for the mirror, took it and turned it in his hand.

"It's Roman, isn't it?" He looked at Paolo, who nodded.

"Yes, but don't ask its provenance. You are aware of the legend of Diana and Acteon depicted on the obverse?"

Klaus looked closely at the back of the mirror. "You mean when Diana turns Acteon into a stag to be killed by his own dogs?"

"Quite so. She was wise and set duty before love."

As he spoke, Paolo looked directly into Klaus's eyes. After a few moments, Klaus averted his eyes and looked down. Paolo was sure he had grasped the message, but he noticed that Rosanna seemed to draw a discreet veil over this aspect of her heroine goddess, choosing to be absorbed in the exquisite artistry of the ancient work.

"It must remain a secret." Paolo took back the mirror and returned it to the old chest.

"But why have you shown it to us, *Papà?*"

"So you know where it is hidden." He turned the key in the lock of the chest. "In case anything happens to me."

"Don't be so morbid, *Papà*." Rosanna chided her father. "Nothing will happen to you."

"One never knows."

Rosanna shrugged aside the somber thought, as if she did not wish to contemplate it.

"Klaus, I never did show you the old Via Sacra. Let's go and see it." She had already turned towards the museum door. Klaus made to follow her, but he caught Paolo's meaningful glance and waited for the old man to nod his acceptance.

"And his name is Carlo!" Paolo shouted after her as they left the museum.

One hour later.

Paolo filled his pipe for the third time as he peered through the window at the couple sitting on the wall outside the museum. He knew he should ration the tobacco, but it had been so long since he had enjoyed a decent smoke. Besides, he felt happy. Quite why he should feel happy he did not know, but the war seemed so far away as his hand swept away the smoke to look at them. Rosanna was waving her arms excitedly as she talked, a broad smile on her face. Yes, she was happy, and Paolo was pleased. He saw Klaus smile, too, nodding at Rosanna's words; yet the German still sat stiffly. He would have to talk to him, otherwise his disguise would not work: no Italian sat like that.

But he felt he could trust Klaus; he was a fine man, a principled man. And he had someone to whom he could talk about the ships - like the tobacco, that pleasure had rarely been enjoyed lately. He wondered if there were other good Germans like Klaus; the tales he had heard of the atrocities in Rome made it hard to believe. Maybe Klaus was a freak happening, someone unusual tossed up by the tide of war.

As he puffed on his pipe, he wondered what young people found to talk about for so long. He closed his eyes and remembered that day in the gardens of the *Villa Borghese* just after the last war, when he and Maria had gazed out on the city of Rome lying before them. They had talked incessantly then. About what was to come, about the hopes and joys that lay in the future.

He opened his eyes. Those hopes were there, sitting on the wall, smiling at the young man by her side. What hopes were there for Rosanna in this war-savaged world? Was there any place in her future for the young man beside her? He knew an old man should not trample on the hopes of the young, but he was filled with apprehension. He tapped the final ashes from his pipe.

He knew he should tell Maria, but he also knew he could not. She would not understand and there would be all manner of scenes; it would upset her if she knew. He was lying to himself. If she found out, there would be hell to pay; if she found out, he'd have to face it out, but there was no need to stir up a hornet's nest by choice. With luck, maybe the usual prying eyes of Nemi would be looking elsewhere.

"*Signor Giraldi, Signor Giraldi.*"

The thin reedy voice cut across his thoughts and he turned to see Gianni's frail form framed in the doorway.

"*Signore,* why has the German officer come back? Why hasn't he got his uniform? Has he brought some more sandwiches with him?"

Paolo grabbed the urchin and tweaked his ear. "Ssh! It's a secret." He would ask Rosanna to talk to the rascal. He would listen to her. Otherwise, he saw a long period of bribery before him.

The same day. Late evening.

"Who is he? What's he doing at the museum?"

Paolo sighed and shrank into himself. There would be no escape from his wife's probing.

"I suppose that Gianni has been telling tales."

He had hoped Rosanna would have been able to sweet talk the boy.

Maria did not pause as she pounded the washing in the sink, but she turned her head, her eyes ablaze with her anger.

"That little good-for-nothing? Nearly every word he says is a lie!"

She wrung the wet sheet in her hands as if she were breaking the rascal's neck, her knuckles whitening.

"As a matter of fact, Francesca told me after mass." She slapped the sheet on the draining board. "It seems her husband heard from someone who was collecting firewood down by the lake."

Paolo picked up his book and tried to hide behind it. There was always some busybody poking his nose into other people's business. He hoped his web of lies would not ensnare him further.

"And don't think hiding behind that book will help you!"

"He's just a refugee from down south."

His remark was intentionally casual, but he knew, once he had spoken, that it was a red rag to a bull.

"What, one of those useless ne'er-do-wells that live in the caves? You'd better watch him!"

"No, actually, he's very keen to do some work in the museum. In fact, he's staying there. I thought we might spare him some blankets to keep him warm at night."

"Work?"

The sheet slapped loudly upon the draining board, and Paolo began to realize that he was not a good liar.

"And what are you going to pay him with? With the way prices are at the moment, our life savings – such as they are – will be gone in a few weeks."

Paolo decided to be silent, in the hope everything would die down.

"And blankets, is it? You're letting him stay in the museum? You'd better be careful – he'll steal your precious ships!"

He winced. Silence clearly did not work. He looked for any words to stop the tirade.

"He doesn't want paying. He's got money. He just wants to lie low. He's not one of the usual refugees - he's a professor from the University of Naples, on the run from the Germans. Something political, I guess, but I didn't think it right to ask."

The huge lie he had agreed upon with Klaus was let loose.

Maria stopped the pounding and came over to him, wiping her hands on her apron.

"A professor? Why didn't you say so? I thought he was one of the riff-raff who lives in the caves."

Paolo felt relieved. 'Professor' had worked.

"We must help this professor – as we would any good Italian on the run from those German swine."

She lifted the pan from the stove and tipped the brown fluid into two cups.

"Did he give you this wonderful coffee?"

Paolo nodded, pleased that her anger had passed. "I told you he had money." He would tell her about the sausages tomorrow.

Later, Paolo lay restless in his bed, sleepless as he wondered why he had lied to his wife. Perhaps he had gone too far; he wished he had not started the masquerade. He should have sent Klaus on his way.

"Paolo?" His wife's whisper came from her bed.

"Yes?" He yawned, hoping to keep the conversation short.

"Perhaps, if he is a professor, he might be able to do something for Rosanna. After the war, you know."

"Of course, *mia cara*, go to sleep."

After the war, he thought. When would that be? And he wondered what his wife would say when she found out the professor was not some old intellectual, but a fine–looking young man. And, Heaven help him if she found out he was a German.

The next day. January 20th 1944.

"**S**it still – stop fidgeting!"

Klaus looked up briefly from his drawing pad as his pencil brushed lightly across the paper.

"But it's freezing!"

Rosanna pulled her coat tightly around her. She had difficulty holding the pose, stamping her feet to keep out the cold.

"Don't you understand that I am immortalizing you?" Klaus chuckled, mischievously. "One has to suffer for the sake of art!"

"Mona Lisa didn't have to suffer this cold – that's why she's smiling." Rosanna craned her neck. "Can I see it yet?"

Klaus shook his head. "No, you know it's bad luck."

He reached for a softer pencil to trace the line of her jaw. Although the late January sun gave little heat, it had climbed enough to paint her face with light and shade, as it did the statue of the goddess Diana in the background. His fingers fought against the cold, the pencil working assiduously, caressing her image onto the paper. God, she was beautiful, he thought; she made the statue little more than an afterthought. He despaired of capturing the proud, haughty angle of her head, of setting the warm whiteness of her face against the contrast of her long, black hair. He desperately wanted to do justice to the sketch, but his fingers were beginning to be betrayed by the cold.

"Just another couple of minutes. And stop pouting. Goddesses do not pout."

"I was thinking about the Mirror of Diana that *Papà* showed us yesterday. What did you think about it?"

He recalled how he had turned the treasure in his hand, holding it at an angle so he and Rosanna could see each other; he remembered how she had run her hand over the sculpted obverse. He also remembered Paolo's thinly-disguised message about duty and love, but he decided not to mention it.

"It is a magnificent work of art – it must be kept safe until the war is over."

She blew on her fingers. "Will the war be over soon, Klaus?"

"Yes."

A lie needed only one word; the war could go on for years, but he did not wish to dampen her hopes.

"Did you know I did a sketch of Gianni yesterday? Somehow, I managed to keep him still for a few minutes."

He rummaged in his knapsack.

"Here it is." He handed it to her.

"It's very good. You show him as the scamp he is. Can I see mine now?"

"No, you know you must wait until tomorrow. I think I'll give Gianni this sketch – it will be something to remember me by after the war."

He pushed the drawing back into his bag.

Rosanna jumped up from her seat.

"Remember you? You are going? You won't come back?"

Klaus realized he was treading on dangerous ground.

"Of course I'll come back."

He changed the subject abruptly. "Your father tells me that he has told your mother about me."

"Oh, yes." The smile returned to her face, and to the dimple on her chin. "She's very impressed that you are an Italian professor from Naples – do you know she wants *Papà* to invite you to the house?"

He laughed, but did not answer; his fingers moving quickly as he sought to put the final touches to the sketch.

"Klaus?"

"If I am to come to your house, you'd better start calling me 'Carlo,' unless you want your mother to have a nasty surprise."

"She wants you to come, but she is ashamed because there is so little food to offer you."

"But you have forgotten that I am a refugee. I am used to privation." He held the pencil in front of him, slanting it to get the right angle. "You must remember the story, or there will be trouble."

He tutted to himself as he struggled to get the line of her chin correct.

"Besides, I have helped out by giving your father some sausages."

"Sausages? Did you say 'sausages,' Klaus?"

"*Carlo* said 'sausages.' Don't open your mouth so wide – I'll lose the charms of your face." He pointed down to the drawing.

"Where did you get the sausages?"

"They're a present from the Fuehrer."

"A present? Stop making fun of me," she paused, deliberately, "Carlo."

"But it's my birthday tomorrow. You're pouting again."

"You're still making fun of me, Klaus. Birthday, indeed!"

"Carlo is making fun of you – but January 21st is Klaus's birthday." He made a last few lines with his pencil and closed the pad.

"You can't just tell me like that – what am I going to give you for your birthday?"

He stood up and put the pad in his bag.

"Perhaps one of those lovely smiles when you see the drawing."

"It's finished?" She leapt up and clapped her hands. "Let me see."

"No."

He enjoyed teasing her. She came over to him and slipped her hands under his jacket, around his waist. He felt her warmth against him.

"Please, Klaus, show it to me." Her brown eyes pleaded with him,.

"No. Carlo will show it to you. At his birthday party. Tomorrow."

He leant forward and kissed her gently on her forehead.

The next day, January 21ˢᵗ. Early afternoon

Maria's spoon stirred vigorously. She had managed to persuade Sofia Ruffo to part with a cupful of semolino. It had cost her heavily, forcing her to dig into her meager savings to get it from the old crow, but it would be worth it. She had to have something to serve with the sausages, and baked *gnocchi di semolino* seemed right.

The sausages! Her eyes feasted again on the dozen *cotechini* lying on the table. Paolo had said they were a gift from the refugee professor; heaven knew how he had got them and she wasn't going to ask. The ache in her stomach returned as she looked at the sausages, their smooth skins plump to bursting with pork. She forced herself to return to preparing the gnocchi, checking that her apron protected the black high-collared dress that she had recovered from her old chest.

Maria felt she had been right to agree to her husband's request to treat the professor to a birthday dinner; she could do little else, given that the guest had provided the main course. Another sidelong glance at the sausages proved irresistible and she crossed herself for yielding to the temptation. She wished she had a little more cheese to add to the gnocchi, but beggars could not be choosers and, even if he were a professor, he was still a refugee.

Maybe he could do something to help Rosanna after the war – pull a few strings, something like that. Her spoon moved to the other pan to stir the *pappa col pomodoro*; a bread soup was a poor dish to set before a guest, but along with a little fried onions and garlic, together with the jar of tomatoes she had preserved at the end of the summer, the humble ingredients could be transformed into a thick and delicious *zuppa*.

She looked in the mirror and fussed with her hair. They had neglected Rosanna's education. Paolo had done much to teach her himself after she had left school, but it had been all airy-fairy notions, not suitable to stuff into a young girl's head. The girl was intelligent and bright, but she was almost twenty and still lived in a dream world of her own. Maria's sinewy hands turned the pestle to grind the rosemary in the mortar.

It hadn't turned out at all the way she thought it would. She had hoped that Rosanna would marry one of the better young men from nearby, one with prospects. But the war had taken them all away, and, anyway, Rosanna had shown not the slightest intention to settle into the way of life that had been her mother's lot. It was like that with young people nowadays. The war had changed everything.

Perhaps the professor – she sought the name Paolo had told her – Carlo, yes, that was it – perhaps Professor Carlo could help find a place at the university after the war.

She tipped the rosemary onto a saucer and pulled on the handle of the water pump, washing her hands and wiping them on her apron. Perhaps Rosanna could learn languages – she always had her head stuck in a foreign book. Or maybe medicine. Yes, a nurse, she would make a fine nurse. Maybe after the war...she stopped suddenly and sighed, her chin falling onto her chest.

She had been daydreaming. After the war. It might be ten years away. Father Berutti had whispered after Sunday mass that it could be over soon: the Allies had reached Cassino; soon the German swine would be gone forever. But they had said the same after the landings at Salerno the previous September, and the Germans were still in Nemi four months later. In fact, it was worse. Now the Germans stole whatever they wanted – food, wine, whatever they took a fancy to, and woe betide anybody who tried to stop them. And young Italian men just disappeared from the streets; some said they were sent to slave camps in Germany. What had she been dreaming of? What hope was there for them, for Rosanna?

The latch of the door startled her from her thoughts. She quickly took off her apron as her husband's head appeared around the door. She called anxiously to him.

"Is he here?"

"No, he's finishing some sketches of the ships; he'll be here soon...."

He stopped and looked at her, his mouth agape.

"Where did you get that dress?"

"You don't remember?" Her eyebrows arched.

Paolo smiled to cover his confusion.

"I haven't seen it since before...."

"Well, you're seeing it again now. Don't stand there gawking like

an idiot. Get a bottle of wine from your secret store and help me prepare the table."

She crossed the floor and shouted up the stairs.

"Rosanna, hurry up – you can help me with the dinner."

CHAPTER 31

Later that day. Early evening.

Maria jumped at the knock on the door. A knock on the door usually meant trouble; she had heard of many people who had answered the knock, only to lose their food, their furniture, even their husbands and sons, never to be seen again.

"It's alright, *mia cara*, it's only him." Nevertheless, Paolo had jumped up instinctively and anxiously. "The professor." His mind wrapped quickly around the story he and Klaus had concocted. "*Professore* Carlo." He glanced at Rosanna, an eyebrow raised, to remind her of the ruse they had planned.

"*Perbacco*, I'm not ready." Maria quickly pulled off her apron and stuffed it into a drawer. Her hands brushed down her dress, then rose to primp her hair as she looked in the mirror.

"Maria, he is but a professor," Paolo sighed, "not the King of Italy."

But he is the King of the Forest, thought Rosanna, as she put down her book and hurried to the door.

"No, no, it is not proper." Her mother's reproach stopped her in her tracks. "Your *Papà* should welcome the guest."

Paolo opened the door to a sheepish-looking Klaus, his drawing pad in one hand, and a small package in the other.

"*Prego, si accomodi, Professore.*" Paolo extended his hand before realizing that Klaus had both hands full. Klaus put down his pad and shook hands firmly. There was a brief pause before Maria coughed gently. Klaus's eyes joined briefly with Rosanna's before they turned to find her mother's.

"I'm sorry," Paolo tried to cover his embarrassment, "we don't entertain very often. Please let me introduce you to my wife, Maria."

"I am honored to meet you, *Signora*," he took her hand lightly and offered the package with the other. "This is a little something for you. I'm sorry it is not gift-wrapped, but the war...."

"Thank you very much, *professore*." Maria held herself stiffly, as if in the presence of a dignitary.

"Please call me Carlo." He looked at her inquisitively. "Aren't you going to open it?"

She began to unwrap the gift carefully. "But it is your birthday, *professore*, not mine."

"Carlo, please. It is a little gift for preparing our meal."

"*Mamma mia, cioccolata!*" Maria almost dropped the packet with shock.

"*Cioccolata?*" Paolo and Rosanna cried out, almost with one voice.

"Where on earth did you get it?" Her hands put the bar on the table almost reverently. "Did you steal it from the Germans?"

"Mother, you ought not to ask such questions!" Rosanna spoke to her mother, but her eyes were fixed on the chocolate.

Klaus chuckled inwardly at how close Maria was to the truth. He would tell Gunther the story when he got back.

"Ask me no questions and I'll tell you no lies." He tapped the side of his nose.

"Carlo, it is a wonderful gift," Rosanna broke the silence. "Mamma, perhaps we can all share it for dessert? You wouldn't mind, Carlo?"

"Of course not, if your mother doesn't."

"Well, shall we get on with the birthday dinner?" Paolo did not want to mention how the aroma of the sausages was churning at his stomach; even the sound of the sizzling in the pan was driving him crazy. He tossed a log onto the fire.

"Yes, yes, please sit down," Maria paused, "Carlo."

Maria ladled the soup into bowls as Paolo opened the bottle of wine.

"It's the best Frascati," he smiled as he poured, "from my secret store."

"We have to hide everything from those German swine." Maria grimaced as she passed the cut bread.

Rosanna looked nervously across the table at Klaus, who smiled to hide the pain the words caused.

"They steal everything. Nothing is safe." Maria brought the four steaming bowls of bread soup to the table and sat down. Paolo and Rosanna said nothing.

"This is delicious, Signora." Klaus spoke to break the silence as he sipped the soup. "You must give me the recipe for my mother."

"Where does your mother live?"

Alarm bells sounded in Klaus's head at Maria's question; Paolo and Rosanna looked anxiously at him.

"She lives in a little town just outside Torino – I don't suppose you know it," his mind rapidly turned the pages of his old guidebook. "Pinerolo – I was born there."

"I thought as much." Maria's response surprised Klaus. "I thought I could detect it in your accent. Besides, you don't have the complexion of a Neapolitan."

"As it is your birthday," Rosanna looked teasingly at Klaus as she tried to divert the conversation, "how long ago were you born in Pinerolo? How old are you?"

Too old, thought Klaus; born at the wrong time, and in the wrong place.

"As old as my tongue and a little older than my teeth!"

Paolo gave a belly-laugh as he topped up the wineglasses.

"That's one in the eye for you, *bambina*."

Rosanna pouted as Klaus's laughter echoed that of her father, who returned to savor the remains of his sausages and the gnocchi, rich in delicious juices.

"But you are young to be a professor, Carlo." Maria brought her napkin to her mouth. She was deliberately eating slowly; it would not do to stuff the sausage into her mouth, despite the insistence of her hunger.

"It's nothing nowadays." Klaus thought of his young fellow professors in Berlin, and then pushed the image from his mind, lest it betray him.

"But the war has ruined your career, obviously. How long have you been on the run from the Germans?" Maria's fingers caressed the plate with a crust of bread, mopping up the last remnants of the dish.

"Long enough." Klaus desperately needed to move the conversation down other, safer channels. He took a mouthful of wine from his glass. "I haven't shown you the drawings I have made." The empty plates were pushed aside as Klaus reached for his pad.

"Yes, yes," Rosanna clapped her hands excitedly, "show mamma and papa the drawing!"

Klaus smiled as he opened the pad teasingly to reveal a sketch of the ships in the museum.

"It's very good, Carlo. You have captured the classical lines of the ships perfectly." Paolo spoke through a dense cloud of smoke emanating from his newly-lit pipe.

Maria was about to express her view of the ships, but said nothing, sighing as she cleared the plates away.

"It was an excellent meal, Signora Giraldi." Klaus beamed his thanks.

"What about *my* classical lines? Show them the other drawing!" Rosanna was incapable of hiding her impatience. She gently kicked Klaus under the table.

"What other drawing?" Klaus pretended ignorance deliberately and Rosanna glowered at his teasing. "Oh, you mean this one?"

He turned the page to reveal his sketch of Rosanna. Maria leaned forward to look.

"It's wonderful. You are very talented, Carlo. A perfect image."

"No, it isn't. My nose is too big." Rosanna jumped up from the table.

"I always said it was." The wine had given Paolo a mischievous twinkle in his eye and Klaus struggled to contain his own laughter.

"It's absolutely perfect." Maria allowed the mirth to die away. "You've captured my daughter perfectly." She nodded, as if she were seeing her own image. "You have a great talent, Carlo. It's a pity that the war has prevented you from practicing your gift every day."

"War, war, let's stop talking about this horrid war." Rosanna ignored her mother's disapproving eye.

"Shall we talk about your nose instead?" Replete with sausages and wine, Paolo continued with his joke.

Klaus leapt to his feet, holding the sketch before him. "Rosanna, this work of mine, with all its imperfections, is yours." He handed it to her. "I would like you to keep it as a memento of me and my stay here."

Rosanna looked at him, seeking the depths of his eyes. He saw her mother reach for a handkerchief and dab her eyes. Rosanna turned, put down the drawing on the table and walked across to the sideboard. She pulled a package from the drawer.

"It is your birthday, Carlo, yet it is you who are handing out presents." She smiled as she handed over the package. "This one is for you. From the family." Her mother and father glanced at each other with raised eyebrows, waiting for the mystery to be revealed.

Klaus sat down and began to unwrap the gift. His fingers told him it was a book, but he took his time, removing the wrapping gently. He undid the silk ribbon binding the book and took off the gift paper that had clearly graced at least one previous gift.

It was, indeed, a book. The cover was worn and there was some cracking down the spine. He opened the well-thumbed pages to find penciled notes in the margins, written in a neat, tiny hand. It was clearly her hand and it was obvious that the book had been hers for many years; he sensed it was part of her life, if not, along with her family, the basis of her life. She had caressed these pages; she had drawn life from them.

She looked at him anxiously as he raised the spine to examine the title. *The Golden Bough* by Sir James Frazer. He had read it before, at university, but he could not explain how the power of the book that he held in his hand flowed into his body.

"You will find the true tale of the King of the Forest in there – and much more." Rosanna searched his face for his feelings. "Happy birthday."

Paolo said nothing. He knew the value of the gift his daughter was giving.

"I shall treasure this book for the rest of my life." He glanced at Maria and Paolo and then held Rosanna's eyes for several seconds.

"Let's have some music!"

Paolo broke the silence as he went to the cupboard and pulled out their old gramophone. Within moments, the moving sounds of Puccini's 'Chrysanthemums' filled the room, and Paolo could not resist standing in front of the hearth to conduct his imaginary orchestra. He picked up a twig from the wood box and began to wave it in the air, trying to match the rhythm. At one point, his left hand made a wide, sweeping motion.

"Did you see how I brought in the violas at that point?"

"You are a silly old fool." Maria tried to hide her face behind her hands in embarrassment, but she could not resist breaking into a giggle as Paolo continued his performance, his face a mask of solemnity.

"I should be invited to La Scala." His hands moved more quickly as the piece progressed to its climax. Then the spring began to wind down; Paolo slowed his arm movements as the gramophone slowed, and the room rang with their laughter as he ground to a halt, like a marionette whose strings have been cut.

"Bravo, bravo!" Rosanna clapped enthusiastically, despite being almost doubled over with laughter. "You are so funny, *Papà*."

Maria smiled. She felt happy. Maybe it was the wine, but she hadn't felt so happy for a long time. It was almost like the old days. She looked across at Carlo's face and found him smiling as he watched

Rosanna. Surely as a professor he could do something to help Rosanna's education after the war. She would talk to Paolo about it tomorrow. She broke the chocolate into portions and put it on a small antique dish.

Paolo and Rosanna stared at the rich, brown color but resisted the urge to snatch at the plate, gently lifting it to their mouths as if they had chocolate every day. Rosanna, however, could not prevent the look of bliss on her face as the flavor exploded on her tongue.

Paolo wound the gramophone up again, changed the record and they all sat silently listening again to the moving piece, each lost in thought and the enjoyment of the chocolate. As the last notes crackled through the horn, Klaus stood up, aware that Rosanna and her parents were nodding and sighing in their appreciation of the afterglow of wine, music and chocolate.

"And now I must be away." He felt an urgency to escape the emotions of the moment.

"Go?" Paolo looked at him, surprised.

"Aren't you aware of the curfew here, Carlo?" Maria spread her arms wide in disbelief.

He had forgotten about the curfew. It did not apply to Klaus. But it did apply to Carlo.

"I'll take my chance. I've done it before." He lied convincingly, but he thought about the irony of being shot by his own comrades.

"Nonsense, you can't take the risk." Paolo shook his head. "We assumed you would be staying here. We've got an old cot in the cupboard – you can sleep down here, close to the fire."

Maria nodded. "I regret it's not a proper bed, *professore*, but it will be more comfortable than sleeping in that smelly museum." She ignored the disdain on her husband's face. "And it will be warmer, too."

Klaus knew he had no option. "You are too kind, *Signora*."

"Let us have a drop of this before we go to bed." Paolo removed a brick by the hearth and pulled out a bottle. "It's grappa. Too good to hide anymore."

"Don't you think you've had enough?" Maria's voice was sharp. "You'll be sorry in the morning!"

"*Mia cara*, we have one good night in three years!" Paolo leaned forward and patted his wife on the rump. "Let us enjoy it!"

She slapped his hand and eased him back into his chair. "It's time for your bed!" She looked across the room to Carlo and Rosanna and was not surprised that they were lost in each other.

"Hey, big nose!" Paolo teased again. Rosanna turned on her father, but softened as he pointed to the book. "You must really like him to give him that book, don't you?"

Her mother caught her daughter's embarrassment and sought to change the subject quickly.

"Come, it's definitely time for your bed." She eased Paolo out of his chair and led him toward the door to the stairs.

"*Buona notte*." The old man's hand waved loosely in the air.

"*Buona notte*." Klaus looked at Maria and smiled. "Thank you for a wonderful meal, Signora Giraldi. It is a birthday I shall always remember."

"It was nothing. Thank you for the sausages. I hope you sleep well." Maria smiled, but her aspect changed as she turned to her daughter. "Do not be long, Rosanna." She pushed Paolo through the door; Klaus and Rosanna heard the uneven steps shuffling on the stairs.

Rosanna waited until she heard the bedroom door shut. At the sound of the drop of the latch, she grabbed Klaus's arm.

"Quickly – come with me." She pulled her cloak from the hook by the door. Klaus stumbled against a chair as he followed her to the front door.

"Sssh!" She raised her finger to her lips and leaned forward to whisper in his ear.

"I must show you the three moons of Diana. We shall go to the well."

"But what about the curfew?"

Her hand waved his objections away as she dimmed the oil lamp and opened the door.

Klaus wanted to ask about the three moons, but she bundled him through the door and gently dropped the latch behind them.

CHAPTER 32

The well was only fifty yards away, but the climb was steep; they took care as they navigated the cobbled path. As they reached the tiny piazza that clung to the hillside, Rosanna put her finger to her lips and moved forward around the well to peer down over the wall. She scanned the streets beneath, before beckoning Klaus to her side.

"It's alright, there's no one about," she whispered. "We get an occasional visit by a guard from Genzano, but that's all. Most of the Ger…" she hesitated, choosing her words, "Most of them have been moved down south."

"I know," Klaus spoke quietly, "I've been there. I'm a German, too."

"No, you're not, not to me." She took his hand. "To me you are the King of the Forest." A faint smile crossed her lips. Klaus was not sure whether she was poking fun at him or not.

"That was a wonderful present you gave me. I shall keep it with me wherever I go – just like this icon of Diana." He reached beneath his shirt and showed her the icon on the chain around his neck.

Rosanna smiled, but she wanted to banish the thought of Klaus's departure from her mind.

"Look, look," she pointed out over the wall, across the lake, "you can see the three moons."

Klaus looked skywards. In the cloudless sky, the moon was well past its first quarter, its clear luminescence washing the land with a cold light. Below, the lake, undisturbed by even the slightest breeze, amplified and returned the light, the crescent reflection a perfect image of the moon hanging in the dark heaven above.

"But can you see the third moon, Klaus?" Rosanna's finger pointed to the west, over the far rim of the lake crater. Her face turned up to his.

Klaus looked over the western side of the hills, and he could just discern the coastal plain that ran down to the sea. He picked out the coastline and, beyond it, the Mediterranean Sea; halfway to the horizon, its form changing in the waves, was the third moon.

"It's so wonderful, Rosanna. The war is so far away. I wish I could stay here forever."

He put his hand on her shoulder and looked down at her. Her fingers crept around his waist, but she avoided his eyes, her face pressing down against his chest.

"You *can* stay here forever, Klaus."

She raised her head, her eyes fixing on his face.

"Please kiss me, Klaus."

Her lips were upon his and he heard the rustle of her dress as her arms slid around him before he had time to think. But the kiss was not demanding and, although he felt the soft warmth of her body against him, it was not insistent. His hands came up and rested lightly upon her shoulders as their lips parted. Her breathing was uneven, but she moved slowly, almost reluctantly, away from him, her eyes dancing over his face.

"You can stay here, Klaus," she smiled eagerly, "with us."

"You know I cannot." He dropped his hands from her shoulders and half turned away, breaking the eye contact as he looked down distractedly at the bell tower of the church below.

"Why not?" Her face fell in disappointment. "You speak the language perfectly; you could become just one of the thousands of refugees." She reached for his hand. "Until after the war."

Klaus held her hand, but he did not look at her, although he was tempted by what she had said. He could burn his uniform, lie low until the war passed; he could draw, he could study the ships; and, above all, he could be with her. But from the reflection of the moon emerged the vision of his father and mother, their faces haunted by shame as they received the official notification of his absence from duty, presumed deserted. He looked out at the distant image in the sea and other faces emerged: Gunther and the men of his unit suffering the jibes about the captain who had run away.

He turned to her, but his eyes were still downcast.

"It is difficult for me to say why I cannot stay." He raised his eyes to hers to see that she was watching his face very closely, looking at every line as if it gave the key to his heart's thoughts. "It is a question of honor – and duty." He shrugged his shoulders, as if he could do nothing about it.

"Honor?" She almost spat the word out. "You're no different from the puffed up braggarts who strut around the streets of Genzano." Her voice was low, but it carried a tone of anger that he had never heard before. "What does honor bring you? Death, that's what honor brings you. What does it matter if you die with honor? You die, you go to the grave, and your honor dies with you. And duty? Do you not remember my father's tale of Diana and Acteon? How Diana, *my* goddess, put duty before love – what did it get her?"

Her voice faltered and Klaus looked up to see she was crying. She did not avert her eyes; she looked at him beseechingly, as if her look could impart her pleas into his mind. He saw the tears stream down her cheek, her face pale and sad in the moonlight, its silver cast giving a cold, ghostly hue to her warm, olive-brown skin. His heart felt for her anguish, but he remained silent. There was nothing he could do, nothing he could say.

"I'm sorry, Klaus, but I thought you understood how I felt."

She held him close to her. His hand ran through her hair as she wept on his shoulder.

"I think I do know. I think you feel the same way as I do."

Her head came up from his shoulder, her moist eyes pleading with him.

"Then stay, Klaus." Her plea was loud, echoing in the cold night air, and he put his finger to her lips to hush her. For several moments, there was no sound except the running of the water from the well, a bubbling and splashing as it fell, timelessly, onto the stones. "Do you want duty and death, or me, alive, with all the love in my heart?"

"The gift you gave me told me how you felt." He tried to shift the talk to other grounds. "That book represents your life, doesn't it Rosanna?"

"It is only a book." She moved her face closer to his, and he felt her body against him again as she clung to him even more tightly. "You know the present I really want to give you."

His body began to throb, but the memory of his promise to her father leapt into his mind, unbeckoned, to conflict his emotions and subdue them. Duty, always duty. Why did he think this way? Perhaps Rosanna was right: the moment should be seized. Yet, as gently as possible, he eased their bodies apart. He held her by the hands as he looked down at her anxious face. "Why don't we go down to the temple tomorrow?"

He knew he was postponing the decision, pushing aside the conflict between his desires and his conscience. He pulled gently at her hand, trying to lead her away from the scene of his anguish, but she stayed his hand.

"Look one last time at the three moons of Diana." He detected an air of resignation in her voice. "And remember our time here together."

They looked silently at the heavens, the lake and the sea, their forms bathed in a light that seemed almost like daybreak.

"Come now, before your mother finds out we are gone." He took her hand and led her down the street towards the house.

Dawn the next day. January 22nd 1944

Klaus was standing in the front pew of the church, his chest pushing out against his full dress uniform. Behind him, he heard the snickering of the old Italian women, talking scornfully behind their hands, but it did not matter to him. It was the happiest day of his life. He turned to look down the aisle as he heard the rustle of her dress at the church doors.

His mouth dropped. Why was she wearing a black bridal dress? He could not remember his agreement to such a strange dress. Maybe it was a Roman tradition, or some temple rite of Diana. The veil and train were also black; even the bouquet was of black roses.

But where was Paolo? Klaus peered into the light streaming into the church doors, surrounding Rosanna. Surely, his eyes were deceiving him. Behind Rosanna came a cortege, the coffin swaying on the shoulders of the pallbearers. At the front of the cortege was a black uniformed man, a swastika emblazoned on his sleeve. It was Dressler, his face creased with a smug smile. Suddenly, the church doors slammed shut, but there was, at first, a gentle tap, and then he could hear his mother's voice and a hammering on the door.

"Klaus, Klaus."

There was knocking. Klaus sat up quickly on the cot, clawing at his clammy undershirt, willing his conscious mind to banish the nightmare.

"Klaus, are you awake?"

He sighed in relief as he recognized Paolo's voice, whispering, but urgent, demanding. Klaus swung his legs over the side of the cot and struggled quickly into his pants. He was pleased to be awake, the nightmare gone. He rubbed his eyes and noticed that there was a hint of daylight coming under the door.

"*Sì, sì,* I am awake, Paolo."

The door leading to the stairs flew open and an agitated Paolo raced across the room to the cot. Klaus sat up, still rubbing the sleep from his eyes. The old man stopped, put his finger to his lips and listened for any noise from the floor above. Satisfied, he leant forward and whispered in Klaus's ear.

"Klaus, the Allies have landed. At Anzio."

Klaus smoothed down his hair, a bemused look upon his face as his tired mind tried to come to grips with what Paolo was saying.

"How do you know?"

"Because they can be seen from the window. Didn't you hear the guns?" He beckoned to Klaus. "Come, come. Quickly."

The old man walked over to the window. Klaus leapt from the cot, pulled on his shoes and followed him across the room. Surely the old man had made a mistake. But Paolo was excited and agitated as he led him to the window that overlooked the lake and pushed back the half-opened shutter. Klaus peered out into the growing gray light of the breaking dawn, looking beyond the lake to the sea in which, but hours before, he had seen the third moon. He rubbed his eyes again, as if his own sight were deceiving him.

There were ships, little dots bobbing like corks beyond the coast-line. From some of the bigger dots came flashes of light, followed by plumes of smoke. After a few seconds, there were eruptions just behind the coastal town. A few seconds later, the noise of the blast reached their ears, as if time itself were out of joint.

"It's the Allies!" Paolo's shout was filled with happiness. "Soon the war will be over!"

He started a little dance of glee, his slippers shuffling on the stone floor as he turned, his hands held above his head. Suddenly he stopped, realizing that Klaus was still staring at the landing beaches, not sharing his joy.

"I'm sorry." Paolo's dropped his hands to his side and struggled to find the right words. None came.

Klaus said nothing, his eyes fixed on the men swarming over the beaches like scurrying ants. For him, the landing did not bring the joy that Paolo felt; it brought an agony that he felt physically inside of him, as if his very soul were being torn apart. Was it only yesterday that they celebrated his birthday, only hours since he had held Rosanna to him? He wanted to stay, to draw, to talk of the ships, to laugh, sing and dance with her. His eyes closed, in the hope that the ants and the bobbing corks would go away, that they were all part of his bad dream, but the explosions of another salvo assailed his ears and he knew that this nightmare was real. He opened his eyes and sighed, a deep sigh that rattled in his throat, as if part of him were dying.

"I have to go." His voice was mechanical, like a condemned man accepting his fate.

"Go?" Paolo looked at him incredulously. "But the war will soon be over. You can stay here. We can hide you." The old man knew at once that he had said the wrong thing. The young man had nowhere to hide.

Klaus shook his head. He could not explain. He had wondered why his father and mother had appeared in his nightmare; now he realized that he could not throw away his guilt like some old coat for his mother to pick up. Why hadn't he gone home to Berlin instead of coming here? There was no choice.

"I don't expect you to understand, but I must go."

Paolo followed him as he ran down the stairs. Klaus pulled on his shirt and jacket.

"Please let me have the key to the museum. I need to collect my uniform. I will leave the key in the lock."

Paolo shook his head, but reached into his pocket and thrust the key into Klaus's hand. Klaus turned as he made his way to the door, but was unable to look Paolo in the face.

"Paolo, you know that I must do what I have to do. But I want you to know that I have kept my promise about Rosanna. Please tell her...."

The latch on the stairway door rattled, and both men turned as Rosanna came into the room, clutching her nightdress around her.

"What's going on? Where are you going, Klaus?"

She looked up as Klaus opened the front door. In the brief meeting of their eyes, she saw the guilt on his face. He went out and pulled the door shut. Rosanna stood, unbelieving, as the sound of his running footsteps receded.

"No, no, Klaus." Rosanna's shout filled the kitchen as she ran to the door. "Klaus, don't go, don't go!" She pulled on the latch and looked out, but he was gone: there was only a faint echo of his boots on the cobbles below. The early morning frost clutched at her as she slowly closed the door, the tears beginning to well in her eyes.

"Klaus?" Paolo jumped at his wife's voice and turned to see her in the doorway to the stairs.

"Who, in God's name, is Klaus?"

Three weeks later. February 18th 1944. Velletri.

K laus wondered why Dressler had sent for him. There was a fear inside him that the commanding officer had learned about his visit to Nemi; Dressler seemed to have spies everywhere. Klaus had been back with the division for over a week; why had Dressler waited so long? The anxiety showed on his face as he crossed the piazza and made toward the headquarters building. He should not have gone to Nemi; it wasn't just the question of his own personal safety: he felt he had betrayed Paolo, Maria and Rosanna. Above all, Rosanna. Even now, he could hear her shouting his name as he had hurried from their home, unable to look back because of his shame, and for fear of seeing the look on her face. She would never have understood why he had to leave. His mind drifted back to the night of the three moons....

The rumbling of artillery fire to the west brought him back to the present. He had been lucky to escape after leaving Nemi. For some reason, the Allies had not pressed their advantage after landing at Anzio; there was virtually no opposition in front of them, yet they just sat there, in the beachhead. He had managed to hitch a lift in a truck heading back south down the Liguri valley. Everywhere was confusion, the roads choked with refugees and troop movements. He had discovered that his division and artillery unit had been pulled out of the line and had been moved north to contain the bridgehead. It had taken him almost two weeks to find his unit back at Velletri.

The town was not the same as when they had left it five months before. Klaus looked down the street; already the Allies' artillery fire had crumpled several buildings; the streets, littered with debris, were deserted. Most of the Italians had long since gone, fleeing the destruction that was hurtling their way. An emaciated cat peered at him, and then slunk away, in the hope of food, towards a gun emplacement dug into the basement of a demolished house. The animal leapt and scurried for cover as the gun belched flame in retaliation against the incoming shells.

Klaus returned the guard's salute as he ducked into the headquarters building. The adjutant led him through the big doors into the old council chamber and he noticed how the huge mirror was now cracked, the windows were blacked out and dust covered everything. Dressler looked up from the papers lying on the desk.

"Forgive the décor, *Hauptman*," Dressler's right hand waved around the room, "soon we shall have to move to better quarters."

Klaus snapped to attention, fighting to keep his face impassive, as he sought to control the anger and loathing within him. He realized that most of the anger came because of his own fear, from his inability to challenge the arrogance of the man seated before him. Dressler fixed him with his sharp eyes. He leaned back in his chair, his arms behind his head, the smug smile disguising the menace that Klaus could almost feel, as if it seeped from the black uniform.

"Things are much better now, Schmidt." The thin lips barely moved, but Dressler moved his face back from the light of the desk lamp and Klaus was no longer able to discern its features. "Now that you are behaving like a German officer and not as a protector of *untermenchen*. You may stand at ease."

Klaus adopted the stand-easy position, relieved that somehow Dressler had not heard of his visit to Nemi. Yet he felt his body was still rigid, the muscles taut as he struggled to contain the strange combination of dread and hatred that consumed him. He looked down at Dressler, who was adjusting the swastika armband on the sleeve of his black tunic. Dressler was the worst sort of Nazi: not only did he believe all the 'master race' propaganda; he was prepared to act upon it. And he was no fool; he knew the levers of power, and he knew how to operate them. Klaus looked at the smug face sitting atop the Iron Cross that hung at the neck.

"How was Berlin?" The question caught Klaus off guard.

"My parents are well." His mind desperately searched for some extract from his mother's last letter. "There are more and more air raids, sadly."

"Those Allied *schweinhunden*!" Dressler brought his fist down on the table. "They will pay, Schmidt, mark my words." Dressler's face reddened with rage. "I have heard that the Fuehrer is about to launch a new, secret weapon. Then they will dance to another tune!"

The rage left him as quickly as it had come.. A hint of a smile crossed Dressler's face, increasing Klaus's fear.

"Of course, we must all do our duty to gain the final victory. Which is why I sent for you, Schmidt."

Klaus felt apprehensive as Dressler stood up and reached for a drawer of the desk.

"Now, *Hauptman*, I have a job for you and your considerable talents as an artillery officer." He pulled out a map and laid it out on the desk.

"We have contained the Allies' bridgehead, here, at Anzio." His long finger stabbed at the map. "Although why they did not advance inland after they landed last month is beyond comprehension. Do you know they were virtually unopposed?"

Klaus feigned surprise as he recalled his view of the landing from Paolo's window.

"Yes, Schmidt, they could have cut right across the rear of the Tenth Army." Dressler's pencil slashed across the map.

"But they did not. Their generals are dim-witted sheep." His smile widened as he tossed the pencil aside. "Which is why we shall win the war."

Dressler looked up from the map.

"Do you believe we shall win the war, Schmidt?"

"Of course, *Standartenfuehrer*." Klaus knew it was not the truth. All the events in Italy, the news of the defeats on the Russian front told him otherwise.

"Well, your job in helping to win this great victory is simple."

The smile returned to his face as he picked up the pencil and leaned over the map again.

"The Allies' bridgehead is here." He drew a rough circle around Anzio, its boundary encompassing Aprilia and Campoleone.

"We have managed to contain the bridgehead, but supplies continue to come ashore. It is necessary to harass them, to bombard the beach continuously, until we bring more reinforcements from France. Then we shall drive them back into the sea."

He peered more closely at the map, narrowing his eyes as he searched for a particular spot.

"I want artillery fire brought down upon the landing area, Schmidt. Your unit will help in the barrage. You will take your guns and locate them…" He raised his eyes to meet Klaus's as he drove his finger down onto the map. "…there!"

Klaus broke from Dressler's stare and looked down where the neatly-manicured finger was pointing. He looked back into his superior's eyes, disbelievingly. The finger hovered over the lakeside at Nemi.

"But…" Klaus tried to bring his thoughts together, but Dressler ignored him.

"You can see it is an ideal place. The crater of the lake will provide you with cover. If you place your guns by the side of the lake, it will be very difficult for the Allied gunners to locate you."

The thin smile returned to Dressler's lips.

"But then, I do not have to teach you anything about artillery, do I, *Hauptman*?"

Klaus could see that Dressler was enjoying his cruel ploy. The artillery officer within Klaus told him that Dressler was right. It was an ideal position, but it was located alongside the museum.

The Allied gunners would find it difficult to locate the emplacement, but his experience at the front told him they eventually would sniff him out with air reconnaissance. A stray shell and the museum….

"Sir, I beg you to reconsider."

Klaus saw Dressler's body stiffen, his fingers tossing aside the pencil, which rolled across the map with a dull clatter.

"Reconsider? You ask your superior officer to reconsider an order?"

The black uniform came quickly to the front of the desk and Dressler put his reddening face right in front of Klaus. "Come to attention!"

Despite himself, Klaus snapped to attention like an automaton. Dressler fixed his eyes on Klaus's.

"On the Russian front, I had men shot for much less. Are you frightened that the Allies will shoot at you?" The voice was heavy with sarcasm.

Klaus knew Dressler had the power of life or death over him, but he stood his ground.

"With respect, sir, it's not that. I will put my record under fire before any man."

"Then you will not be afraid to locate your guns…" Dressler turned back to the desk and picked up the pencil. "…precisely here." He drew a small circle at the lakeside.

"Sir, the position is right next to the museum – the museum that houses the ships of Caligula. Two thousand years of history could be destroyed by a stray shot. Even the *Reichkommisseriat* has declared them objects of culture."

He had hoped the appeal to authority would work, but Dressler brushed it aside.

"Like *Reichmarschall* Goering, when I hear the word 'culture,' I reach for my gun, *Hauptman.* The past is of no importance. We are fighting for the next thousand years – for the thousand-year Reich." He lit a cigarette and blew the smoke towards Klaus.

"The ships of Caligula. Whatever next? Of what use to the Reich are they? Just shriveled pieces of wood. If we have to destroy all the artifacts of the Roman Empire to win the war, we will. Do you think we are making war in a museum?"

Dressler looked pleased with his irony as he returned to his desk, and leant back in his chair.

"Perhaps I could locate my guns here, sir." Klaus leant over the map and reached for the pencil.

"Enough!" Dressler leapt to his feet, the flat of his hand slamming down on the map.

Klaus jumped back in shock and reverted to attention. Dressler came round the desk and pushed his face within inches of Klaus's. The mixed odors of tobacco and brandy assailed Klaus's nostrils.

"You will obey orders, Schmidt!" Dressler shouted, his face again contorted with rage.

The fear returned to Klaus. He had made the mistake of trying to compromise with the devil. He should just refuse the order, but the words would not come to his lips. Dressler might carry out the threat to shoot him; at best, there would be a court-martial. His parents' faces, their heads shaking at the shame, came to his mind.

"Yes, *Standartenfuehrer.*" Klaus's voice was little more than a whisper.

"That is better, *Hauptman*, but you do not sound very convincing." Dressler eased away and put his hands behind his back, peering arrogantly down his nose at Klaus.

"You are riddled with the disease of modern society, Schmidt – the cancer of liberalism. Do you think it is somehow noble to protect these useless pieces of historical refuse?"

Klaus remained silent, holding himself to attention despite an almost uncontrollable trembling in his left leg.

"So that's it, is it? So noble. Such scruples." Dressler's cold, sardonic laugh rang around the room, as he walked slowly across to the fire in the huge hearth.

"You should know by now that men are driven by fear, greed and lust. All ignoble base instincts, my noble friend." He tossed his cigarette into the fire and ran his fingernails along the mantelpiece.

"Tell me, *Hauptman*, do you think, on the other side of the front, among the Americans and English, and the other mongrel races, do you think there are noble people" - Dressler spat out the word 'noble' - "who think their role in the war is to preserve historical monuments?" He did not raise his head, his gaze still fixed on the fire. Again, Klaus made no reply.

"Then let me ask you this, Schmidt." He turned suddenly from the fire and returned to stand in front of Klaus. "Do you know of Monte Cassino?"

Klaus nodded. He had seen it often when his guns had been in the front line. The magnificent monastery, founded by St. Benedict in the 6th century, sat astride the mountain, the early morning mists caressing the walls that housed over a thousand years of books and historical treasures. He saw Dressler was smiling malevolently.

"Well, *Hauptman*," Dressler's voice assumed a mocking, sarcastic tone, "the noble warlords of America and England bombed the monastery to heaps of rubble three days ago."

Klaus was dumbfounded. His jaw dropped and he shook his head. He could not believe that such a thing of beauty was now nothing but rubble. Dressler pressed on, savoring the moment.

"Of course, there was not a single German soldier inside. The Allies killed a few pious monks and several civilians, that's all." He wheeled away on his heel, his acid voice continuing to cut into Klaus. "And now they are bombing Rome. The so-called Eternal City." He laughed as he poured a glass of brandy and raised it in a toast.

"To the noble culture lovers of the liberal democracies." He downed the drink with one swallow and looked across at Klaus. "Now you know what these mongrels think of your culture!" He toyed with his glass, put it down.

Klaus said nothing, for he knew he had no answer. The war was reducing all men to barbaric savagery, defiling them, and forcing them to defile other men and the beauty of the world. And he was part of it; part of the war, part of the corruption, part of the descent into barbarism. Was there no escape? The vision of Rosanna swam before him, the vision of her innocent hope. He longed to share that hope, but he knew that he was imprisoned in the maelstrom of war: there would be no escape until the madness was over, until the bloodlust was sated.

"And they are right, Schmidt!" Dressler's shouted voice boomed in his ears. "The only use for all this so-called culture is to ship it back to the Reich for the pleasure of the Fuehrer and Reichfuehrer Himmler. Unfortunately, we cannot do that with your precious ships!"

Dressler waved his hand dismissively. "I expect your guns to be in position by the day after tomorrow. See to it."

Klaus saluted perfunctorily and made for the door, eager to escape. As he reached for the handle, Dressler spoke again.

"I am sure you will find Nemi a better place than the front. I am told it has its attractions."

Klaus closed the door behind him, wondering how much Dressler knew. He felt uneasy as he walked across the piazza.

CHAPTER 35

February 20th 1944. 2.30a.m.

"**S**ignor Capitano, Signor Capitano, come quickly, quickly!" Klaus's mind did its utmost to filter out the intrusive noise as his body turned in the lumpy bed, craving the return to the sleep it desperately needed. But the voice did not go away.

"*Signor Capitano*, it is urgent – come quickly!"

The voice was accompanied by a rapid, insistent knocking on the door. Klaus half-raised himself on an elbow, his eyes blinking as he struggled unwillingly into the waking world. He fumbled for the pocket of his tunic on the chair by the side of the bed, brought out his lighter and flicked the wheel. The sudden light forced him to screw up his eyes as he peered at his watch. Nearly two-thirty. What the hell was going on? Surely his unit hadn't arrived yet? He had moved to Nemi with Gunther in advance of his guns to prepare their billets, but his men weren't expected before dawn. His face creased in drowsy puzzlement as he swung his legs from the bed.

Still the voice continued, raising itself to a plaintive whine.

"*Signor Capitano*, come quickly, please."

"Is that you, Gianni?" Klaus felt annoyed as he recognized the boy's voice. "What are you doing out at this hour?"

"*Sì, sì, Signor Capitano, eccomi.*" The relief in the boy's voice was evident, but the urgent strident tone returned at once. "It's the ships, Signor Capitano. There is danger. Signor Giraldi wants you to come at once."

Klaus applied his lighter to the bedside candle. As its pallid flame gave a meager light to the room, he padded across the bare floor to the door and turned the key. Gianni burst into the room like a small tempest and immediately grabbed at Klaus's hand with his small bony fingers. Klaus resisted the youngster's tug.

"This isn't another of your tricks, is it, Gianni?"

Gianni looked up at him, the flickering candle flame painting ghostly pictures about his face and his pleading eyes.

"*No, no, Signor Capitano.* Signor Giraldi sent me. He thinks some people are going to attack the ships."

Klaus remembered seeing Paolo the previous evening. He had been sorting out billets for his troops when he had seen the Italian across the street. Neither had spoken, but Paolo had looked at him with shock and then averted his eyes. It was what Klaus had dreaded; he had hoped not to see Paolo.

Klaus detached himself from the young boy's fingers. He leaned over and gripped the boy by his upper arms.

"Attack the ships? You're talking nonsense, Gianni. Why would anyone want to attack the ships?"

Gianni looked bewildered and frightened.

"*Non so, Signor Capitano, non so*. I am staying with Signor Giraldi – my mother is ill – and he wakes me up. 'Get *Signor Capitano* at once,' he says. 'The ships are about to be attacked.' He tells me you are staying here, and then he starts to walk down the path to the museum."

The words came quickly, the pace broken only by the deep gulps of air the youngster sucked into his lungs.

"And he takes his hunting gun with him."

"His hunting gun?"

Klaus became anxious as Gianni nodded. He moved to the chair and began to pull on his boots hastily. To break the curfew was a capital offence, and Paolo would not be mad enough to do that unless he really felt the ships were under threat. Klaus buttoned up his tunic and checked his sidearm. And Paolo had a gun. He shuddered with the fear that a guard might see the Italian.

He handed the candle to Gianni and motioned to the boy to follow him along the landing. At the top of the stairs he turned and rapped on the door of another room. A protesting mumble of disturbed sleep answered. Klaus knocked again, louder.

"Gunther, it's me," he shouted, "come quickly!"

The protesting continued. "What in hell's name is going on?"

Klaus pushed open the door, the meager beam of the candle revealing Gunther searching under the bed for his boots. The sergeant squinted into the light.

"My first chance of sleeping in a proper bed for weeks and you wake me up at this god-forsaken hour. What's the problem?"

"Gianni says there's some problem at the museum. Meet me in front of the house as soon as you're dressed. And bring your Schmeisser."

Gunther looked at the boy carrying the candle.

"If that little bugger is playing one of his tricks, I'll flay him alive." Klaus did not bother to frighten Gianni with a translation as they went down the stairs.

Fifteen minutes later.

"My god, he must have the eyes of a cat! Here am I, Gunther Mattheus, an expert at night fighting, and the kid sees better than me!"

Gunther cursed as he made his way behind Klaus through the undergrowth on the narrow path that led down from the town to the museum. Klaus said nothing as he struggled to keep up with the boy leading them down the hillside in the darkness. The night was clear, the three-quarters moon offering some light, picking out the small ghostly clouds of their breath as they panted in the crisp night air.

"*Venite qua* – mind the fallen branch."

Gianni turned to urge them on. The moon painted the white, pasty face sitting atop his angular body, from which emerged little sticks of arms and legs. Klaus wondered what drove the urchin. He seemed emaciated by privation, yet had small but well-formed muscles and limbs that could scale the crater's side like a gazelle if need be - or if the reward were worth it.

They emerged from the trees into a clearing by the lakeside. The museum, a hundred meters away, looked like a sepulcher in the moonlight.

"Wait, slow down, Gianni." Klaus called to the lad, who stopped to allow them to catch up. "Where is Signor Giraldi?"

"Probably in the museum. Now come quickly." Gianni tugged at Klaus's hand, but the German gently placed his hand over the youngster's mouth and raised his index finger to his lips.

"Shush. Wait, listen." Klaus peered into the darkness. A figure lay on the ground by the museum. Gunther had seen it, too, for Klaus heard the snap of the safety catch on the sergeant's Schmeisser. Klaus raised a hand behind him to restrain Gunther. Suddenly, there was another movement, but Gianni slipped his hand and moved forward unconcernedly.

"Come on," his spindly arm waved them forward, "they're only refugees."

Klaus sighed his relief. "Refugees? I thought they lived in the caves and grottoes."

"They are everywhere now – there are so many. They're supposed to get seven lira a day from the government, but there are no pickings there." Gianni shrugged his shoulders as they edged their way towards the museum. Klaus translated in order to calm Gunther, who mumbled under his breath. As Klaus approached the museum he saw a few other shapes huddled in blankets on the steps, ignorant of his presence in their midst.

"Thank God you have come!" They were all startled by the sound of Paolo's voice coming from the shadows at the entrance of the museum. "Follow me – the ships are about to be attacked by partisans. Gianni, stay here!"

Klaus was puzzled as to why anyone would attack the ships, but he told Gianni to stay where he was before following the old man as he made his way around the wall to the back of the museum.

"What's going on, boss?" Gunther's voice was urgent in his ear.

"I'm not sure. Do nothing unless I give the order."

Gunther nodded. "And what's the old fool got there?" He pointed to the weapon Paolo held. "I don't know who he intends to frighten, but he sure frightens me. He's out after curfew and he's carrying a gun. Shouldn't we arrest him?"

"I'll explain later, Gunther. Just do as I say for now." Klaus wondered how he was going to explain, but took the old hunting rifle from a protesting Paolo.

"It is better that you leave this business to us, Paolo." They crouched at the back of the museum, peering out across the clearing to the edge of the trees. "How do you know there is going to be an attack?"

"There is little that is not known in the town. Word travels faster than the birds." Paolo whispered, his eyes remaining fixed on the trees.

Klaus had no reason to doubt him, but after fifteen minutes of listening to the silence of the forest, he began to question his judgment. Gunther, too, became restless.

"To think I could be dreaming in bed, undressing Marlene Dietrich, instead of out on this wild goose chase. It's not as if the American army is out there. Besides…"

His voice was cut short by a gentle crack that came from the trees. Klaus wondered whether his senses were playing tricks in the dark, but, after a few moments, there was another footfall. Then there was a murmuring of Italian voices, one predominate, urging others on.

Gunther listened intently for several seconds, before lifting his hand and raising three fingers, then a fourth, to Klaus. Three men, maybe four, no more. Klaus interpreted the sign, nodded, and made a sweeping gesture with his right hand. Gunther was to move out to the right and get in behind them. The sergeant slipped away noiselessly and disappeared into the trees about fifty yards to the right of the voices.

The voices still came on. Klaus made Paolo lie down and leveled his pistol across the clearing. Suddenly, the moon picked out a figure moving out of the trees; after waiting for some moments, it turned, calling to others. "*Senti - è molto facile, non è vero?* Now let's get the stuff and get out of here."

Two others, just visible in the pale light, followed into the clearing. Klaus became a little nervous. What had happened to Gunther? The men kept advancing. There was no way Klaus could tell whether they were armed, and they were less than fifty meters away.

"*Hande hoch!*"

The three men turned, surprised at the German voice, to find themselves looking straight at Gunther's Schmeisser.

"Don't fire, Gunther!" Klaus switched on his flashlight, blinding the intruders, catching them frozen in its beam. He moved toward them, leveling his machine pistol at the leader of the men, who looked terrified as he discerned Klaus's uniformed figure behind the light.

"Do not move!" Klaus had switched quickly to Italian. "Throw down your weapons!"

"We have none - don't shoot." The man's voice was plaintive, pleading. Suddenly, there was a shriek of pain from another man as the butt of Gunther's gun hit him between the shoulder blades.

"It's alright, boss, they have no weapons."

"I know, Gunther, he's already told me that. Just bring them over here."

Gunther kicked the man on the ground to his feet and prodded the three forward with the his gun. "The fools are carrying sacks!"

Klaus grabbed the first man, whose breath reeked of liquor.

"What are you doing here?" He shouted into the downcast face. "Do you know that the penalty for breaking the curfew is death?"

Klaus turned his head to one side. "Do you know these people, Paolo?"

Paolo got up from his hiding place. Klaus could sense that he was reluctant to show himself.

"They are nobodies – just brigands and thieves! *Ecco*!" His finger pointed to the sacks the men carried. "They have come to steal from the museum."

One of the men laughed and spat on the ground.

"So the old fascist gets the German army to do his dirty work!"

"Silence!" Klaus thrust his pistol and his flashlight in the Italian's face.

"Did you come here to steal from the museum?" He turned his gun to the other two men.

Klaus wondered if they knew about the Mirror of Diana and the other treasures that Paolo had locked in his wooden chest, but the brigands said nothing and looked down at their feet.

"Gunther – keep them under guard in the museum and have them shipped down to Velletri when our men arrive in the morning."

Gunther did not much fancy spending the rest of the night looking after three Italian thieves, but he clicked his heels and prodded the men forward.

"What will happen to them?" Paolo had waited until they had disappeared behind the wall of the museum. There was an edge of anxiety to his question.

"They will probably be shot for attempted robbery." Klaus's voice was unemotional, matter-of-fact. "If not, they'll be shot for breaking the curfew."

"They're bastards for wanting to steal from the museum – but I didn't want that to happen." Paolo sat down on the steps of the museum, his body shaking.

"What did you think would happen?" Klaus turned on the old man, angrily. "Did you think we should have said 'Don't be naughty boys again' and sent them away?" Klaus's palm smacked against his leg in exasperation.

"I don't understand you, Paolo. You asked me to come to protect the ships – which could get me into more trouble – and when I do, you don't like the consequences. I know why you want to protect the ships – they're your life. But why did you risk the life of Gianni? He's only a boy."

Paolo looked down at the steps of the museum to avoid Klaus's eyes.

"I am sorry, truly sorry, Klaus. But there was nothing else I could do. You see, I didn't expect these thieves. I believed there would be communists coming to destroy the ships."

"Communists? Destroy the ships? Why would they – or anyone – want to destroy the ships?"

"You don't understand, Klaus," Paolo shook his head. "These ships represent one of the triumphs of Mussolini. It was he who ordered the recovery of the ships from the lake. Of course, for him, it was political – the old glories of the Roman Empire recovered as a showpiece for his new Italian empire."

He spat on the ground and cupped his hand to light his pipe. Klaus could see that his hand was shaking.

"Mussolini himself opened the museum four years ago," he looked at Klaus and then averted his eyes, "and I was there, too."

He drew deeply on his pipe and sighed out the smoke into the night air.

"So, you see, the communists would like to destroy the ships. Just to get at Mussolini. They would destroy two thousand years of history – simply to get at that *figlio di puttana*."

"But didn't you support Mussolini?" Klaus peered at Paolo from under the peak of his cap. The Italian shuffled uncomfortably.

"Yes, the brigand was right. I was – theoretically still am – a member of the Fascist party. I make no apologies – everyone was a member, particularly if you wanted a job of some importance. I went the way the wind blew."

There was weariness in Paolo's voice.

"For me, it was a question of the ships." He sighed. "For others it was a need to get by. Life goes on, whatever the politics. Do you have any tobacco?"

"Only cigarettes. Help yourself." Klaus offered his silver case to the old man, who pulled out two cigarettes before breaking them down to plug the tobacco into his pipe. He cupped his hand across his face to shield the match, the light of which played grotesquely across his face.

Klaus shivered. A cold wind was beginning to swirl around the lake and he wished he had put on his greatcoat. It was strange, he thought, that, before the war, he had always pictured Italy as a country of sun, light and warmth. Yet here he was, chilled to the bone amidst the long darkness of night. Perhaps he would come back, after the war, when the sun shone, lighting the smile on his face. And on Rosanna's. After the war.

"Do you support Hitler?" Paolo's question caught him unawares and angered him.

"I am fighting a war for my fatherland." His terse reply brought a nod from Paolo. Klaus knew it was a lame answer; he was caught up on the same treadmill as the Italian.

He did not support Hitler, or Dressler, or any of the others the monster had spawned. But he was fighting for his country, for his father and his mother. What could he do? He had done what Paolo had done: he had gone the way the wind blew. He wanted to be away from this hell, to be with Rosanna, to hold her in his arms.

"She is well, but she has been very upset."

Klaus jumped as Paolo anticipated his thoughts.

"I am sorry, but you know why I had to leave." Klaus nervously lit a cigarette. "It is an impossible situation. You must tell her to keep away."

The old man got up and looked up at the first streaks of dawn.

"Another day. I wonder how many more there will be before it is all over." He looked over his shoulder as he shuffled off toward the path back up to the town. "I shall tell her what you have said. I agree that it would be better if she didn't see you."

Klaus threw his cigarette to the ground and stamped it out.

Three months later. May 15th 1944. Noon

Klaus pushed open the flap to his command tent and looked out over the lake. There was hardly a sound, only the gentle, rhythmic lapping of the water at the lake's edge and the isolated cry of a gull, swooping down from the sun. Klaus walked toward the edge of the lake, brushing aside the myriad puff balls that confirmed spring's arrival after the departure of the foulest winter he had known. Renewal was in the air. He could feel it in the burgeoning warmth of the sun on his face, see it in the buds that had emerged for their place in that sun. He looked out across the placid surface of the lake, ruffled only by the faintest of breezes, a hazy mirror for the towns of Nemi and Genzano that hung high on the hillsides above the water.

He picked up a large stone and hurled it angrily into the water. What hope was there in this spring? It was difficult to imagine from the scene before him that, barely twenty miles away, men were locked in a life-and-death struggle, where the air was rent with shrieks of agony and the cries of death.

He strode back towards the emplacement. Beneath the camouflage netting that made them appear part of the forest were his four guns. For almost two months, they had bombarded the beaches at Anzio and Nettuno, but now they were silent. A shortage of ammunition. Problems with the supply lines, divisional headquarters had told him. The army was beginning to feel the pinch. Despite all the shelling, despite the frenzied infantry attacks around Campoleone and Aprilia, the Allied bridgehead was holding. Now he had no shells. And he had heard reports that the Allies were about to move onto the offensive: Velletri was now under heavy artillery fire and there were rumors that the divisional headquarters would soon have to pull out. Still, at least the allied *Jabos* hadn't found them. Some planes had flown over the lake, but, thanks to the camouflage, or some miracle, the guns had not been spotted.

Klaus saluted the guard as he entered the gun emplacement. He was pleased that he had set up the tents under the camouflage and moved all billets down to the lakeside. The refugees had been sent away – some had been lodged in the town, the rest had gone God knew where – but he now had his guns and his men, together as a team.

He and his men did not now have to visit the town. It had been a good move. On the few occasions he had visited the town, he had literally felt the hatred from the Italians. None did or said anything, but their eyes spoke of their enmity, their disgust. He knew he had been right to keep his men away from any possible danger. It had definitely been a good move.

It wasn't the only reason he had moved the unit down to the lakeside, and he knew it. He made his way under the camouflage netting, threw aside the flap to his command tent and sat down on the camp bed. Of Paolo, he had seen little since the incident with the brigands. Whether the Italian regretted the arrests, or whether he feared some action would be taken against him, Klaus knew not.

There had been one visit, just after the incident, when Paolo had arrived just after sunrise, looking furtively back up the hillside at the town. Klaus had not understood why Paolo, at the end of the visit, had repeated his request to protect the secret of Diana's mirror and the other treasures. He had thrust a key to the trunk into his hand; perhaps there was no longer anyone else the old man could trust.

Klaus felt for the key that hung at his neck on his I.D. chain, and felt his hand move from it to the amulet that also hung there. He had glimpsed her twice since his return: the first time, when he had been attending to the removal of the refugees from the museum to the castle, he had seen her walking across the piazza, and he had ducked behind the fountain to avoid her; the other time, he had been returning from Genzano in the staff car when he had seen her pushing her bicycle by the side of the road. She had looked up at him and had half raised a hand in greeting, before she saw that he had deliberately turned his head forward to look at the road ahead. She had dropped her hand, stuck out her chin and walked on, as if to show her contempt. Didn't she realize that he was trying to protect her? That there was only danger if anyone saw any hint of feeling between them?

Klaus got up from his cot bed, angry with himself for having allowed her to occupy his thoughts. He flicked through the papers on his field desk. The war. The damned war. When it was over.... He refused to allow his mind to follow that path. Who knew where he would be when the war was over? Maybe he wouldn't survive. If he did, he could be over a thousand miles away, left with only a dream of her. Maybe their meeting had been a dream, too. His fist slammed down onto the desk and he swore loudly.

The tent flap lifted as Gunther's face appeared, his brow furrowed.

"Everything alright, sir?"

"The Allies are about to break out of the beachhead, Velletri is getting pasted, and we have no shells! Of course everything is alright!"

Gunther was taken aback by the sarcastic outburst, but said nothing.

"I'm sorry, my friend." Klaus sighed apologetically. "I'm off to Genzano to see if I can get the ammunition supplies sorted out. It's a waste of breath talking on the telephone."

"Kick a few butts for me." Gunther smiled.

"I'll take the motorbike. Back around four o'clock."

The same day. 3.30 p.m.

Gunther squinted at the sun as it began to fall away from its zenith into the cloudless afternoon sky. At least the winter had gone. He was used to the cold in Bavaria, but not the perpetual freezing damp, snow and rain that had persisted since the previous November. He longed to be back on his father's farm; it would be calving time now and everyone would be helping in the barns.

He shook his head at the memory and returned to cleaning his machine pistol. The boss was getting very edgy lately. The outburst that morning had showed he was getting more and more wound up. It was unlike him: he was usually calm and in control. Gunther chuckled as he remembered how the boss had rescued him from an angry brothel keeper in France, telling him to submit his bill to the address on a piece of paper he gave him; Gunther often wondered how Reichfuehrer Himmler had reacted to the bill.

The war was clearly getting to the boss. Maybe it was Dressler, he thought. He was a mean son of a bitch, and he knew he had it in for the captain since that business about the report on the Italian woman – a big mistake, that. You had to get on with the war and shut your eyes to a lot of things, or you would end up going mad. Obey orders; it was the easy way.

Perhaps it was the woman – he had seen how the boss had gone all soft when he saw her at the museum. Women were always bad news. When would men ever learn? The bull serviced the cow and moved on. That was Gunther's motto: fuck 'em and forget 'em. He was indulging in the memory of some he had not forgotten, when a great din made him stop cleaning his weapon and get up from the chair in front of the large tent that served as the unit headquarters.

The noise got worse: protesting squeals, interspersed with a babble of Italian he did not understand. He looked out across the other camouflaged tents that surrounded the gun emplacement at the edge of the lake. He shielded his eyes against the glare of the sun. There was no doubting the source of the noise: one of his men had his arms under the armpits of a young boy who was screaming and kicking for all he was worth.

"Look what I found out there."

Gunther beckoned the soldier to him. "Bring him over here. What was he doing?"

"*Vaffanculo! Vaffanculo!*"

The torrent of indecipherable words continued to flow from the young boy's lips as he continued to try to dig his heels into the soldier's shins.

"He was messing about at the edge of the camp. Heaven knows what he was up to. What the hell is he jabbering on about?"

"How the hell do you think I know? But I don't suppose it's very nice." Gunther walked towards the soldier and the boy, and stopped suddenly as he saw the boy's face. It was the urchin he had tossed in the air at the museum when he had visited the lake with Klaus six months ago: he recognized the angular body, the tousled hair. It was the little bastard who had stolen the sandwiches.

The soldier, anxious to avoid further damage to his shins, dropped the boy, but held onto his arm. "What shall I do with him? Headquarters has said we can't trust any of these Italians, even the kids."

Gunther laughed. "No, this one's on the scrounge. I've seen him before. Mind you, this one might steal the guns if we turned our backs. Send him over to me."

The sergeant beckoned the boy with a deliberate movement of his index finger. "*Janni.*" His tongue struggled with the Italian name. "*Janni, hergekommen.*" The lad looked anxiously for a moment, then recognized Gunther's face and moved cautiously toward him.

"Would you like some cheese?" Gunther produced a small piece from his pocket. Gianni's eyes widened. He leapt forward to grab for the morsel, but Gunther lifted it high above his head as the little boy jumped up in a vain attempt to secure the food. Gunther amused himself with the game for a few moments before relenting, tossing the scrap to the lad.

"My God, you're hungry!" Gunther watched with surprise as the boy clamped his teeth around the cheese and devoured it in a few moments. He wiped the back of his hand across his mouth and looked up at the sergeant, who ran his hand through the boy's dark matted hair.

"Dov' è il Signor Capitano?"

Gunther looked down quizzically at the boy, who began to tug on his sleeve.

"Dov' è il Signor Capitano?"

The sergeant shrugged his shoulders. Why didn't these people speak German? "There is no more food. *Ich habe nichts!*" He opened his hands. "*Nichts!*"

The boy persisted for a while, tugging at the soldier's sleeve again, then stood back and raised one hand above his head, rotating it in a circle; his other hand he held at an incline slanting down from his forehead. Gunther looked bemused until the lad made an exaggerated movement, as if taking off a hat. Then he raised his fingers to his shoulders, tapping each in turn.

Gunther grasped the meaning. A cap and shoulder flashes. An officer.

"Ah, der Hauptman! Hauptman Schmidt?"

"Sì, sì, il Signor Capitano! Dov' è?" Gianni spread his spindly arms wide.

"Er nicht hier ist." Gunther looked into the boy's uncomprehending face, and then raised his arm, his finger pointing across the lake to Genzano. The lad made as if to run off towards the town, but Gunther grabbed him. Gianni began kicking and shouting, but Gunther pulled him to him and held him in a firm but gentle bear hug.

"Verboten! Sperrstunde!" The boy continued to struggle. Gunther wondered how he could tell him about the curfew. He turned Gianni so he looked away from him, holding him with one arm as he used the other to point at the sun, which was beginning to fall toward the western rim of the crater. As he did so, he saw the motorcycle coming down the hill toward the lake and heaved a sigh of relief.

Gianni wriggled free from Gunther's relaxing grip and ran towards Klaus as he brought the motorcycle to a halt.

"Signor Capitano! Signor Capitano!"

Klaus killed the engine and dismounted from the machine, raising his goggles onto his cap.

"What's all this about, Gunther?"

"I don't know, boss. He came scrounging for food, then said he wanted to see you."

"Gianni, you know it is forbidden for you to be here." He spoke harshly to the boy. "You can get into serious trouble."

"Sì, sì, but I have come with a message."

"A message? From whom?" Klaus's brow furrowed.

The boy looked up at Klaus, then looked across at Gunther and began tugging on the captain's sleeve. "It's a secret." His voice was little more than a whisper.

"But Gunther doesn't understand a word of Italian."

"I know, but he might recognize names."

Klaus pulled the youngster to one side. "This is a silly game, Gianni."

But he nodded to Gunther. "I'll be with you in a moment. I need to teach him the dangers of coming into our encampment." Gunther turned and disappeared into the command tent.

"Now, Gianni, what's all this about a message?"

"It's from Rosanna." Klaus started anxiously at her name.

Gianni sensed Klaus's anxiety and hesitated.

"Go on!" There was a sharp edge to Klaus's voice.

"She wants to see you." The boy hesitated again. "Tomorrow. At the temple. Four o'clock." Gianni raced through the last part of the message and turned to go. Klaus grabbed him before he could run off. He held Gianni tightly by the upper arms and squatted down in front of the boy so they were face to face.

"Gianni, listen carefully to what I'm going to say, because I want you to repeat every word to Rosanna."

The lad nodded apprehensively.

"Tell her…" He struggled with the words. "…tell her that I cannot come – tell her that it would put her and her parents in grave danger. Are you listening to me, Gianni?"

"*Sì*." The boy looked into Klaus's eyes, then down at where Klaus's hands held his arms tight. Klaus sighed, shook his head and released his grip.

"And tell her not to send you here to the camp. It's very dangerous for you, Gianni."

He waved a finger of admonition in front of the youngster, who replied with a cheeky grin.

"I'm serious, Gianni!" He grabbed the boy again and shook him.

"*Sì, sì, capisco.*" He wriggled free of Klaus's fingers. "Can I go now?"

Klaus nodded and the boy scampered to the edge of the camp.

"Tell her one more thing." Klaus called after him and the boy stopped and turned. "Tell her that I…" He felt an aching void, a pain that seized him, filling him with despair. Gianni peered at him, curiously. "…that I will come back for her after the war."

The boy nodded and took to his heels. Klaus shook his head. It hadn't been what he had meant to say, but he felt he had said more than enough. After the war: some glimmer of hope. It was a false hope, probably as false as his promise to return. He kicked at a stone on the ground. There was no hope. Only the war.

The next day. 3.30 p.m.

"I'm just going to have a look around."

The guard saluted Klaus as he made his way to the perimeter of the camp.

"If that little rascal shows up again, just box his ears and send him home."

Klaus raised his hand to his cap to return the salute. The soldier smiled and continued his patrol.

Klaus began to walk away from the museum, through the small patches of cultivation that dotted the flatter land which bordered the lake before it swept up in a steeper incline towards the forested hills. A few people tended the strawberry beds in the afternoon spring sunshine. The dictates of Nature, of the seasons, Klaus thought. It was as if the war were a thousand miles away instead of just beyond the hills at the southern end of the lake.

He breathed deeply of the afternoon air, savoring the smells of the ripening strawberries, before he stooped to pick one, crushing it between his teeth to let the wonderful taste dance on his tongue. As he began to meet the rising ground, he turned to look over the lake, shining like a mirror as the wind held its breath, the reflection of the towns of Nemi and Genzano shimmering on its surface.

The tranquility was disturbed by a slight rumbling in the distance and he knew that this apparent haven of peace would soon be rent asunder by the maelstrom of war hovering over the horizon. His ammunition would arrive tomorrow, but he knew it would be too little and too late. The noise he could hear was the Allies pasting Velletri; the Americans and the Tommies could no longer be contained in the Anzio beachhead. It could only be a matter of days before he and his men would be forced to pull out as the army retreated northwards.

One of the people tending the beds looked up at him. Klaus could see the sullen hatred in his eyes, but he also detected a knowing smile. The peasant knew, too, that it would not be long now before he could tend his patch in peace. Klaus heaved a sigh; he held no hatred for the man; he, too, wished the war were over. He pictured the University in Berlin and conjured up a vision of taking coffee on the Unter den Linden. If anything was left of it; he hadn't been home for nearly a year, and, from his friends who had, he had heard that the city was being heavily bombed day and night.

A swish of branches farther up the hill broke his train of thought. He looked for a few moments, but saw nothing. Perhaps a small creature of the forest, nothing more. He fervently hoped it was not Gianni. The lad did not realize the dangers he faced. If Gunther hadn't known him, he would already have been in serious trouble. Rosanna should not have sent him.

Klaus grimaced as his own hypocrisy hit him. He knew where his feet were taking him, slowly, but inevitably. Every part of his brain, all his rational thought was screaming at him to turn back, but his feet continued to move up the hillside towards the temple. He glanced at his watch. A quarter to four. He took a small path and entered the forest.

He should not have come. It was foolish and dangerous, for Rosanna as well as himself. But something drove him on, something he could not control. He felt, instinctively for the little icon at his neck and caressed it, as if he were caressing her. He had to see her, to explain why he had left her, to promise her that he would return after the war.

Perhaps she would heed his message and not come. Part of him hoped that it would be so, but his heart wished otherwise. The battle with himself consumed him; twice he stopped and turned to go back, only to turn again to follow the path upwards. The shade of the trees ended and he emerged into the sun at the edge of the temple site.

The tranquility of the site overwhelmed him. Only a solitary bird's cry broke the silence. He shrugged off the irrational feeling that there was some supernatural force surrounding him; he was letting Rosanna's fairy tales get to him. But it was eerily quiet: there was not a sound, not a breath of wind. He walked forward a few paces and listened again. Not a sound. There was no one. She had heeded his words, and he wondered if he had hurt her by casting her aside a second time. He turned to retrace his steps.

"I knew you would come."

He turned, startled. She was there, a dozen feet away, sitting on top of an old wall. Her eyes sparkled and her lips were parted in a broad smile.

"I was sure you'd come."

She leapt down from her perch, her blue dress billowing up. She stood looking at him for a moment before running across to him, her arms spread wide. As she neared him, she stopped briefly and drank in his face with her eyes. Then she hurled herself at him, her arms and her lips feeding hungrily upon him. He tried to will his arms to remain at his side, but he found they had a will of their own; she looked up at him and he crushed her to him, both hostages to a power greater than themselves.

CHAPTER 38

Afterwards, they watched the progress of the sun, which was falling slowly toward the hills on the western edge of the lake. Klaus could feel her warmth as they lay on the grass, her head across his chest, gently rising and falling as he breathed. He ran his fingers through her long black hair and softly kissed the top of her head. He wanted time to stand still, but, inch by inch, the golden disc moved, inexorably pressing reality back into their lives.

"You know I can't stay here with you."

He answered her question before she asked. He propped himself up on one elbow as he looked down at her. He had not wanted to break the spell of the moment, but he knew it had to be done. His eyes dropped briefly, but the smile returned to her face after a moment as she nestled her head under his chin.

"Too many people here know me as a German soldier."

"I know." He was surprised that she acquiesced so quickly, without any protest. "My mother would kill you. After you left, she didn't speak to papa for days. But I understood why you had to go."

She came up to him and brought her lips to his, easing back after a few moments to look into his eyes.

"It doesn't matter. From now, we shall be together forever." Her hand reached up to caress his face.

"What do you mean?" His brow furrowed. "You know I cannot desert. I have to go back to my unit." His voice fell away. "To the war."

She said nothing, but reached under his shirt and pulled out the icon of Diana. With her other hand, she pulled out its twin from between her breasts. She placed the pair together, touching.

"You see," her soft brown eyes looked up, "we shall be together forever."

She eased herself up onto her arm, lying half across him, and held up his icon.

"Wherever you go, I shall go."

She lifted her icon to her lips and kissed it.

"And wherever I go, you will go."

Her lips moved to his and she kissed him, unlike before, but with such a tenderness that he could feel his heart break. He pulled her to him, holding her, hugging her, in a vain hope she would never go away.

"I love you, Rosanna."

She gently broke from his grip and held his face in her hands.

"And I love you, Klaus."

She could see the tears in his eyes and moved her lips to kiss them away.

"I shall come back after the war."

She smiled, but said nothing, turning her eyes to the horizon. Dusk was less than an hour away.

He sat up, and she heard him sigh.

"I know. We can't stay any longer." She got to her feet. "But let's take one last moment."

He got up and stood beside her. They gazed at each other and she slipped her hand in his as they turned to look down over the lake. There was still no wind, but the light was different, the hues darker as the sun began to slip away.

"See how still the water is!" She clutched at his hand, waving her free arm toward the lake. "It is like a mirror – yes, like my father's mirror - Diana's Mirror!" Her eyes started to fill, and Klaus put his arm around her, wishing that he could stay her tears.

"The mirror has captured our souls and will hold us together forever." She held his hand even tighter as they walked back to the edge of the wood.

Klaus did not want to dispel her dream, but he felt the reality of the world beginning to grind again as the sun kissed the hilltop, lengthening their shadows.

Suddenly she became agitated, her eyes desperately seeking his. "I know what you're thinking – that the war will cast us apart, that we shall not see each other again."

"No, no..." He knew there was a hesitation in his voice, despite all his hopes.

"But you are wrong!" Her voice was almost a shout. "Diana will bring you back to me. It will be so!" She reached for him and kissed him. "Diana, her icons and her mirror, they will all bring you back to me. After the war, you will return for me."

She did not linger with the last kiss, but broke quickly from him and ran to the edge of the clearing, to the path that led up to the town. Suddenly, she stopped, turned and looked back at him.

"You will come back." She held out her icon. "Remember the mirror." She waved. "And remember me."

She turned and was gone. Klaus gazed at the path for a few moments, in the vain hope she would return. He wanted to go after her, but he knew it was futile. He vowed to himself that he would come back, after the war. They would be happy once more, after the war. He looked one last time across the temple site, then turned and started to walk back down the path to his guns, wondering how he could keep his promise when he did not even know what tomorrow would bring. The old man tending his strawberry patch looked up at him again, the hatred still burning in his eyes.

CHAPTER 39

Two weeks later. 3.30 p.m. May 31st 1944

Rosanna tried to read her book after lunch, but the noise from outside distracted her. She walked across to her bedroom window and cautiously opened the shutters. German voices rose up to her, and she could see that the piazza was a hive of activity. The soldiers were scurrying about, some leading horses, as a troop marched down the street, their boots clumping in unison on the cobbles. A car arrived, bearing the swastika pennant, delivering several officers at the entrance to the German headquarters at the Ruspoli palace.

Rosanna understood at once. They were leaving. The hated Germans were leaving. She knew she should be celebrating, but an ache tugged within her. She looked across at the wall where she had hung Klaus's sketch of her. He was about to go, too. Perhaps she would never see him again. Her hand reached for and fondled the icon at her breast.

Her thoughts were distracted by a truck that passed beneath, belching its fumes. Orders were being shouted and soldiers were beginning to climb into the trucks. They really were going. And Klaus would be going with them. She shielded her eyes against the afternoon sun and peered down to the edge of the lake by the museum. She knew he was there. So near, and yet, by tomorrow, he could be gone. She had to see him.

The wind gusted, snatching at the shutter. The old clock on her dresser chimed three. She had to move now, before the curfew. The voices of her parents in the kitchen below were subdued. She took a sweater out of her closet, slipped it over her shoulders and eased open her bedroom door. From the sound of her parents' voices, she could tell they were at the front window, curious themselves at the bustle in the piazza. Her feet moved noiselessly down the stairs. She paused, holding her breath so they would not hear her, and then slid silently through the side door into the street.

She knew she had to hurry, so she ran quickly around the corner of the street leading to the piazza and the town gate. The hands seized her roughly, crushing her arms to her side. Another hand came up to clamp her mouth and stifle her cry. Fear seized her as she struggled vainly;

she turned, trying to see her attackers, but the sack came over her head, plunging her into darkness, and the string tightened around her neck until she could scarcely breathe.

"Now, German lover," the unseen voice hissed in her ear, "it's time to pay the price for playing around with those swine!"

CHAPTER 40

It was a sound Klaus knew only too well. The whine of the shell reached its culmination; the whine became a whistle, then an ear-piercing scream, driving fear into all who lay in its path. For a second, the briefest of moments, there was silence, then the explosion. As the blast hit, the noise burst in the ears and the skeleton shook within the body. The explosion hurled flying branches, clods of earth, and stones into the air; the shards of the shell whistled through the air, seeking vulnerable flesh.

"They're getting closer, boss." Gunther shook off the debris and looked out from under the camouflage netting that the blast had half torn from the gun emplacement.

"They're firing from closer range, now. Any minute now, the bastards will have the accurate range, and...." The sergeant drew his fingers across his throat. "It's time to go!"

Klaus picked himself up from where the blast had blown him, re-trieved his cap and grimaced at the sight emerging from the dispersing smoke of the gunfire. One of his men came staggering toward the camp, trying to hold his shattered arm against his body, the blood arcing from the severed artery until he collapsed, twitching as his life's blood drained away; there was a final shudder, then the stillness of death.

"Get him out of here!" Klaus screamed at the men who had been momentarily transfixed at the sight of their fallen comrade. Two other men had flesh wounds, and he sent them to the dressing station up in the village. The carnage among the horses was devastating; a lieutenant took his pistol to the screaming injured beasts and released them from their pain.

Gunther was right: it was time to go. Why he had not received the formal order to withdraw was beyond his understanding; he wondered why Dressler and the other fools in the headquarters in Nemi hadn't issued it. Surely they could see what was going on. Probably there was another 'fight to the last man' directive from the madman in Berlin.

Klaus looked to the southern edge of the hills above the lake; be-hind them – who knew how near – the Americans were advancing. Four months of ceaseless bloody battle had failed to hold the Allies at

Anzio. With the fall of Velletri two days ago, Klaus knew that they had broken out of the bridgehead. The game was up. He looked to the west, where the sun was beginning to fall in the sky. He hoped his unit would be able to chance a withdrawal under cover of darkness. If someone gave the order.

The crump of another shell carved another swathe in the woods, but this time it was higher on the hill. Klaus looked across to the museum, as yet undamaged, apart from a few windows blown in by shell blast. The museum was only two hundred meters from the gun position; any stray shell could consign the ships and their two thousand years of history to oblivion. His hand went to his neck, feeling for Paolo's key, as another shell came in, falling into the lake, sending a huge plume of water into the air.

Klaus could sense the anxiety of his men as they fretted around the guns. The ammunition had run out two hours before and they were stuck there like sitting ducks. Why didn't the order to withdraw come? He brought up his field glasses and leveled them at the town high above. Men were running around by the western gate as horses and a few trucks were being gathered in the piazza. Preparing to evacuate? Klaus swung his glasses higher, into the hills, trying to pick out his artillery spotter. He had heard nothing from the observation post since his ammunition ran out, except for a brief message that the Americans were closing up on the outskirts of Genzano, and that, off to the east, enemy troop movements could be seen on the road coming north from Velletri.

He whipped around at the sound of a dull explosion at the southern end of the lake. Everyone turned as a sheet of flame rose above Genzano, lighting up the sky, dancing violently in the growing wind. The refection, like some macabre early sunset, played upon the lake's wind-tossed surface.

Klaus grimaced. "Gunther, I think you're right." He lowered his field glasses. "It's time to go." He cranked the field telephone, but there was no response.

"To hell with them." He slammed the receiver down and told his gun commanders to prepare for withdrawal. As they left he called Gunther to him.

"Gunther, with half the horses dead, we're stuck here unless we can get replacements – or trucks. Take your men and get up to the northern end of Genzano as quickly as you can. Bring back four trucks to limber the guns. And get as much gasoline as you can."

Gunther saluted and turned to leave, but Klaus called after him.

"Tell them it's on my orders. And if that doesn't work, steal them! Off you go, *schnell, schnell!*"

As Gunther and his men disappeared beyond the museum, Klaus hurried about the gun emplacement, as the gunners pulled off the camouflage sheets. The stability legs were removed and the gun elevations were depressed to prepare the weapons for transport. He looked over his shoulder. The flames over Genzano had abated a little, but he could hear the sporadic chatter of small arms fire. He hoped Gunther would be in time.

"I present *Standartenfeuhrer* Dressler's compliments, *Hauptman* Schmidt."

Klaus turned sharply at the shock of the voice. It was Schneider, Dressler's ass-kissing adjutant. A half-pace behind him, in a similar black uniform, stood an SS corporal, a Schmeisser machine pistol held across his chest.

"So, you've brought the order to withdraw at last." Klaus turned away off-handedly. "How good of you to come down the hill to bring it to me personally, Schneider. I thought you had forgotten us." He began to move away to urge on his men.

"You must understand, *Hauptman* Schmidt," Schneider's voice had a supercilious tone, "that *Standartenfuehrer* Dressler wishes to discuss the matter of withdrawal with you...personally." The last word was said slowly, the voice full of menace.

Klaus's anger exploded.

"Look!" He pointed to the flames hanging over Genzano. "The Americans are knocking on the door, I have no ammunition, and Dressler wants to *discuss* things with me?"

Klaus saw Schneider stiffen and the SS corporal's knuckles whiten as his grip on the machine pistol tightened.

"*Hauptman* Schmidt, I think that present events are clouding your judgment." The escort's machine pistol dropped a few degrees from the normal position. "Please follow me."

Klaus recalled that Schneider had cold-bloodedly shot some peasant who had refused to hand over his livestock. He bowed to the inevitable. Better get this nonsense over as quickly as possible so his men could get out of this rat trap. He shouted orders to his gun crew commanders and followed Schneider's black uniform as it scrambled up the hillside towards Nemi. The goon with the gun followed behind him.

Dark clouds began to obscure the sun as they climbed the steeply ascending path, plunging the lake into the gloom of an early twilight. The growing wind plucked at Klaus as he followed Schneider. He knew he had to stand up to Dressler, but for some unknown reason, he felt a premonition of disaster. His hand grasped at the icon hanging around his neck.

"Something's up!" Paolo's frame was bent over the window, the curtains lifted as he peered out.

"I think they're going, Maria." He clapped his hands, almost involuntarily. "I think they're going at last!"

"Put that curtain down, you fool! You're asking for trouble"

"They've got enough on their plate than to bother about us." There was a happy tone to his voice, but he lowered the curtain, peering around it to look down on the piazza.

"Yes, they're loading trucks. Running about like headless chickens. The bastards are going!"

He left the window and began to dance and skip around the table at which Maria sat impassively.

"The Germans are going! The Germans are going!" He kissed his wife on the top of her head. "Aren't you happy?"

Before she could answer, they both heard the crump of a shell not too far off. Paolo raced back to his vantage point. He pulled back the curtain carefully, frightened of what he might see. He heaved a sigh of relief when he saw the explosion was high on the crater wall, well away from the museum.

Paolo's emotions were confused: he was happy that the Germans were leaving, but he was anxious for the safety of his ships. Why didn't they leave now? One more day – that was all that was needed. One more day, and his ships would be safe. Just one more day, please God.

The explosion on the other side of the lake caused him to jump back from the window.

"My God, Genzano is on fire!"

Maria's chair clattered to the floor as she pushed it back and rushed across the kitchen floor, thrusting her husband aside to see for herself the flames engulfing Genzano.

"Holy Mother of God!" She crossed herself as the reflection of the flames flickered across the window. "Pray God everyone is alright!"

Paolo leant over her, grasping her shoulders, pulling her away from the window. He held her to him, trying to comfort her, trying to draw her mind away from the flames consuming Genzano.

"Not long now, *mia cara*." He felt her body heave against him, sobbing with worry and anxiety. "Soon the swine will be gone."

He was alarmed as she suddenly pulled herself free of his grasp.

"And will that swine, Carlo - or Klaus – whatever you want to call your German friend," she spat out the word 'German,' "will he be gone with them?"

Paolo saw the temper in her eyes, fighting its way through the tears. Perhaps the anger was there to fight off the tears. He felt unable to defend himself.

"Probably." He slumped into his chair. "But he wasn't a bad man, Maria." His hands went fumbling for the pipe in his pocket, as they did at times of stress. "He did save Rosanna from…."

"What if he did?" She turned on him sharply. "He soon bought you with his tobacco!" She glowered at him from across the table. "And he fooled me with his lies, his damned lies that you connived in."

Paolo sucked on the empty pipe; he had no answer. All he wanted was a pipe of tobacco, a little peace and quiet, and his ships. He moved once more to the window. The flames over Genzano still licked at the darkening sky and, by their light, he could just pick out the shapes of the museum way down below him at the water's edge. Just one more day, he muttered to himself again. Just one more day and the ships would be safe.

"Still worrying about your precious ships?" His wife clung to her argument, like a dog with an old bone. "What about Rosanna?" She got up from her chair and made her way across the floor towards him. "You, her own father, almost laid her on a plate for that blond German *porco*." She swung her arms, beating her fists against her husband's chest. "Our only child and you…."

Paolo grabbed her and pushed her away, holding her at arm's length to avoid her blows. Suddenly, she stopped and threw herself against her husband, sobbing on his breast.

"Oh, Paolo, Paolo, what has become of us?"

He stroked the back of her neck. "Ssh, *mia cara*, Rosanna will hear you."

Her sobbing slowly subsided and she slipped from her husband's grasp.

"You're right – I'm sorry." She pulled a handkerchief from her pocket and wiped her eyes. "It's just that…."

He waved his hand in front of him to tell her there was no need for explanation. She moved across to the sink and splashed water on her face. She dried herself on the towel and walked across to the door leading to the stairs.

"I'll call her down." Her fingers rattled at the latch. "She can help me prepare dinner, such as there is."

There was no answer to her call.

"She's probably dozed off."

Paolo heard his wife's footsteps on the stairs as he turned to look once more through the window. The fire at Genzano cast an eerie light over the lake as if the flames of hell were licking at the water. He heard the scream of a shell, and heaved a sigh of relief as it fell short into the lake, throwing up a huge plume of water. Just one more day.

"Paolo, Paolo, she's not there!" His wife's voice reached him as she ran down the stairs; he turned to see her in the doorway, her face full of fear and anxiety.

"Mother of God, Paolo, she's gone! Do you know where she is?"

He shook his head. "I thought she was in her room. Perhaps she slipped out."

Maria wrung her hands. "No. Stubborn as she is, not even she would go out just before curfew with that racket and all those Germans in the street."

"But she must be somewhere, *mia cara*." He reached up to the hook on the door and took down his jacket.

"What on earth are you doing?" Maria ran across the floor and grabbed at the jacket. "No, no, you must not go out. It will soon be curfew. They'll shoot you!"

"I have to take the chance." Paolo gently eased her fingers free. "I must find Rosanna!"

He turned, cradled his wife's face in his hands and kissed her gently. He could see the fear in her eyes.

"Bring her back, Paolo. But please be careful." She pulled him to her, briefly, before he moved away and put on his jacket.

"I am always careful." He blew her a kiss as he closed the door behind him.

There was no sentry at the entrance to the old palace as Klaus, breathless after the steep climb from the lake, followed Schneider through the gate. Everywhere was chaos. Hobnailed boots clattered across the piazza; engines screamed as trucks maneuvered in the narrow streets; a troop of soldiers led a dozen whinnying horses toward the western gate of the town; everywhere, officers shouted, striving to bring order from the unfolding chaos. Black clouds now covered the sky and the whole scene danced in the glow of the flames from Genzano across the lake.

"*Schnell, schnell!*" Schneider urged Klaus across the palace courtyard and through the door that led to the great hall. Klaus's eyes first fell on the fire blazing in the hearth, the flames roaring up the chimney. Several men fed the fire constantly with files and dossiers.

"So good of you to come, *Hauptman* Schmidt!"

The nonchalant clipped tones of Dressler startled Klaus and he turned quickly to see the black uniform leaning over a map set on a long table. Despite Dressler's disinterested air, Klaus felt he could detect a hint of anxiety on the cold features of his face.

"I see you have still forgotten how to salute, Schmidt!"

Klaus snapped to attention, but his hand came up to his cap in the traditional military salute. Dressler looked at him, but did not comment on Klaus's veiled insubordination. Instead, a smile spread beneath the ice-blue eyes and Klaus heard alarm bells in his head.

Dressler looked down at the map. "It seems we must make a tactical withdrawal to…" his fingers made a circle on the map, "…Frascati."

Klaus wondered if Dressler believed it was a tactical withdrawal or whether he was deluding himself about the real situation. Now that the Allies had broken out of Anzio, there was little to stop them. Frascati tomorrow, then Florence, Turin and Milan, until the Allies would be knocking on the door of the fatherland itself. Didn't Dressler realize that the whole house of cards was crashing down?

"If we have to make a tactical withdrawal, why have I not yet received the orders to evacuate my unit?" Klaus was surprised with his own boldness. "Because of my position by the side of the lake, my men can only get out by way of the Via Appia." He traced the route on the map. "And soon the Americans will have cut that route."

Dressler waved aside his objection and told his aides to roll up the map.

"My dear Schmidt, in war, communications sometimes get cut."

Klaus recalled the dead field telephone and wondered if Dressler was telling the truth, or had, in fact, intended to abandon him.

"Anyway, the order has now been given." Dressler tapped a cigarette on his silver case before lighting it. "Apparently, your sergeant..." He paused as he drew on the cigarette. "What's his name? Mattheus, isn't it?"

Klaus nodded.

"Well, *Feldwebel* Mattheus has been running amok in Albano trying to commandeer horses, trucks and fuel."

Klaus's gut tightened at the thought of what Dressler had in mind for Gunther.

"He did that on my orders!"

Dressler waved away his protestations.

"There is no need to be alarmed, *Hauptman*." Dressler leant back and blew smoke rings into the air. "I have ordered the release of four trucks to your sergeant, together with, I might add, an ample supply of gasoline."

Klaus was caught off-balance, his mind searching for Dressler's ulterior motive. The black uniform strode across to the fireplace.

"Which, by now," Dressler glanced at his watch, "the sergeant should be delivering to your unit. Why are you waiting, Schmidt?"

He did not shift his gaze from the fire, but his voice became lower.

"Or is there truth in the reports I have read that you no longer want to fight, but wish to stay here in the land of the dagoes with your trollop?"

Dressler turned his head, fixing Klaus with the look of a predator toying with his prey.

Klaus was stunned, dumbfounded. How did Dressler know? Had he put the Gestapo onto him? Had they followed him, watched as he and Rosanna....

He fought the urge to fall upon Dressler, to beat him, to pound the life out of him. He knew it would achieve nothing, except to put himself in front of a firing squad. But he could not contain his feelings. He moved toward Dressler, who tensed himself.

"Listen, *Standardtenfuehrer*." He hissed the words into Dressler's face. Klaus continued before Dressler could say anything. "I am ready to fight. I am willing to fight for my folk, for my mother and father, for my homeland," he leant forward, so only Dressler's ears would catch his next words, "but I will not be fighting for you and your ilk!"

Klaus was taken aback when Dressler did not explode, but smiled and spoke to him in the same harsh whisper.

"Spoken like a true liberal." He spat out the last word. "You intellectuals will always hover around in a miasma of indecision, not knowing which way to move. It will always be people like me who make the decisions. You and your sort will moan about the decisions, whine as only intellectuals can," he reached out and took Klaus's lapel in his hand, "but, in the end, you will go along with the decision. You will obey!"

Klaus was stunned by the calm, clinical way in which Dressler spoke. He stood still, his mind searching for an answer, but Dressler spoke again before he could say anything.

"You see, Schmidt, you liberals can do nothing, and I have nothing but contempt for you."

He turned back to the fire, a smile playing on his lips.

"I have more regard for the Soviets. Don't get me wrong, Schmidt – I detest everything they stand for – but I respect them. They decide what has to be done, and they do it – they don't pussyfoot around like intellectuals, agonizing over choices, before feeling guilty that the wrong choice has been made."

Dressler pulled himself up to his full height, looked down on Klaus and gave a brief condescending laugh.

"The future belongs to us!" He punched the Nazi insignia on his arm. "Or, perish the thought, it belongs to the Soviets. Either way," he prodded his finger into Klaus's tunic, "you and your sort are mere hapless bystanders in the struggle for the world."

Klaus felt he could tolerate the nonsense no longer. He turned to go, to help get his men out of the trap, to leave the madman to his delusions, but he was stopped when Dressler's voice rang across the room.

"And in that struggle, bystanders must learn to obey, Schmidt."

The other officers in the room looked across at Klaus; Schneider and his muscleman watched from the doorway; even the men feeding the fire stopped and cast their eyes toward him. Dressler raised his voice so everyone in the room could hear.

"*Hauptman* Schmidt, there is one final order before you leave, and it is an order you will obey."

Klaus stood, bemused, in the doorway.

"You will find, when you return to your unit, that your good sergeant has more gasoline than your trucks require."

Dressler began to laugh, a guffaw that boomed and echoed around the hall. Everyone in the room stood stock still, waiting as the laughter faded.

"You will take that gasoline, Schmidt," Dressler fixed his eyes on Klaus, "and you will burn the ships of Caligula!"

CHAPTER 43

Paolo slid along the wall in the *Corso Vittorio Emanuele*, edging toward the doorway of the De Sanctis bar. Dark clouds hung in the gloomy sky, and he clung to the shadows thrown across the lake by the fires at Genzano, cowering in a darkened doorway in order to escape the attention of the Germans. He looked up and down the street anxiously, but the Germans were too intent on preparing their withdrawal to notice him.

Only ten more steps to the doorway of the De Sanctis bar. Paolo knew he still had to take care. The noise and the clatter of vehicles and horses were distracting attention from him, but one false move could betray him and put him in the hands of the Germans. He had no defense: the hour of the curfew had already passed.

Paolo breathed deeply to hold himself together as he moved carefully through the shadows. At last, he eased into the doorway. He faced the road, the door at his back, as he looked back towards the piazza, where all the Germans were gathering. They were preoccupied with the preparations for their departure. He closed his eyes and, with his clenched hand behind his back, he knocked four times on the door.

There was no answer. Paolo waited, breathing heavily. Suddenly, he heard the clip of hooves; from the other end of the *Corso*, a German was leading a horse towards the piazza. In twenty seconds, the German would be upon him. He knocked again, four times; there was desperation in his knock.

"*Chi è?*" The gruff whisper from the other side of the door was music to Paolo's ears.

"It's me. Paolo. Let me in, Ernesto, there's a German coming!"

The German had stopped and was examining one of his horse's hooves; then he dropped it and seized the leading rein. The bolt of the door slid open and Paolo slipped quickly into the empty bar.

"I thought you'd never come, Ernesto." Paolo's breath came erratically as he struggled to regain his composure.

"How did I know that you weren't a German?" Ernesto shrugged, his palms turned upwards. "They've taken all of my stock and they keep coming back for more. *Bastardi!*"

The innkeeper moved behind the bar, pulled a chisel from a drawer, and levered a floor board loose. "All except what I have hidden!" He winked at Paolo as his hand emerged clutching a bottle, which he set on the bar. "Let's drink to the departure of the Germans, Paolo!" He filled two glasses and pushed them across the bar.

"Much as I would like to, I cannot." Paolo fiddled uneasily with his cap. "You see, Ernesto, Rosanna has gone missing. I'm very worried. I've called on most of the neighbors, but there's no news. Have you seen her?"

"Missing?" The innkeeper's voice betrayed unease. "No, Paolo, I've not seen her. I saw her this morning, by the fountain, but I've not seen her since the shelling started." He looked down into his glass, averting his eyes.

"But you know something, don't you, Ernesto?" Paolo leant across the bar. "What's going on?"

"No, there's nothing." He again avoided Paolo's eyes. "Now, I've got things to do."

He started to turn from the bar, but Paolo grabbed him by the front of his shirt.

"There is something, Ernesto." Paolo hissed into the innkeeper's face. "Tell me."

"Ok, ok!" He struggled from Paolo's grasp. "But it isn't pleasant."

Paolo waited patiently as Ernesto refilled his glass and emptied it in one swallow.

"Sometimes, we don't even know our own children, Paolo." He wiped the drops of wine from his mustache with the back of his hand.

"What do you mean, Ernesto?" Paolo moved around the bar to confront the innkeeper.

"Well, there's been a story going around the town for a few days now." He tipped the bottle into the glass again and drank quickly.

"Story? What story?"

"That Rosanna has been seen..." he fumbled for his words "...with a German officer."

Paolo stepped back, dumbstruck.

"I don't believe it!" He gasped.

"It's hard to believe such a thing about a lovely girl like Rosanna," Ernesto looked down at his empty glass, "but she was seen at the temple by...."

"Who saw her? He's a liar!"

"Does it matter? She was seen by more than one man! Some of the women are angry that she went with one of those swine." He spat into the fireplace.

Paolo shook his head in disbelief, but his own guilt still gnawed at him. If only he'd done things differently.

"Where is she, Ernesto?" The anger in his voice trailed away, as he began to sob. He sat down at a table, his body shaking as he held his head in his hands. "For pity's sake, tell me where she is!"

"I don't know, Paolo, I honestly don't know!"

Suddenly, Paolo leapt up and made for the door.

"I have to find her!"

Ernesto grabbed the old man from behind and held him in a bear hug.

"Don't be a fool, Paolo. It's past curfew. You'll be shot. Stay here until tomorrow. They'll be gone then."

Paolo shook himself free. "It will be too late. I have to go now. I must find Rosanna!"

CHAPTER 44

For a few seconds, no one in the room moved. Klaus's senses reeled, his mind numb as it attempted to grasp the enormity of Dressler's order. Destroy the ships? At last, his tongue found words.

"You are mad," he screamed at Dressler, "completely mad!"

He strode across the chamber toward Dressler, who clicked his fingers; two black uniforms snapped to attention, their machine pistols held across their chests. Klaus stopped short, in front of Dressler, who waved his hand to stay any further action by his men.

"I am not mad, Schmidt," his voice was soft, like an adult gently chiding an unruly child. "I am merely obeying my orders." He lowered his head, looking directly into Klaus's eyes, then shouted with venom. "Just as you will obey!"

Klaus began to recover from his initial shock and shouted back.

"This is an outrage! It is not a justifiable order!"

"Since when do orders have to be justified? War would be a very long process if orders had to be justified!"

Dressler laughed at his sarcasm, and his laughter was echoed by Schneider and the others in the room. Klaus felt his face flush with anger; he fought with his emotions as Dressler's supercilious smile inflamed his temper.

"Where is the order? By whose authority is this monstrous crime proposed?"

Dressler walked away from Klaus, sat himself behind the long table and lit a cigarette.

"Authority? Crime? You studied too much law at university, my dear *Hauptman*."

A collective snigger came from all parts of the room, and Klaus realized that Dressler was playing to the gallery.

"It is not a valid order. The ships are protected. Even our own Heritage Commission has declared them protected!" Klaus shouted in his anger. "No one can order the destruction of two thousand years of history. Such an act would be a crime. Only a philistine, a savage, a madman would make such an order!"

Dressler threw his head back and laughed.

"The order comes on the authority of the Fuehrer himself!"

The murmur of chatter in the palace's grand hall died away. Only the crackling of the fire could be heard as the room became a frozen tableau. All eyes turned to Klaus; sweat trickled down his ashen face.

"I demand to see the order!" Klaus knew Dressler was lying, but did not know how to call his bluff.

"You demand to see an order of the Fuehrer?" Dressler's eyebrows rose in astonishment. "Really, Schmidt, have you lost your senses?"

"I refuse to obey such an order!" Klaus could hardly believe the words that came from his lips. A low whistle emerged from one of the soldiers by the fireplace. Dressler, his face reddening, looked at Klaus for several moments.

"So, you refuse to obey the order of the Fuehrer." He motioned to one of the black-uniformed guards. "Remove his side arm!"

The guard removed Klaus's pistol from its holster.

"I could have you shot now, Schmidt."

Klaus felt the shudder of fear and wondered why the confident smile still played across Dressler's lips. The smile persisted as Dressler walked across the room and eased himself into a chair by the side of the hearth. He tossed his cigarette into the fire.

"However, if I did show you the authority for the order, would you obey it?"

Klaus felt a dryness in his mouth and throat. He knew Dressler was probing him, enjoying his sadistic mind game. If he didn't carry out the order, someone else would and he would pay with his life for ruining the *Standardtenfuehrer's* joke. But the ships were things of beauty, treasures of history that belonged to all men for all time. Yet if he destroyed them, it would not merely be a victory for Dressler's sadism, it would mean a lifetime of anguish and torment for him.

"No."

The word came quietly, without anger or contempt. All eyes in the room turned to Dressler.

"Enough of this nonsense. Bring him this way."

He snapped his fingers as he turned on his heel and made his way toward a small door set at the back of the hall. Klaus felt the prod of the butt of the guard's rifle and he staggered through the door.

Dressler led the way through a long, dark corridor. Portraits of princes long since dead gazed down on Klaus as he followed the black uniform. He would soon join them, Klaus thought. He tried to control his thoughts, but they were scattered. An image of his mother leapt to his mind, to be replaced in an instant by himself at his graduation, his father shaking his hand. Then there was Rosanna and himself at the temple. His actions were mechanical, as if predetermined. He looked down to see his boots walking along the carpet, thinking they were not his boots.

"Right, in here!"

Dressler pushed open a door leading off the corridor and stood back as the guards pushed Klaus into the room. It was a small chamber, probably a servant's room, Klaus thought, but it had been stripped of all furniture and Klaus's boots echoed off the wooden floor. He looked around, but there was no other exit, only a small curtained window. He turned to face Dressler and his guards, who looked at him with faces that did not show a flicker of emotion.

"So, you wanted to see the authority for the order?" The malicious smile returned to Dressler's lips. "If you look through that window," he pointed towards the curtain, "you will see all the authorization you could possibly wish!"

Klaus knew it was a ploy, a trick to get him to turn his back on the guards so they did not have to look at him as they gunned him down. He turned to the window, his body shaking as he awaited the chatter of the weapons and the thud of bullets tearing into his flesh.

CHAPTER 45

There were no gunshots. Nothing. Klaus heard only Dressler's evil laugh echo around the empty room.

"Well, my dear Schmidt, why don't you look through the window? You do want to see the authority for the order, don't you?"

Klaus leant over the window, his hand shaking as he pulled back the curtain. It was an internal window, looking down on a large room that had probably once served as a kitchen, but there was no fire in the hearth. He saw a guard standing just inside the door, his rifle hanging at his shoulder. The soldier was looking towards a recessed corner that was just out of Klaus's sight. Klaus craned his neck so he could see into the half-hidden corner of the room. Suddenly, he gasped, his eyes widening.

It was Rosanna. He could barely recognize her. She was slumped across a table. Her head was half shaven, short tufts of her once magnificent hair protruding in clumps from her scalp. Klaus pressed his cheek to the window, but Rosanna could not see him. She lifted her head. Her left eye was swollen, almost closed by a huge bruise, and on her right cheek were streaks of blood where someone had dragged fingernails across the flesh. Her dress had been torn down the bodice from the neck and her left hand held it together. Her body sobbed uncontrollably and tears ran from her eyes.

Klaus reeled back from the window in shock, hatred beginning to course through his veins.

"You swine, Dressler, you swine!"

He hurled himself toward the black-uniformed figure, but he was stopped in his tracks as one of the guards slammed the stock of his weapon into his stomach. The pain made him fall to his knees, winded, and the guard stood over him, pointing the muzzle of his gun at Klaus's head.

"There will be no need for that." Dressler waved aside the guard and leaned over Klaus.

"Did you think, Schmidt, that I did that?" He pointed toward the window. "Do you think I am a barbarian?"

Dressler's smile broadened. Klaus raised himself unsteadily to his feet, his lungs still fighting to regain his breath. He thought of the shooting in Russia of which Dressler had boasted. A young boy killed on Dressler's whim. He wondered what new sadistic game the S.S. man was playing.

"You need the full story, *Hauptman*." Dressler carefully placed his hands behind his back and began rocking on the balls of his feet. "The injuries to this woman were inflicted by people from the town of Nemi."

Klaus shook his head in disbelief.

"Yes, *Hauptman*, I am afraid so. If it hadn't been for some of my men searching outhouses for hidden provisions, her injuries could have been worse. The perpetrators – mainly women, I might add – fled from their act of violence. My men brought the unfortunate girl to headquarters."

Klaus looked to the window, then back to Dressler

"Why?" His eyes dropped to the floor as a glimmer of understanding began to force its way into his mind. "Why did the people do that to her?"

"Apparently, because she had been…" Dressler paused as he lingered over his choice of words "…granting her favors to a German officer."

Klaus's head dropped, his mouth agape. Dressler reached forward and grabbed his chin, lifting it so he could see his face.

"You must look at a commanding officer when he addresses you."

A wretchedness seized Klaus. A pain like no other he had ever felt. It burst from his heart, its tentacles quickly finding their way to his head. He was responsible for all this agony: the violence, the disfigurement of Rosanna were the result of his actions. The physical pain inflicted by the guard subsided but he could do nothing about the mental anguish. His face was expressionless, his mind stunned, barely able to notice that Dressler was circling him like a predator.

"Of course, she has committed no crime as far as I am concerned." Dressler's hand reached inside his tunic pocket for his cigarette case. "As far as I am concerned, her sleeping with a German officer deserves a medal."

He lit his cigarette, blew the smoke toward Klaus's face and smiled. Klaus felt the clamminess of his own palms as he began to grasp the gist of Dressler's intentions.

Dressler walked to the window, lifted the curtain and looked into the room below.

"Poor girl!" There was no trace of irony in his voice as his hand let the curtain fall. "She has done no wrong. I shall have to release her."

Klaus's mind reeled as the full import of Dressler's decision filtered through his dazed state. To turn Rosanna back onto the streets of Nemi was tantamount to a death sentence; once the army had left, the savage vengeance of the mob would be completed.

"No, no," Klaus voice was little more than a plaintive murmur, "you must not, *Standartenfuehrer*, I beg you."

Dressler beamed, beginning to savor his unfolding victory.

"Perhaps you are right, Schmidt." He let his cigarette fall from his fingers and ground it out with his heel. "I have half a mind to take her into protective custody and bring her with us as we retreat."

Dressler looked carefully at every aspect of Klaus's face, watching as the agony played upon it. "Perhaps, Hauptman, you could convince me of this course of action?"

Klaus looked down at the floor to avoid Dressler's triumphant eyes. The choice was stark, brutal: Rosanna's life or the death of the ships; either he would burn the ships or Rosanna would be turned over to the violence of a hate-fueled mob. He could not trust Dressler, but he knew he had no choice. His head sank to his chest.

"I shall do as you say."

"Excellent!" Dressler clapped his hands in his triumph. He turned to the guard. "It is my order that the girl be placed in my staff car when we depart!"

He placed his long, black-uniformed arm around Klaus's shoulder. "You see, I have kept my part of the bargain, Schmidt." He led Klaus toward the door. "Now you must keep yours."

The scream and crump of a shell hitting the hillside made Dressler start.

"But you must hurry – there is not much time!"

Klaus half turned to look toward the room where Rosanna sat. He felt his body shaking, as if his very being was held in a tightening vice, squeezing until nothing remained. He shook his head and followed the black shape of Dressler down the corridor.

CHAPTER 46

The darkening gloom hung over the town as Klaus walked from the palace into the piazza. The light of the flames of Genzano still played on the walls of the houses of Nemi. The acrid smell of the burning buildings, borne on the stiffening wind, assailed his nostrils. All around him was the clamor of a war machine preparing to move. Horses bridled and whinnied at the smell of fire; trucks snorted and belched their noxious fumes into the air; everywhere the stamping of weary boots resounded on the cobbled street.

Klaus felt apart from it all. The thought of what he had to do built a wall in his mind. He looked at the flame-washed chaos, but he did not see it; the shouts and brutal noises reached his ears, but he did not hear them. His mind dwelt on the horrendous vision of Rosanna, savaged and brutalized; on the inhuman sadism of Dressler; and, above all, on the act of barbarism that he, himself, was about to commit to save Rosanna.

He turned away from the piazza and walked down toward the old town gate set in the western wall of the town. His movements were mechanical, automatic, as if his mind did not wish to concede that every pace was taking him closer to the death of the ships, that every single step was taking him to the flaming torch that he would use to consign the mighty relics of antiquity to ashes. He passed through the gate and came to the low wall that looked far down over the lake. He saw, in the gathering dusk, that his guns had gone, and his men with them. Below him, the waters of the lake, agitated by the wind swirling around the hillsides of the crater, danced with the ebbing flames of Genzano.

Klaus's hands were shaking as he cupped them around his lighter to shield the flame from the wind. He drew deeply on the cigarette, exhaled, then drew deeply again, trying to dispel the specters haunting his mind. He could not do it; he must not do it. He stamped his feet on the cobbles, as if trying to strengthen his new-found conviction. Was any life worth the glory of the ships? The vessels came down from antiquity, from time immemorial, reaching across a score of centuries; an individual's life was brief and brutal - in comparison with the ships, worthless. The intellectualization held sway in his mind for a moment.

His own life he knew to be worthless; yet the images of Rosanna gnawed at his rational thought. He saw her face, angrily bruised, her body sobbing with pain; then he saw her smiling, her face beaming back from the wondrous Mirror of Diana that Paolo had shown them.

The mirror! He remembered the message of the mirror: duty over love. But his duty to the ships was as nothing compared with his love for Rosanna. He knew that the mirror was hidden in the museum, tucked away in the old chest under the table in the back room. Perhaps he could....

His thoughts were broken by a familiar whine that grew to a high-pitched scream. Instinctively he flinched, but saw the shell fall short, plunging into the lake, just short of the shore in front of the museum. A huge spout rose, then fell back into the waters already troubled by the wind. Fate was against him, he knew. If the enemy gunner had pitched his range higher – a mere fifty yards – it would have blasted the museum and the ships to smithereens. He tried to grasp the tormented logic of his fevered mind. The shell would have destroyed the ships he longed to save; but he would have been absolved of the crime, free of blame. Perhaps he was seeking only to salve his conscience, to save his sanity. Perhaps the destruction of the ships was not what really troubled him; perhaps it was the guilt he would carry for the rest of his life.

Klaus lit another cigarette from the butt of the first, as the growing wind tore at his tunic. The wind whipped around the hills of the crater, moaning as it tormented the treetops.

What had he done to deserve such a fate? His mind searched for answers that would not come. Others had determined that he come to Italy. All he had done was to come to look at the historical ships he had longed to see. And he had fallen in love. Were any of his actions crimes? Men had fallen in love for centuries – even before the ships had been built – but they had not been punished as he was being punished. He had done nothing, yet the woman he loved was shorn of the hair through which he had once run his fingers; she was now in the hands of a sadistic monster, again because of him. As for himself, he had sold his soul: he was about to put the torch to the ships of antiquity, to reduce Paolo's life work to ashes.

Klaus's mind began to clutch at straws. If only he hadn't read about the ships; if only he hadn't come to see them; if only he had walked away when Paolo had asked him. The mental hammering in his mind was interrupted by a noise on the path leading up from the outer gate of the town. He peered into the gathering darkness to see Gunther, his breath labored, bracing himself against the wind as he struggled up the path.

"Damn it, boss, it's a hell of a climb from down there!" He spat on the ground, cursing under his breath as he approached Klaus. Still panting, he looked up at his *Hauptman* and stopped short.

"Hell, boss, what's the matter with you? You look terrible!"

"It's nothing, Gunther." Klaus's voice was weary. "I'm just very tired."

The sergeant shrugged his shoulders. "You and me both, boss. Anyway, it's done."

"Done? What's done?"

"The ships have been dowsed with gas. Didn't you know? I received the order when I got the trucks in Albano."

Klaus realized that Dressler had planned everything down to the last detail. There was no escape.

"It needed plenty, boss." Gunther blew the smoke from his cigarette into the air. He shuffled his feet and looked uncomfortable.

"I wondered why I wasn't asked to burn them myself, but I was told you were the one who was going to apply the torch. I couldn't figure out why, particularly as you like 'em so much. But I obey orders – it's the easy way. You do understand, *Hauptman*?"

Obey orders. The easy way. Klaus understood only too well.

"It's ok, Gunther. I have to obey orders myself." Klaus gave his sergeant a pained smile.

"You've been ordered to burn the boats?" Gunther's face screwed up in astonishment. "There's something fishy here. Do you want me to burn them for you?"

A brief sense of relief came to Klaus, but it died almost immediately. It would be easy to ask Gunther to burn the ships. His sergeant would put the ships to the torch with no more feeling than tossing away a cigarette stub, and would think little of it for the rest of his life, perhaps occasionally sharing the moment with his friends in a bar after the war. Klaus knew it would be an easy solution for him: to pass on the guilt, to distance him from the heinous crime which, no matter how he disavowed it, was his responsibility. But he knew he could not ask Gunther to burn the ships; he had to accept that he was responsible for the consequences of his own actions. Besides, Dressler would have made sure to have him watched. He turned to look through the arch of the gate, back along the street that led to the piazza. Schneider, Dressler's toady, stood in the street, ostensibly playing some part in the evacuation, but Klaus knew he had been sent to spy on him. Dressler needed to be sure of his pound of flesh.

"Well, I can't hang around here any longer." Gunther interrupted Klaus's thoughts. "It's beyond me, but I suppose you know what you're doing." The sergeant shook his head, unable to understand what was happening. "I've prepared the torch for you – it's leaning against the door of the museum."

The mention of the torch brought home the immediacy of his crime to Klaus. His hand would grasp the torch; his hand would apply the light to the torch; his hand…. He shuddered, but he knew now that he had to complete the act. He felt driven by a perverse compulsion invading his mind, strangling his will.

"I must go now, Gunther. Take care."

The sergeant gave an informal salute and turned to go. Klaus started out on the road leading down to the outer gate. A shout born of desperation stopped him in his tracks.

"Klaus, Klaus, where is Rosanna? Where is Rosanna?"

K laus turned to see Paolo running towards him. It was a halting but urgent run, the run of an old man driven by fear.

"My god, Paolo, what are you doing? It's way past curfew. It's a wonder no one saw you. If they had, you'd be dead now. They would have shot you."

Paolo approached Klaus and stopped, gasping for breath. Klaus looked down on Paolo's face, haggard in the dying light of day. There was fear on the face; the cheeks were damp with tears.

The old man grasped at the lapels of Klaus's tunic.

"Rosanna, where is Rosanna?" His eyes pleaded with Klaus. "Do you know where Rosanna is, Klaus?"

Klaus gently shepherded Paolo into the darker shadows of the town wall and signaled Gunther to keep watch.

"She is safe, Paolo, she is safe."

How safe she was he did not know, but he fed the lie to the old man, whose face brightened for an instant before fear seized it again.

"Where is she? Where is she?" Paolo pulled on Klaus's tunic.

"She is in the palace."

"I must see her." Paolo turned to go back through the town gate, and struggled as Klaus grabbed him.

"Don't be a fool, Paolo, they'll shoot you on sight!"

He pushed Paolo against the wall, the old man fighting to free himself from Klaus's grip.

"Please, Klaus, I must find Rosanna."

"Later, Paolo, you can see her later, I promise." Another lie. Lie after lie seemed to flow from his lips, as easily as wine from a bottle.

Paolo, his face a haunted gray skull, ceased struggling and looked up at Klaus. The gusting wind tugged at the white wisps of his hair. His eyes fixed on Klaus's.

"Klaus, I believe you. You know I trust you."

The words stabbed into Klaus, and he felt his guilt cutting deeply at his conscience. He looked down into Paolo's moistened eyes. The old man had trusted him with his ships. Betrayal. He had trusted him with his daughter. Betrayal. Everything that was dear to the eyes that looked at him trustingly he had betrayed. Klaus felt his soul screaming within him.

"Car coming, boss!"

Gunther's warning startled Klaus. He pushed Paolo into a dark recess of the wall, barely visible beneath the dark clouds and the gathering dusk. He beckoned Gunther to his side so that the two of them would conceal Paolo.

"Stay still, Paolo – don't make the slightest sound!"

The shaded headlights of the car came nearer, approaching the gate. Klaus prayed that the car would pass by, but he saw the insignia flag on the mudguard and his heart sank. It was Dressler's staff car.

The vehicle eased to a halt in front of Klaus and Dressler's highly-polished boots rapped on the cobblestones as he got out, slamming the door behind him. He waited for Klaus to snap to attention before answering his unasked question.

"She is asleep." His high-peaked cap nodded to the back of the car. "She's been given something to ease her pain and help her sleep."

Klaus craned his head to see Rosanna on the back seat. She lay awkwardly, her legs tucked up under her. Somehow, she had found a towel that she had tied around her head to try to hide her mutilated hair, but it did not fully cover her partly-shaven head. The lacerations on her face were still painfully red and the half-closed eye now had an angry black and purple hue. Even Gunther winced as he saw her injuries.

Klaus gave Gunther a meaningful look and held his position so that Paolo could not see what was going on; he was thankful that the Italian could not understand one word of German.

"You see, I have kept my side of the bargain." Dressler's face broke into a supercilious smile of triumph. "Why have you not yet kept yours?"

"It was necessary to complete the preparations. *Feldwebel* Mattheus," Klaus inclined his head toward Gunther at his side, "now assures me they are finished. I am about to go down to the museum to complete the task."

Dressler's smile broadened. "Good. I shall have my driver stop on the road above the crater to watch the flames."

He moved a few paces back to the car and stopped, pointing to the door handle.

"*Feldwebel?*" Klaus shuddered as Gunther moved obediently to open the car door; Paolo now had a clear view of the car.

The scream was unlike any Klaus had ever heard, even from men with limbs severed by artillery shells. He grabbed Paolo before he could reach the car.

"Rosanna!"

Paolo's shout was stifled as Klaus clamped his hand over his mouth. He pulled the old man away from the car and back toward the town wall. Their legs tangled and they both fell in a heap at the side of the road. Paolo, winded, struggled for his breath.

"I trusted you, Klaus – you said she was alright!"

"She will be alright, Paolo." Before he could concoct further lies, Dressler's voice rang out.

"Well, well, what do we have here?" He turned to the car. "Flashlight!"

The driver leapt to obey the order. He searched quickly under the dashboard and handed a flashlight to his commanding officer. Dressler flicked the switch and pointed the beam at Paolo and Klaus. The old man was sobbing, his hands covering his eyes, as if trying to block out the images he had seen. Dressler turned the beam on Klaus, who raised his arm to shield his eyes.

"Get to your feet, Hauptman Schmidt!" Dressler's voice was harsh, insistent. "A German officer does not lie on the ground with scum!"

Klaus struggled to his feet; he felt numb, his mind dazed by the day's events.

"Who is this man?"

Klaus said nothing. He felt he was falling apart, stunned by the blows that Fate was raining upon him. Had his actions brought about this catastrophe? He looked down at Paolo's wretched face, then back at the form of Dressler, hazy behind the beam of the flashlight. He heard Dressler stamp his boot on the pavement.

"Well, Hauptman Schmidt, who is this man?"

Klaus did not answer. Only the purring of the car engine and Paolo's weeping challenged the wind's embrace of the trees. The snap of the safety catch on Dressler's pistol broke the sad rhythm of Paolo's sobbing. Dressler waved the pistol under Klaus's nose.

"Perhaps this will aid your memory, Schmidt!" Dressler shouted his threat, his face reddening.

Still Klaus said nothing, staring sullenly into the beam of the flashlight. He did not care if he died; perhaps it would be better if he did. The cold steel of the pistol's muzzle pressed against his left temple.

"*Feldwebel!*" Dressler turned his head toward Gunther. "Do you know who this man is?"

Klaus sensed the workings of Gunther's mind. It was a simple choice: either his captain's life or the information Dressler wanted.

Obey the order, or suffer the consequences. Gunther would obey the order. It was the easy way.

"The man is the curator of the museum, *Mein Herr*. The young woman is his daughter."

"Ha!" Dressler could scarcely contain his delight. He removed the pistol from Klaus's temple. "Now we have the full story."

Paolo looked up, unable to comprehend what was unfolding before him.

"Get that wretch to his feet, Schmidt!" Dressler waved his pistol in the direction of Paolo.

"Tell him his daughter is under my protection because of the injuries inflicted upon her by his own people."

Dressler put away his pistol and lit a cigarette as Klaus lifted Paolo to his feet and told him of Dressler's intentions. The old man listened sullenly, barely able to comprehend what his ears were hearing; between his sobs, he uttered one word, over and over: "*Perchè? Perchè? Perchè?*"

Dressler's head went back as he laughed. "I know enough of their miserable language to understand that word." He smiled maliciously. "Tell them that his own people did it because they took exception to his daughter's granting her favors to a German officer." He dwelt on the final phrase, as if savoring it.

Klaus stood immobile, his senses barely able to accept what Dressler was demanding. The black uniform moved toward the rear of the car, the pistol again unholstered. Still Klaus remained silent, his eyes looking at the ground. Dressler glanced at the pathetic bundle on the back seat, still locked in her drug-induced sleep and then he looked menacingly at his pistol, before his eyes moved to Klaus.

"Do not try to fool me, *Hauptman*. I shall know from his reaction if you have told him what I wish."

Klaus knew there was no escape. His hand went instinctively to feel the amulet Rosanna had given him. He forced himself to look into Paolo's eyes as he translated Dressler's message.

For a few moments, a look of disbelief passed across the Italian's face, his lips mouthing the word '*Che?*'; then the features hardened, the brown eyes narrowing as they fixed upon the guilt in Klaus's. Paolo's head went back and came forward sharply as he spat in Klaus's face. "So it's true. *Bastardo!* You betrayed me! Worse, you betrayed Rosanna!"

Klaus felt only guilt. He saw the hatred in Paolo's eyes, yet felt none himself. He wiped the spittle from his face. The events of the day had drained all emotion from him. Was the man in front of him the same man who had laughed and joked with him as they had talked of the ships? Was it only two weeks since he and Rosanna had lain in the sun at the temple, planning what they would do after the war? Or was it some cruel dream, some strange universe he once used to inhabit? He felt empty, crushed. Only his love for Rosanna gave him the spark of hope that had been swept to the farthest reaches of his soul. Otherwise, there was nothing but guilt, the guilt that pulled him toward the abyss into which he would soon fall. The ships yet awaited him. There was no redemption, no straw at which his conscience could clutch.

"That was a fine reaction!" Dressler laughed, looking at his fingernails briefly: a gesture of triumph, as if playing with people's souls were a bagatelle, an amusing game.

"Now let us see his reaction when you tell him that you are going to burn his ships."

Klaus felt as if Time had stayed her hand. The wind that had been tugging at his tunic died away. Down on the lake, he saw a tormented image, the reflected flames of Genzano licking at the walls of the museum as a portent of what was to come.

All was still; all eyes, Dressler's, Gunther's, Paolo's, were upon him. Only the purring of the car's engine marked the passing of time. His heart ached, his soul cried within him. There was nothing left. Suddenly, the wind picked up. Klaus raised his head and looked at Dressler.

"No." The word came quietly from his lips. "I shall not tell him what I am about to do. I will keep my part of the bargain and you will keep yours. There is nothing more."

Dressler pointed his pistol at the rear window of the car. "I will give you five seconds, Schmidt!"

CHAPTER 48

Klaus turned away from Dressler and walked, slowly and stead-
ily, along the cobbled road that led towards the path down the
hillside to the museum. He at last began to understand the evil
that was Dressler: he was insane with the lust for power, and for using
that power to satisfy his lust. He would not shoot Rosanna. To do so
would end his game; by taking Rosanna's life, Dressler would lose his
power over Klaus. Only brute force would remain to Dressler, and even
his enjoyment of violence would not be enough to give him the satis-
faction for his perverted lust.

"I warn you, Schmidt!"

Klaus walked on. One step, two, another, and another. There was
no shot. If Dressler killed Rosanna, Klaus knew that Dressler had to kill
him, too. Klaus no longer cared. Another step. And another. Klaus
knew he had won. A hollow victory, but he had won. At least Rosanna
would be safe for a while.

Behind him, Dressler could not contain his rage. He rushed to
Paolo, his arms waving.

"Der Hauptman wird Ihre Schiffe brennen!"

Paolo looked at Dressler blankly, uncomprehendingly. Dressler
swore, then ran to open the door of his car and rummaged in the glove
compartment. With a muted cry of triumph, he emerged, his hand
clasping a small black book: the Army's official German/Italian dictionary. His hands were shaking with rage as he flicked through the
pages. He strode quickly towards Paolo, who cowered before the black
uniform.

"Ah, here – *'Schiffe'* – *'Nave!'*" He shouted the translation at Paolo.
His fingers continued their frantic search.

"*Hauptman – Capitano.*" Dressler's free hand pointed at the retreating figure of Klaus. The pages turned again.

"*Brennen – Dare alle fiamme!*"

He screamed the words into Paolo's face, his voice carrying to
Klaus, who stopped and turned to look back up the road. The pronun-
ciation was crude, but the meaning was obvious. Ship. Captain. Set fire
to. Paolo's face was twisted with fear and rage as he ran toward Klaus.

"*No, no, non è possibile!*"

Before Klaus could turn to get away, Paolo threw himself at his body. His hands clutched at Klaus's waist, but his grip weakened as the German tried to struggle free and Paolo slid down until his hands grasped at the ankle of Klaus's right boot, clutching it to him like a bear trap.

"No, no. I beg you. You cannot burn the ships."

He looked up at Klaus, pleading for his life's work. "Not the ships. Not the ships." Tears flowed from his eyes and he howled like a mortally-wounded animal. "Not the ships. Shoot me. Kill me. But do not burn the ships."

Klaus tried to shake his leg free of Paolo's grip, but the old man hung on like a dog with a bone, his body dragging on the cobbles as Klaus sought to escape.

"Please, Klaus. They are not our ships – they belong to the world. Please, Klaus, no."

The wind began to howl again, as if in empathy with the agonized cries of the old man. Klaus ceased trying to escape. He looked back to see Dressler, smiling, savoring his power. Paolo's sobs pounded Klaus's ears; he felt the agony in the cries, adding to his own torment. He reached for his sidearm, forgetting that he had been disarmed in the palace. Dressler's obscene laugh rang back from the town walls.

Klaus leaned down over the sobbing body at his feet.

"Paolo, I am sorry. I didn't mean to betray you. But if I don't burn the ships, Dressler will kill Rosanna. He gave the order to burn the ships. I have no choice."

For a few moments, Paolo continued sobbing. Then, suddenly, he stopped. He hauled himself slowly to his feet, grabbing at Klaus's belt as he struggled upright. He looked into Klaus's face, saying nothing. Klaus searched Paolo's eyes for some glimpse of understanding, but saw only rage and fury. After a few seconds, the old man turned and began to run. Straight toward Dressler.

Klaus called after him, but he continued to run, his rage of desperation giving new youth to his old legs. Within moments, Paolo had reached a startled Dressler, his strong hands grabbing for the officer's throat. Dressler, alarmed and stunned, staggered back under the assault, his pistol flying through the air as Paolo's fingers grasped at his throat. Dressler clawed at Paolo's arms, then brought his fist down on the Italian's face, but still Paolo would not relinquish his grip. Again, he struck Paolo's face. And again. Still Paolo's fingers squeezed.

The surprise shock of the attack had caught everyone unaware, but Dressler's chauffeur pulled his sidearm from its holster. He ran up behind Paolo and brought the butt of the weapon down on the back of his head. Paolo's grip loosened. The pistol came down again on his head. His face battered and oozing blood, Paolo slid down Dressler's greatcoat under the repeated blows until he fell in a heap at Dressler's feet.

The brave but futile attempt by Paolo to save his ships and his daughter had taken but a few seconds. Klaus stood immobile, dazed. Where was his own bravery? Why was it not he who had attacked Dressler, instead of a feeble old man, driven to desperation by the love of his daughter and his ships? His face reddened with his shame.

Dressler's shout echoed back from the walls of the palace.

"Enough of this nonsense!" He kicked out at Paolo who, despite his beating, was struggling to his feet.

"*Feldwebel* Mattheus!" Klaus saw Gunther snap to attention automatically. Dressler lashed the back of his hand across Paolo's face. "This scum, *Feldwebel*, is guilty of breaking the curfew and of assaulting a German officer." Dressler spoke haltingly, still breathless from Paolo's attack, and he waited a few moments until he had fully recovered his breath.

"There can be only one punishment. Shoot him!"

"N o, Gunther, no!" Klaus shouted as he began to run back up the road. His boots slipped as the first heavy drops of rain began to polish the cobblestones. Dressler's driver turned and leveled his pistol at Klaus. Gunther looked at Klaus for a few moments, then shook his head and began to slip his machine pistol from his shoulder.

"Wait!" Dressler raised his arm to order Gunther to stop. "It would be better to teach all these Italian swine a lesson. Take him to the piazza, shoot him there, and leave his body so that all these dagoes can see what happens to anyone who defies the Third Reich!"

"No, Gunther, you must not." Klaus moved forward; Dressler's driver moved to the front of the car, raising and pointing his gun at Klaus.

"It is a direct order, *Feldwebel*." Dressler fixed his eyes on Gunther's. "On my authority as commanding officer."

Klaus moved forward, but he felt the driver's pistol thrust into his ribs. The wind swept up from the lake, howling, as the rain began to ricochet from the pavement.

"*Jawohl, Mein Herr!*" Gunther clicked his heels as he shouted his response to Dressler. He grabbed Paolo under the armpit and hauled the Italian to his feet before half dragging the old man through the gates toward the piazza.

Dressler waited until they were out of sight before turning to Klaus.

"Your sergeant is a fine soldier, Hauptman." The smile had returned to his lips. "And now, Schmidt, it is, surely, time for you to do your duty." Dressler removed his leather gloves from his pocket and pulled them on. "Despite this unfortunate business," he waved a hand toward the gate, "I shall keep my word."

Dressler signaled to his driver. "Come. It is time to go." Both leapt into the car, which eased forward until it stopped alongside Klaus. The wind tugged at the pennant on the hood of the car. Dressler wound down the window and fixed Klaus's eyes, waiting.

Crack.

The shot echoed from the town, defying the wind. Dressler smiled briefly at Klaus, and then tapped his driver on the shoulder. The car sped off into the deepening gloom. Klaus struggled against the wind as he walked numbly towards the path that led down to the museum, the sound of the shot still echoing in his head.

He sought to fathom the workings of Gunther's mind in order to escape probing his own actions that had led to the horror that had unfolded. Good Gunther, who had befriended the young boy Gianni; Gunther, who had stood watch when he had met Rosanna; Gunther, his friend. Obeying orders. It was the easy way.

The dying light clung to the western sky as Klaus began the descent to the museum. His small flashlight gave him little help on the steep path down to the edge of the lake. The rain had died away, but scudding clouds, urged on by the wind, now hid the moon; only the flames of Genzano, given new life by the swirling gusts, offered any light. He could barely pick out the path, half-overgrown with bracken; every few yards a fallen branch or a half-concealed root caused him to stumble. He fell, once, sliding on the treacherous earth until his feet found some purchase. He pulled himself up, cursing.

He clutched at a tree to steady himself, the curses still pouring from his mouth. He was not only cursing at his fall; everything was cursed. The war, Dressler, Gunther, even Rosanna was the object of his curse. He felt as if Dressler were pushing at his back as he stumbled down the path; as if Rosanna were waiting for him at the museum, luring him on to his act of barbarism. But it was his own actions that had placed him at Dressler's mercy; and Rosanna was suffering because of his betrayal of Paolo's trust. And Paolo was dead, because he had dared to befriend him.

Klaus began to sob. There was no one to blame but himself. His body began to shake with his torment. Before that day had dawned, there had been hope - that there could be an 'after-the war.' Now there was nothing, no vision beyond the heinous act to come. He felt impotent, powerless before the hammer blows of fate that bludgeoned him from all sides. He ran blindly down the path, slashing wildly with his arms at the branches that intruded, as if the trees were to blame for his misfortune.

He was surprised when his precipitous descent suddenly ended. One moment he was battling with the trees and then he was clear of the forest, looking across the edge of the lake to the museum. The ships were there, waiting for him. He shook his head. Must he do it? Must he turn the wooden jewels of the past into ashes? Rosanna's tormented face appeared before him as he began to walk toward the museum.

The crack of a twig made him jump. He looked back up the path. There was another crunch, then an oath. In German. Someone was following him. Klaus had no doubt it was Schneider, sent by Dressler to make sure that the ships were burnt. Dressler had probably ordered his lackey to shoot him after the torching of the ships, to make sure that all traces of the crime were hidden. He instinctively felt for his pistol and was again disappointed when he clutched at the empty holster. Perhaps he could lie in wait and ambush Schneider before he had a chance to kill him. He searched around him urgently for some weapon, a rock or a fallen branch, but, after a while he stopped and, despite everything, he began to laugh maniacally.

Was he to be King of the Forest? He tossed the thought aside; he no longer cared what Schneider did. He only knew what he himself must do.

The museum looked cold and forbidding, almost defiant as he crossed the clearance at the edge of the lake. As Klaus approached the building, the wind died away, as if holding its breath in anticipation of what was to come; the moon briefly thrust her way through the clouds to watch.

The torch was exactly where Gunther had said it would be, leaning against the wall at the entrance to the museum. Klaus picked it up and felt the gasoline fumes assail his nose. He was about to reach in his pocket for his lighter when he heard a noise just beyond the small wall surrounding the museum; Schneider was still there, waiting.

As suddenly as it had died, the wind picked up again and began to moan as it swirled off the lake. Klaus could hear the waves tossed by the wind against banks. He crouched in the doorway of the museum, his hand sheltering his lighter as he flicked the wheel. The flame died, but his thumb plucked at the wheel again until the wick shone brightly in the darkness. Klaus looked at the light: such a small flame to destroy the great ships. He put the flame under the torch, which burgeoned, blossomed into a huge flower of light and heat, so much heat that he had to raise it high above his head and shield his eyes from its glow.

Klaus grasped the door knob, pulled the door open and stepped in. He stood in the vestibule and held the torch high. The light played on the walls of the cavernous gallery. He was startled as a sudden gust of wind slammed the doors shut behind him, as if to deny him escape from what he had to do.

He strode through the entrance hall and sensed the pungent smell of gasoline, heavy in the air. He looked up at the ships. They seemed to peer down at him, as if he were insignificant. There was no sound, save the crackle of the torch in his hand. He looked from one ship to the other, as if beseeching some word from them. There was none, only silence, only the mute voice of history ringing in his ears. Klaus hesitated. He could not do it.

Then there was noise: a muted hum that became a whistle, then the familiar shriek. A shell, booming down on him and the ships. Klaus looked to his right as the shell burst just outside the museum. He saw the windows of the museum implode as if in slow motion, before the blast caught him, throwing him senseless to the ground, the torch rolling away from his hand.

CHAPTER 50

It was the sound that brought Klaus to his senses. A shrieking, wailing sound. He felt the heat of the flames as he struggled to his feet, but it was the sound that made him shudder: the ships were weeping. He looked up; although he could have been unconscious for only a few moments, the flames had swept the length of both ships, crackling with fury as they went about their task of destruction. From the ships came a groan as the flames consumed them. The centuries-old timbers wailed in their death throes, as if grieving for the memories of time that were also dying.

Klaus heard the shouts of the spirits of those who had walked the decks of the ships, the cries of those who had labored to raise the ships from the lake. The voices shrieked their agony into Klaus's ears; he raised his hands to cover them, but the cries would not go away.

A flaming piece of timber fell upon him, glancing off his shoulder; then another fell at his feet. The heat of the ships' pyre shrouded him, as if to claim him for the same fate. Klaus kicked away the burning timber and began to run to the door of the museum. He was gasping for breath; the smoke enveloped him as he reached for the handle. He did not care if Schneider was waiting for him outside; he had to escape from the cries of the ships. The handle did not respond to Klaus's grip; the bomb blast had sealed the door. He began to kick at the lock, desperate to escape. Suddenly, he stopped. The mirror. He had forgotten the mirror. The mirror that he and Rosanna had held in their hands.

Klaus turned and ran back, between the ships, the flames reaching out for him, trying to seize him. The sweat ran down his face as he kicked aside the door to the store room. He rushed forward, reaching under the table, throwing aside the old sheet that covered the chest. Smoke filled the room and his eyes as he felt blindly for the lid. He seized the key Paolo had given him, snatching it from his neck. He turned the key quickly and the lid flew open at his touch. His fingers delved deeply into the chest, until they grasped the metal case in which the mirror was stored. He coughed and gasped for air as he pulled the case from the chest. He stumbled to the doorway of the storeroom, but could see there was no escape to the door of the museum. The smoke rose from the flames, the whole hall of the museum had become a roaring inferno.

The dark, acrid smoke billowed into the storeroom, seeking him. It seared his lungs and scorched his eyes, choking and half blinding him. Klaus brushed away the tears and rubbed his eyes as they peered through the smoke seeking a way of escape. Despair was beginning to overcome him when he saw the small window above the workbench. His eyes cast around for a tool, anything to help him. Propped against the wall was an old plank. He hurriedly placed the case containing the mirror on the bench and seized the plank, raising it above his head with both hands. The plank swung against the window, breaking the wooden frame and shattering the glass.

The smoke and hot air rushed toward the hole, pulling at Klaus's tunic as it rushed into the cold air of the night. Klaus knew he had little time; he swung the plank against the window, once, twice and again, until the whole frame had disintegrated. He was fighting for his breath as he leapt up on the bench, pushed the mirror case out of the broken window and started to pull himself through the shattered frame.

Shards of glass still lodged in the window frame cut deeply into his fingers as he pulled himself through, but he did not notice the pain. Desperation drove him as he thrust himself through the gap, his legs kicking behind him as he struggled to be free. The flames licked at his boots as he made a final push.

He fell heavily, winded, but managed to prop himself against the wall, his lungs heaving as they pulled in the sharp air of the night. The moon shone brightly, witness to his crime, and the wind howled about him, as if lamenting the demise of the ships. From within the museum came their death throes: a crackling, and then a roar, as the burning timbers crashed to the floor. Klaus sobbed as he picked up the mirror case and hauled himself to his feet.

A moving shadow intruding upon the moon's light snapped Klaus from his reverie. Schneider! The bastard was circling the museum, trying to check out what had happened. Klaus lay quiet, trying to calm his heaving chest. Perhaps Schneider would believe that he had perished in the flames. The shadow disappeared. Klaus waited a few moments, but decided to get away before Schneider returned. He pushed the mirror case under his tunic and raced for the trees behind the museum. He stumbled over a root and felt the branches spring back at his face. He stopped; he realized that he did not know where he was or where he was going, blind in the depths of the forest where only a few shards of moonlight reached. There was no option: Klaus winced with pain as his badly-cut fingers pulled the flashlight from his pocket and switched it on.

Perhaps Schneider had left; perhaps he would not see the beam of the light. Klaus switched it off and squatted down for a few moments. He listened carefully, but there was nothing except the wind and the crackling of the dying ships. His finger flicked the button of the flashlight and he began to pick his way up the hill away from the museum, his left hand holding the mirror close to his body as the other pointed the beam at the path between the trees.

Klaus knew he had to hide the mirror; he dared not rejoin his unit with it, lest Dressler got to know. Where? Where? His eyes cast about him, looking for some safe spot, some spot that he would be able to find again, heaven knew when. There was a noise behind him on the path. He stopped, switched off the light and held his breath, waiting.

Nothing. Only the swirl of the wind in the tree tops. He switched on the light again and carried on up the path. He recognized the large rock at the side of the path. He had walked here with Rosanna; the tree under which they had sat lay off the path to the right.

His feet swept away the undergrowth as his light swung left, then right, before picking out the tree. The trunk was wide in girth, and Klaus played the light low, looking for where the roots ran into the earth. He picked the north side of the tree; he had to remember: the north side. The north side, the north side, he repeated to himself as his hands began to delve into the earth at the base of the tree trunk: there would he bury the mirror case.

He scooped the soil away, quickly, until he was past elbow deep; two small roots tried to bar his path, but he pulled the earth from under them. Finally, he was ready; he pulled the mirror case from his tunic and thrust it into the hole, his hands pushing the soil back, patting down the earth over the treasure.

Klaus stood back after he had finished burying the mirror. It was over. Rosanna was safe, but still the guilt preyed on him: Paolo was dead; Gunther was his executioner, but Klaus knew that he was to blame.

A noise lower down the path made Klaus cover his flashlight with his hand to dull the light. Schneider? Klaus decided he had to get away. He made his way back to the rock on the path and scratched a mark on it with his flashlight. He would come back.

He looked down at the museum. The ships also were dead. The flames had subsided. Only the dying glow of the embers came from the blackened windows. The wind had dropped to a breeze and the moon, now clear, peered down on the scene of devastation. Klaus turned away and started to climb the path, the cloying smell of the burnt timbers hanging heavily in the air around him.

CHAPTER 51

Over four years later. October 13th 1948

K laus looked around at the peeling paint that hung from the walls of the office of the mayor of Velletri.

"This is a serious matter." The mayor drew on his cigarette, the smoke drifting upwards across his stained moustache.

Klaus nodded. After he had found the swastika daubed on his car, he had wanted to tell the mayor his full story, but he had told him only that he had been in Nemi at the time of the burning of the ships. Of Paolo's death, the mirror, and his role in the fire he had said nothing; nor had he mentioned Rosanna's abduction by Dressler.

Indeed, he had seen neither of them again after the night of the fire. It had taken him two days to find and rejoin his unit at Frascati. Dressler was gone, along with all of his S.S. staff; rumor had it that they had been posted to Warsaw. Gunther, too, was gone; he had been posted as missing in action, presumed dead. Of Rosanna, there had been no trace. He had searched in vain for Dressler's driver, and he had asked everywhere. Everywhere the same answer. No one had seen her. He had prayed that Dressler had not taken her to Poland. Maybe she had escaped and had lain low until the war had passed by; maybe she had returned to her home when the army had been forced to retreat. Klaus had clung desperately to these hopes through the final months of the war and the subsequent years as he struggled to rebuild his life in a ravaged post-war Berlin. He knew it was the real reason for his return to Nemi: his hope that she had survived and would be there. The recovery of the mirror was an excuse, a rationalization; there could be no atonement for what he had done.

"And now you must be very careful!"

The mayor stubbed out his cigarette in the ashtray on his desk, got up from his chair and walked across to the window of his office. Klaus watched as the Italian, deep in thought, looked out over the street. He seemed different from the man he had met in the bar only the day before; the bonhomie was gone, replaced by a taciturn air of formality. His head shook slowly as he weighed the situation. At last he turned to Klaus.

"I must be frank with you, Herr Schmidt."

"Klaus, please, your honor."

"Very well – Klaus." He brushed some cigarette ash from his sleeve. "You are in some danger."

"But, surely, Antonio, the war has been over now for three years, and," Klaus tried to chose his words carefully, "you finished on the winning side."

"Perhaps there are no winners in war."

The mayor sat down at his desk, opened a drawer and pulled out a file, from which he took several sheets of paper.

"Here is a list of people," he spread the papers on the desk in front of Klaus, "who disappeared without trace from Velletri in 1944."

Klaus looked at the list cursorily and said nothing. Although his face was impassive, he shuffled uncomfortably on his seat.

"These people," the mayor tapped slowly and deliberately on the list, "disappeared when you…" He stopped when he realized he had chosen the wrong word. "…when your army shipped them off to Germany for slave labor."

"I am sorry, but…"

The mayor leapt to his feet, and thumped the desk with his fist.

"Sorry? It is not a question of being sorry!"

His face reddened, but he drew deep breaths in an attempt to contain his rage. He slumped back in his chair, shaking his head.

"You see, even I cannot forget what happened. It's not that I didn't want to forgive and forget, but I find it difficult to do either." He raised his head and leveled his eyes at Klaus. "But I thought we must move on. It's a new world now, and we must move on."

Klaus looked down at the carpet.

"So you must understand, Klaus, how other of my countrymen feel. They lost fathers, husbands, and sons. They find it hard to move on. Their hearts are full of hatred."

His hand shook as he offered his cigarette pack. Klaus lit his cigarette, but said nothing. He knew full well that no words could eradicate the past. What did atonement for his crime matter, when his whole nation was awash with guilt?

"The three young men who walked out of the bar yesterday," the mayor picked up the list from his desk, "are probably the ones who painted the swastika on your car."

His eyes scanned the list.

"Two of them lost their fathers in the war. The other is a member of the Communist Party. All are troublemakers."

Although he tried to appear unconcerned, an involuntary shudder ran through Klaus. He had seen what the communists had done in Berlin at the end of the war. They had plundered and raped as they saw fit; he had managed to escape with his parents to the west, returning only when the presence of American troops in Berlin offered some respite.

"Are you going to return to Germany soon?"

There was more than a hint of encouragement in the mayor's voice. Klaus knew he should go. He had stirred up a hornet's nest by coming back. It was the easy way out: to go home, to wash his hands of the whole affair, to forget about the past. But he knew the past would not let him forget.

"Yes, but I shall first spend a few days in Nemi."

It was not the voice of reason, he knew. But perhaps she would be there, perhaps he would see her again, hold her, and swear to her that he would help erase the hurt of her memories, the hurt he had caused.

"Very well." The mayor sighed heavily and eased back into his chair. "Nemi is a beautiful place. I have not visited the town since I took my wife there last spring for the festival of strawberries." He shrugged his shoulders. "My duties here, you know."

He leant forward across the desk. "You do understand, Klaus, that I have no real evidence against these young men? I have no reason to take them into custody." He spread his hands and shrugged his shoulders again to suggest how foolhardy he felt Klaus's decision to go to Nemi was.

"I understand." Klaus stood up and offered his hand across the desk. "I would like to thank you for all your help." He smiled, but felt he was being too stiff and formal; the mayor's description of the Nazi crimes had made him feel awkward.

The mayor looked at Klaus's proffered hand and paused briefly before getting up, as if the past were staying his own hand. But the handshake was firm, and he looked at Klaus warmly.

"Take care."

The next day, October 14th 1948. 8 a.m.

Klaus got off the bicycle and propped it against the wall of the convent on the outskirts of Nemi. He had borrowed the bicycle from the owner of the garage who was removing the swastika painted on his car. He had set out early, soon after dawn, to avoid attention. He looked around him, but saw nobody.

The wall of the convent brushed his left shoulder as he made his way toward the town. At the small piazza in front of the convent, he paused. To his left was the wall where he and Gunther had first looked down on the lake below. Was it five years ago? Or was it yesterday? He walked slowly to the wall. The view was the same. Only the change of season made it different. Then the panoply of the mature summer had painted the lake green with its shimmering reflection; now a few soft yellows and browns of autumn speckled the hillsides of the lakes, punctuated here and there by the evergreen conifers. Below him stretched the lake, untroubled by the wind, basking in the pale early morning sun; a few gulls idled on its surface, which gleamed like a mirror.

The mirror! He swung his head to the right. The museum was still there, squatting at the lake side. Memories flooded back to Klaus: he heard the crackling of the fire that engulfed the ships, the shrieks and groans that rose from the flaming timbers; and the crack of the shot that had killed Paolo. He shook his head and breathed deeply as he fought to contain his feelings.

Even from his position, high above the lake, Klaus could see that the building had been neglected. It looked desolate, forlorn, as if no one had been there since that fateful night when he…. He tried to brush away his thoughts. The concrete walls and roof had survived the flames, but the windows had been boarded up, as if to lock in the secrets of that night. Tongues of soot still painted the walls, evidence of the fire, telling the tale of his crime.

He averted his eyes, looking to the right of the museum, searching for the part of the forest where the mirror was hidden, but his view was blocked by the jutting cliff on which the western part of Nemi stood. Of the exact spot he could not be certain; he would have to go to the gate of the north-western side of the town, to the belvedere outside the gate, where Paolo....

Klaus turned away from the wall and bit his lip in an attempt to stem the tears. What good would retrieving the mirror do for the old man? He tried to convince himself that he was doing it for Paolo's memory, but Klaus knew he was doing it for himself, to try to extirpate the guilt and the nightmares that every night laid his soul to waste.

He walked past the war memorial and saw the new names that had been recently etched upon it. Was that what the future held? Old memorials, new names, each a senseless sacrifice for a cause long-since forgotten? He looked at it again, briefly, and then walked away.

The fountain of Diana greeted him at the southern entrance to the main street of the town. Unwittingly, he felt for the icon of the goddess hanging from the chain at his neck. It was the symbol of their love, the amulet that Rosanna had given him; she, too, had its mirror image about her neck. For centuries, the icons had lain together, until unearthed by Rosanna's hand; was it too much to hope that they would be together again?

He looked along the street, and found it much as he remembered it. Unlike Genzano, which sat directly across the Allies' thrust to Rome, Nemi had been almost unscathed by the war. The street looked the same to him as when he had first walked down it with Gunther, as if Time's demanding hand had not done its usual damage.

The early morning sun slid off the old buildings, casting its shadows across the street. He noticed that there were changes here and there: the fountain, arid during the war, now bubbled with life again; the old coffee shop where he had once sat was now a butcher's shop; and the dull, careworn church tower that had once greeted him when he had climbed to Paolo's house had been repainted.

Klaus began to walk slowly along the street. Of course things were different. Above all, he was different. His step was slow and soft; no longer did his heels clip on the cobblestones. Women did not look at him as if he were the devil incarnate before snatching up their children and sweeping them inside their houses. The fear that had daily stalked the streets had gone, replaced, if not by hope, at least by a normality that allowed people to go about their everyday business without some cataclysm erupting to savage their lives.

Yes, it was different. Now, it was he who felt the fear, the fear of returning, of putting his hand back into the now-stilled pond of time and stirring the mud of the past. It was an irrational fear, he told himself in an attempt to steady his nerves. But he knew it was real; he brushed the sweat from his forehead, although there was yet no heat in the day, the newly-risen sun barely clearing the hill that towered over the back of the town.

His mind told him that he should turn around and leave, but he stood transfixed. He should not have come back; he should have imprisoned his memories in the deepest recesses of his mind. But he could not forget that night: every day his demons conjured up the burning ships, Paolo's face, and the nightmare of Rosanna's pain.

The cobbled street at the side of the church beckoned him. Beyond the church, the path climbed to Paolo's house. What would he find when he went there? Would Rosanna be there? His fear intensified and he stopped as he drew abreast of the church, his feet translating the fear to paralysis.

The church appeared strange with the newly painted walls; how he wished he could hide the past so easily, with a simple coat of paint. His feet began to move again, his hope of seeing Rosanna winning the battle with his fear.

He turned the corner and the house was there. It was unchanged, except the windows were dirty, and the paint was flaking off their frames. Smoke came from the chimney, but the house had an air of neglect, as if no one cared for it anymore. He began to think that the family had moved on. At the side of the house, an old woman sat on a chair, peeling potatoes. Her silver gray hair was bent over the bowl, her eyes looking down at the potatoes that turned in her gnarled fingers. After a few moments, she became aware of his presence. She looked up and stared at him without saying a word. Suddenly, she threw the bowl to the floor and leapt up, her eyes flashing.

"*Bastardo! Porco!*" The insults came from a mouth twisted by rage and hatred. "Why have you come back? Not finished with your torture?"

Klaus was taken aback as the water from the bowl splashed over his shoes. Who was this old woman? How did she know him?

"I'm sorry, but…"

His voice trailed away as the shock hit him. The eyes told him, the eyes and the hatred burning in them. It was Rosanna's mother, Maria. Yes, they were her eyes, but the face in which they were set was not her face. The lines were scoured around her eyes, the brow was deeply creased. The mouth that has once smiled at him was now twisted downwards, soured; the dark hair once flecked with silver traces was now gray, a dull gray, like an overcast winter's sky.

She came towards him, her foot kicking at the bowl, which rattled as it rolled down the path. She stopped, her eyes narrowing; the cold look withered Klaus. He wanted to run, but he could not; her eyes held him paralyzed.

"Why have you come back? Don't you know the pain you caused?"

Klaus could find no words as Maria's stare continued to pierce him. Had he himself etched those deep lines on her face? Was it he who had prematurely deformed the hunched bones of her feeble frame?

"I'm sorry," he mumbled at last. "I should not have come back."

She spoke harshly and quickly as she vented her pain and anger.

"You can be sorry until the end of your days, but you will never remove the hurt you caused."

In her anger, she tried to raise her crooked body erect, to lift her head upright, as if to regain her pride, but after a few moments she fell back into her stooped position.

"The hurt!" She stabbed a finger at her bosom. "Here!"

"But it was the war."

Klaus knew he was lamely casting around for a straw to clutch; he had no answer and, from the scornful look that she cast upon him, he detected that she knew, too.

"I was not the one who gave the order for Paolo to be shot."

"Shot?" The woman started, her face contorting in a look of puzzlement. "Paolo wasn't shot."

Klaus mirrored her amazement. He had heard the crack of Gunther's pistol, the single shot that he had heard every day for the past four years.

"A German soldier brought him back to our door that night."

Her eyes flitted from side to side as she relived the moment.

"The soldier kicked in the door and threw Paolo onto the floor. Then he shouted something in German we did not understand and stormed off."

Gunther! He had not shot Paolo! But Klaus could remember the shot as if it were yesterday.

"Paolo told me later that the German had taken him behind the town wall and raised his gun. Paolo thought he was about to die, but the soldier looked at him, shook his head and fired into the air."

Klaus's eyes widened. Gunther had disobeyed an order; he must have known he would have faced a firing squad if discovered. What had driven him? He would never know. But he had not shot Paolo. Klaus sighed as he felt some of the guilt lift from him; the screams of the demons that Maria had reawakened began to fade. Paolo, at any moment, would emerge from the house.

"He did Paolo no favor."

Her voice was as cold as the crisp morning air. She sat down, pulling her shawl about her.

"It would have been better if he had shot him."

Klaus's brow furrowed. "What do you mean?"

"Turn around."

Klaus was puzzled, but did as she asked.

"What do you see?"

"I see the town, the hills, the lake."

"And the museum? Do you see the museum?"

He looked down, beyond the town to the forlorn building at the side of the lake.

"Yes, I can see the museum."

"Paolo stood on that very spot the night you burned the ships."

Klaus turned to her, to try to offer an explanation, but she raised a hand to stop him.

"He stood where you are standing now. He was already in agony about Rosanna – we were both sobbing, terrified of what had happened to our daughter. His heart was already broken, and then he watched the fire destroy the ships – his ships. The ships were nothing to me, but I knew what they meant to Paolo. It was as if the flames consumed him, too. He screamed. He wept. He fell to the ground, beating his head upon the very cobblestones where you are standing."

Klaus jumped instinctively from the spot. The demons were beginning to regain their voices.

"I would have given my life not to have witnessed that night. When you destroyed those ships," she raised her hand, a bony finger pointing at Klaus, "you destroyed my husband."

The hand fell back to her side and she began to sob, her whole body shaking with her grief and pain. After a few moments, she stopped, wiped away the tears with her shawl and looked at him.

"May you rot in Hell!"

"But Rosanna," Klaus protested, "didn't he tell you about Rosanna?"

She struggled to hold back her tears, her lips quivering.

"Is there no end to the hurt you wish to inflict?" She pulled out a handkerchief from the pocket of her dress. "Don't mention her name again. She is gone. Forever."

"Gone?"

"She has not been seen since that night." Her head fell forward for a moment before she raised her eyes to look at Klaus through her tears.

"Paolo spent six months looking for her, after you and the rest of the swine had gone. He scoured Frascati, Albano, all of the towns. Nothing. He spoke to all the mayors. Everywhere the same: they would shrug their shoulders and say: 'There were so many who disappeared in the war.' We were desolate. Our only child. Gone."

She sighed. She no longer cried, but her frail body seemed to shrink even more.

"Paolo became demented. You have seen the church with its new coat of paint?"

Klaus nodded. He found it difficult to contain his own emotions. Had Dressler taken her away? Was Rosanna gone forever?

"Paolo did that. He organized the whole town to paint the church. He worked like crazy, every day, until it was finished. Then there was nothing. He would sit for hours, just looking at the fire. Or he would stand there – right where you are standing – and pass the whole day looking at the museum. Nothing I did could bring him back. He just looked. Sometimes he muttered 'It's all my fault,' over and over, but, otherwise, not a word. Then, one day, they found him."

The tears again fell from her eyes.

"Found him? Where?"

Klaus knew at once he should not have asked.

"They found him in the museum. Hanging from a beam."

She began to wail, her cries echoing the shrieks of the demons that had returned to torture Klaus. He looked down at the cobblestone beneath his feet, the stone that Paolo had beaten his head against. He needed to escape. He turned to go.

"You cannot go. Not yet." Her voice was cold and harsh again, her grief changing to anger in a moment.

"It was not Paolo's fault. His only mistake was to let you into our lives. You killed him, as surely as if your hands had been the rope around his neck. And you killed Rosanna, too." She bent down to pick up a potato that had spilled from the bowl and threw it at Klaus.

"Now be gone. The fires of Hell are not enough for you!"

CHAPTER 53

The same day. Late afternoon.

The hill somehow didn't look the same to Klaus as he picked his way between the trees. He'd taken a room at the De Victis inn, but he'd sat on the piazza for some hours, devastated by his meeting with Maria. Although it had been late in the day when he had begun his descent to the lakeside, he had felt sure that he would be able to find the hiding place quickly. But everything looked so different and the light was beginning to fail.

Maria's words still rang in his ears. For the hundredth time that day, he wondered why he had come back. Recovering the mirror would not bring Paolo back, it would not erase the memories of that fateful night, it would not make amends for the burning of the ships. Perhaps, he hoped, having taken something precious from the world, he could give something back.

It was difficult to find his bearings. The trees seemed strange, unfriendly, as if deliberately hiding the secret from him. He could find nothing. The large rock that served as a pointer to the gnarled chestnut tree was nowhere to be seen. He turned again to try to assess his bearings, but the view of the museum brought back the nightmare again. The mental filter he had developed over the past few years to preserve his sanity did not seem to be working now that he was back at the scene. The fatal night was replayed in his mind – Rosanna's bruised face and shorn hair, the unspeakable anguish in Paolo's eyes, the ghostly wailing of the dying ships, the lake flecked red with the flames.

Klaus called upon his logical mind to force its way back into control as he measured the coordinates from the lake and the museum. Higher. The tree was higher up the slope. Not only higher, but farther to the west. He needed to retrace his steps, to go back down and find the right path.

He cursed his ineptitude. The light was failing fast; the carpet of dusk was rolling in from the east, and there was, as yet, no moon. His mind snatched at the word 'moon' and would not let it go. He remembered that night when she had shown him the three moons; he had seen her uplifted face shining softly, not only in the light of the celestial body, but also in its sharp reflection of the lake's mirror and the shimmer of the distant image from the sea. Her face had shone, and he had cupped it gently in his hand, afraid it would break like fine china. The cruel mixture of joy, then pain, begged his mind to shut out the image, but it would not.

His feet betrayed him, slipping on the wet soil underfoot, and he fell to his knees. It was no good. He would have to give up and go back to the town. He reached behind him for his knapsack and pulled out his flashlight. His finger was poised above the switch when he heard a noise.

He stood up, listening, not moving a muscle. Only the sound of the breeze ruffling the leaves reached his ears. The light was dying fast. Again, there was a crack, followed by a rustle of leaves. There was something – or someone – in the forest with him.

He was not afraid, although his breathing became shallower, more urgent. He was surprised at how his military training took over his actions. Slowly, he dropped to his haunches and allowed time for his eyesight to adjust in the gathering gloom. The noise was to his left. He resisted the temptation to switch on the flashlight and betray his position. There was another shuffling of leaves underfoot, this time from his right. There was more than one of them. He held his breath, listening for noises, trying to discern voices, but there was nothing. Klaus shook his head; his senses were playing tricks upon him in the darkness. Perhaps some creatures of the forest were setting out on their nocturnal prowl. He stood motionless for a minute, but his ears detected nothing.

He chided himself for behaving like a little child afraid of the dark, but he decided not to switch on his small flashlight as he edged his way back down the narrow path between the trees. Ahead of him, about fifty yards away, he could just see a small clearing. He decided to make for it; perhaps he would be able to get a glimpse of the lake and re-orientate himself, so he could get himself off the hillside as soon as possible.

The light startled him. It came from behind him, fixing him. Then there was another, from his right, the two lights bracketing him. He turned and dropped on one knee, bringing up his right hand to try to ward off the blinding light, as his other fumbled for the switch on his flashlight.

"Who are you? What do you want?"

His shout faded into the darkness of the forest. No reply came. The beams still held him transfixed. One of the lights wavered for an instant, the beam glistening as it bounced off something held in the man's other hand. Steel. A knife.

Klaus leapt up, switched on his flashlight and turned to escape. His light picked out the path amidst the tree roots and fallen branches, but the soft earth was treacherous; several times he slid and slithered, barely succeeding in maintaining his balance.

Behind him, there was a voice.

"*Segui il fascista – figlio di puttana!*"

The beams crossed and crossed again, seeking him out like search-lights hunting an aircraft. He stumbled, his arm flailing out at a tree to regain his balance and propel him forward. Despite all, he was begin-ning to outrun his attackers, as he used all the skills the army had taught him. A plan formed hastily in his mind: once he reached the clearing, he would switch off his flashlight, double back up the hill, and find some place to hide. It was risky, but it just might work.

His plan evaporated as a light suddenly burst upon him from the clearing ahead.

Whoever they were, they had laid their trap cunningly. He had no option: he had to take on the man ahead. His pace increased; ten yards, five yards. He crashed into the man with all the force he could muster, lashing out a hopeful fist towards where his attacker's head should be. The blow was warded off and his assailant grappled with him. For a moment, the beam of his light was cast upward, capturing his attacker's face. The face looked surreal in the light, but Klaus recognized the fea-tures: it was one of the young men who had been in the bar the day before, one of those about whom the mayor had warned him.

He drove his knee up into the youth's groin. He could see the pain in his attacker's eyes, but before Klaus could wrench himself free, the youth swung his flashlight, bringing it crashing against his temple. Klaus staggered, fighting to hold onto consciousness, but he slid slowly to the ground. The youth raised his flashlight again.

"*Basta*. Wait, Alessandro."

The torch was slowly lowered as the other two attackers caught up, breathing heavily, their lights seeking out Klaus's face.

"This bastard must suffer. We must teach him a real lesson. He must know what it is to suffer, to wait, knowing he is going to die."

The voice was cold, emotionless. Klaus shook his head, trying to shake off the effects of the concussion. He squinted into the light and saw again the flash of steel.

"Well, fascist swine, how is the master race this evening?"

The others laughed as the tallest of the three leaned forward, waving his knife under Klaus's nose, but the man to his right was anxious.

"For Christ's sake, Vittorio, let's get this over and go."

"There is no hurry, Giorgio." The leader spoke unhurriedly, as if savoring each moment. "He must suffer, as my father suffered in the labor camp. Before they killed him."

He spat out the final words, slowly, deliberately. For some reason, Klaus felt that he wanted to see the man's face, to give form to this man who hated him, but the beam of the flashlight made him a shadowy figure, unseen. He wondered why he felt so detached when his life was in peril.

He grabbed wildly at the man's ankle. Briefly, he had a grip, but his tormentor shook his foot free and kicked Klaus in the ribs. Once, twice, three times. Klaus gasped as the air was kicked from his lungs. He looked up helplessly as the man on the leader's right raised his flashlight above his head.

"Not yet, Giorgio."

The leader's hand came out to stay the falling arm. He leaned again over Klaus's heaving frame.

"You thought you would try your luck, *tedesco*? That you might have a chance?"

There was emotion in his voice now.

"We shall give you the same chance as you bastards gave my father. Or Alessandro's brother. None."

He grasped Klaus's hair and twisted his head to one side. The tip of his knife cut at Klaus's cheek, and then slid slowly down toward his mouth. Klaus felt the stab of pain and tasted blood as it ran down into his mouth.

"For God's sake, let's finish him off now and get out of here!"

One of the accomplices spoke from the darkness behind the lights.

"Not yet, I've not yet fin...."

The shot startled them all. The explosion was loud, echoing around the clearing.

"Drop that knife, or the next shot will be for you."

A torchlight beam snapped on from the edge of the clearing. All eyes turned to the light, the leader of Klaus's attackers pointing his own beam toward it. Even in his confused state, Klaus could see that it was the mayor. The shotgun he held waist high was waving in front of him.

"I told you to drop the knife."

He pointed the gun at the leader. The young man stared at the mayor for some moments. and then let the knife fall from his grasp, the blade glinting in the light as it fell onto the leaves.

"Are you alright? Can you get up?"

The mayor's remarks were addressed to Klaus, but he did not take his eyes off the attackers.

"I think so."

Klaus spluttered out the words, his mouth full of blood. He spat it out and raised himself unsteadily to his feet. His hand reached for his cheek; he looked at his bloodstained fingers as his other hand dug into a pocket for a handkerchief to staunch the flow of blood.

"Why are you protecting this Nazi scum? He and his kind killed my father."

The leader had recovered from the shock of the mayor's sudden arrival. His eyes glowered.

The mayor came closer, his gun still leveled at Klaus's attackers.

"I know of no crime he has committed."

The two younger men edged backward, but the leader held his ground. Klaus saw his breath, caught in the beam of the flashlight, snorting from his nostrils.

"What about all the round-ups, all our people who disappeared to Germany to die in labor camps? What about the murders? What about the atrocities? Have you forgotten about the slaughter in the caves of Rome?"

"You cannot blame someone for the crimes of others. I have no evidence that this man is guilty of any crime."

Klaus's mind saw the burning ships, and he lowered his head. That was his crime.

"However, I have seen a crime committed here tonight."

The mayor spoke in a matter-of-fact voice, but there was a hint of menace in his voice.

"Now, go home. I shall deal with you all tomorrow."

He motioned them away with his gun. The two younger men moved uneasily to the edge of the clearing, but the leader held his ground, leveling his eyes at the mayor.

"So, fascism still lurks in Italy." He gestured obscenely. "Nazi lover!"

He turned, beckoned his accomplices to follow him and they trudged away from the clearing, their footsteps fading.

"*Signore*, I cannot thank you enough."

Klaus stepped forward into the beam of the mayor's flashlight and offered his hand. The mayor looked at the hand, shook his head, then uncocked his gun and cradled it in his arms.

"Why have you come back here, making all this trouble?"

There was an angry edge to the mayor's voice. "The past is the past. It is best forgotten." He paused and looked at Klaus. "If it can be forgotten." He nodded in the direction of the departing men. "For some, it is difficult to forget."

Klaus understood. He knew *he* could not forget. He let his hand fall limply to his side.

The mayor came closer and raised his light to Klaus's face.

"Now, we must find a doctor to attend to your wound."

Klaus turned to make his way down the path, but the mayor gripped his arm.

"Tomorrow, you will leave and return to Germany."

The tone of the voice suggested it was an order rather than a request.

"And you will forget."

The next day. 7.30 a.m.

Klaus sat on the wall overlooking the lake. The pain was still bad. He resisted the temptation to put his hand to the dressing on the side of his face. The doctor had stitched up the wound, but there had been no anesthetic, other than several glasses of grappa. There would be a scar, the doctor had said. He winced at the memory.

Despite the drink, he had not slept at all. At the first glimmer of dawn he had got up; he needed to escape brooding over the events of the previous day. Breakfast had been out of the question: it was painful enough just drawing on a cigarette, so he had taken a walk. From his perch on the wall, he looked back down the street. Outwardly, it all seemed the same as four years ago, but he knew it was different, as if he had returned to another town, another country.

A cock crowed dementedly, but otherwise it was quiet, the street waiting patiently for the start of another day. He gazed at the cobblestones at his feet, but he saw only the returning images of his nightmare; only the ghosts of the past inhabited his mind. His head fell to his chest, and he began pounding it with his clenched fists, as if he could beat the images and sounds out of his mind. There was no salvation, no atonement for him here. He could search for the mirror, but he knew it would offer no hope, no redemption.

He threw down his cigarette and ground it underfoot. He would go, leave this cursed place. He would cycle back to Velletri, pick up his car and go back. Back to Germany, to try to find some normality in his life, perhaps a future that would eradicate the hateful images of the past.

The squeak of a bicycle wheel cut across his thoughts. A youth with an awkward limp was pushing his bike across the piazza, heading for the western gate. Klaus shrank into himself, feigning unconcern; the last thing he wanted was further trouble. The lad - Klaus thought him barely in his teens - looked at him as he went by. He was tall and gangling, loping from side to side as he limped across the piazza. Klaus could not make out his features clearly, except for a huge shock of black, curly hair atop his head.

The youngster passed by, his gait uneven, with a slight drag of his left leg. After a few yards, he stopped, turned and looked back, staring.

Klaus got to his feet and prepared to leave; there must be no more trouble before his departure. The lad began to call at him, but Klaus continued to walk away.

"*Signor Capitano?*" The voice caused him to stop and turn.

"*Signor Capitano?*" The limping gait was hurried as he approached Klaus. "Is it you?"

A glimmer of recognition came to Klaus's mind as the boy came near.

"It's me – Gianni!"

He leaned his bike against the wall and came toward Klaus, whose eyes widened. The figure before him was two feet taller than the little urchin who had brought messages from Rosanna.

"It *is* you, *Signor Capitano!*" The curly hair and the brown eyes came closer. "Have you come from Germany?" Suddenly, a look of concern came to his face. "What have you done to your face?"

Klaus raised an index finger to his lips and pulled Gianni back to the bench on which he had been sitting.

"Talk quietly, Gianni – I don't want anyone to know I've come back."

He turned his eyes toward the street; already a few people were about. When he looked back, he found Gianni still staring at the bandage on his face.

"It was an accident." He shrugged his shoulders. "But how are you, Gianni? Why do you limp?"

The smile disappeared from Gianni's face and he looked down.

"It was after the war. A mine."

The lad looked up at Klaus. The devil-may-care luster that had been in the boy's eyes three years ago was no longer there. Despite the hardship then, the joy of life had shone there; now the eyes were dulled with regret, wistful of times gone.

"We were walking – my friend, Giuseppe and me – along the path that leads to the Velletri road."

Gianni looked blankly toward the lake, as his eyes recaptured the event he longed to forget.

"There was a big explosion. Giuseppe had stepped on a mine. He died. His guts were strewn all over the road."

He gagged on his words. Klaus wanted to look away, but could not.

"The shrapnel broke my leg."

He leaned forward, his hand running down the afflicted limb.

"It was not set properly. It has never been right since."

Klaus grimaced and shook his head. Wherever he turned, the war and its aftermath leapt up to scorn and mock him.

"But why have you come back, *Signor Capitano?*"

Klaus turned away and looked down on the morning blanket of mist cocooning the lake. He knew he had no real answer. To find Rosanna? To recover the mirror? After Maria's damning words, it no longer mattered.

"I do not know, Gianni. For some, the past beckons."

"At times it beckons me, *Signor Capitano.*"

He looked down at the path that snaked its way down the hill through the mist to the lakeside. A glimmer of a smile crossed his face, then his eyes fell to his leg.

"But sometimes it doesn't." Gianni looked wistfully along the street, empty except for two old women on their way to church. "It is all so different now."

Klaus knew what the lad meant. The town had not changed for fifty, perhaps a hundred years. Yet it was a different town from the one he had seen but four years ago. For Gianni, too, it was different; it was as if time had warped their senses.

"I live in Rome, now. My mother moved us all there after the war, after the accident." He glanced down at his leg.

"I don't like the city, but at least there is work there for my mother. I come back here now and then to visit my aunt." The lad looked at the lake again; the early warmth of the sun was beginning to chase the mist away, giving glimpses of the surface beneath.

"To think I used to run down there. Like the wind. No one could catch me."

The shock of hair shook sadly at the memory, but that memory brought forth another, happier moment.

"*Signor Capitano*, do you still see the big soldier who used to throw me in the air and give me sausage?"

A smile played across his lips and his eyes brightened.

Gunther. Klaus recalled the image of the ox of a man, tossing Gianni into the air. It was the first day he had seen….

"He is dead, Gianni. Killed in the war."

Klaus cursed himself as soon as the words left his lips. He should have told the boy a lie, that Gunther was back on his farm, tending his animals; that the big soldier often talked of the little boy in Italy; that he would come back to see him one day. Instead, he had shattered Gianni's reverie, bringing more bitterness to a young life already soured.

Gianni's eyes saddened, but he did not cry; he had not cried since Giuseppe had stepped on the mine.

"The war brought much death, *Signor Capitano.* You know that Signor Giraldi is also dead?"

"I know, Gianni."

Klaus's mind brought forth the image of Paolo's body hanging in the soot-stained museum. What had Maria said? That he had killed her husband as surely as if the rope around his neck had been his own hands. He looked down at his hands, then sought Gianni's eyes.

"Maria – Signora Giraldi told me. She said that Rosanna had not been seen since that…" his voice caught on his words as he felt the vise clutch at his heart, leaving it empty, void, "…since that night when the ships were burnt."

He saw the towel wrapped around her shaven head, the bruises on her face.

"Gone. Forever. That's what Signora Giraldi told me. Gone. Forever."

Gianni averted his eyes from the tears welling in Klaus's and shuffled uncomfortably on the seat. He opened his mouth as if to say something, but then shook his head and stood up.

"I must go now, *Signor Capitano.* I must ride down to the station. I have to catch the early train back to Rome." He looked up at the church clock, its hand climbing to mark eight o'clock. "*Ciao, Signor Capitano.* I hope you come back again some day."

The bicycle squeaked as he wheeled it away.

"I shall try, Gianni. *Ciao.*"

After a few paces, the lad made to mount the bicycle, but stopped and turned back to Klaus. His words came hurriedly.

"She is not dead, *Signor Capitano.* Rosanna lives in Rome with…"

Before he could finish, Klaus had leapt to his feet and rushed forward, grabbing the handlebars of Gianni's bike.

"Where is she, Gianni? Take me to her now. I'll get my bicycle."

Gianni wrestled the handlebars from Klaus's grasp.

"I can't do that, *Signor Capitano.* I've told you too much already. I must go."

He turned to go, but Klaus gripped his arm.

"But how, Gianni? How? I do not understand. Her mother says she has not been seen since that night. Why didn't she come back to her family?"

Gianni averted his eyes and tried to pull himself free.

"Tell me, Gianni!"

Klaus's shout echoed off the walls around the piazza. He saw the innkeeper come to the door of the bar and look across at them.

"Please tell me."

Klaus lowered his voice, but his tone was still insistent, pleading. Gianni looked down at Klaus's hand, still holding the youngster's arm in a vise-like grip.

"You're hurting me."

"I'm sorry." Klaus relaxed his grip. "But please tell me."

The lad's eyes scanned Klaus's face, as if searching for something, as he decided whether to tell more.

"She couldn't come back, *Signor Capitano*. The shame would not let her return."

"Shame?"

Gianni's eyes fell, looking down at the cobblestones.

"There was a child."

"A child?"

Klaus reeled back at the shock. Gianni seized the chance to mount his bike, his game leg swinging awkwardly over the saddle. He pushed away, then turned his head back to Klaus.

"I'll tell her I've seen you. I'm coming back tomorrow afternoon. If there's a message, I'll bring it."

The bicycle wheeled away, then stopped. Gianni turned in the saddle.

"There's something else you should know, *Signor Capitano*. The evil one is back. He's been seen in Albano."

With a kick of the pedals he was off, the wheels bumping over the cobbles as he made his way out of the piazza toward the western gate. Klaus ran after him for a few paces and stopped. The innkeeper watched him for a few moments, then turned and went back into the bar.

October 19th 7.15 a.m.

Klaus had gotten out of bed at first light. He had barely slept. Since the meeting with Gianni the day before, his mind had churned in turmoil. He pulled back the curtain and looked out over the lake, again covered by a blanket of mist vainly trying to protect it from the probing light of a new day's sun.

Perhaps he had made the wrong decision. He had chosen to stay an extra day, despite the mayor's warning. The innkeeper had looked at him suspiciously, but Klaus knew he had to stay. There was the chance of a message from Rosanna; perhaps he might see her again. Then despair overwhelmed the brief hope in his heart; maybe, after all that had happened, she would not want to see him again.

He sat in the chair by the window, looking out, but seeing nothing. The questions were asked again, the questions that had preyed on his mind since his meeting with Gianni.

The child. All night long, he had tried to picture his face. His son was out there, in Rome, tugging on his mother's skirt. He would be three now, Klaus thought. He shook his head. He had not had time to ask Gianni whether the child was a boy or girl. Or even when it had been born. Suddenly, he shuddered. What if the child....

Dressler. His mind jumped again, as it had done so often over the past day. Why was Dressler here? Why had he come back? For Rosanna? Did he know about the mirror?

Klaus sensed danger. He should not have stayed. He should have taken the mayor's advice and left. He slammed his fist against the wall. He would leave. It had been a mistake to disturb the ghosts of the past. They should be left in peace.

He walked back across the room and lay on the bed, gazing at the ceiling. He would leave – the decision had been made – but he would retrieve the mirror before he left. Even if there were no message from Rosanna, he would give Gianni the mirror. For her. For the child.

The pillow beckoned him and he pressed his head to it. He saw her face beside him, as it had been that day at the temple of Diana. Perhaps there would be a message. He held the vision of her to him as sleep, at last, claimed him.

12.30 p.m.

Despite his jacket, the wind still felt cold. Klaus cursed himself for sleeping so late; it had been almost noon when he had started out down the hill; the innkeeper had eyed him suspiciously again.

But he was sure he had found the right path. He looked back toward the lake, now bathed in the pale light of the autumn day, and checked his position. The sights of that night came back to him as he tried to verify his position on the path. The flames leapt again in his mind. He shook his head to dispel the thoughts. It was time to put them aside, time to retrieve the mirror, and give it to Gianni for Rosanna. Time to end the agony.

The mirror was close by, he was sure. He shielded his hand from the cold wind to light a cigarette as he squatted by the side of the path. The lake was placid, like a mirror itself. He remembered when he and Rosanna had gazed over the water and he had seen her eyes, the eyes that still pierced his soul. He had to find the mirror, he told himself again. For her. For the child.

He pulled himself up, tossed his cigarette away, and began to climb the path, the fallen leaves crackling beneath his boots. After a few steps, he stopped. There was a noise behind him. Had his attackers come back? He turned his head, but saw nothing. The events of two days ago had made him jumpy. He shrugged away his paranoia. It was an animal of the forest, not some ogre come to claim him.

Where was the rock? The rock by the side of the path, the rock that bore the mark he had made that night, the rock that would point to the mirror's hiding place. He looked back at the museum once more to double-check his position. He was sure he was right. Not far now. Perhaps a little higher. His breath became labored as he resumed his climb.

Another noise. Ahead of him this time. His eyes searched among the trees, but again saw nothing. He stopped, steadied his panting breath and listened. Nothing. His mind was deluding him again. He moved up the path again, hurriedly, urgently. Perhaps, if he found the mirror, he could lay his ghosts to rest.

There was still no sign of the rock and doubt began to creep into his mind. Perhaps he was wrong; perhaps it was not the path he had taken that final night when he had slipped away from the pursuing Schneider and buried the mirror. Perhaps it had all been a dream, a nightmare – the war, the ships, Rosanna, Paolo, Dressler, Schneider. He shook his head, as if he could shake away the memories.

His breath billowed before him as he struggled up the path. It was time to give up, to go home, to let go of the past. But he knew it would not let go of him.

It was there. The rock. It sat at the side of the path, half overgrown, but there was no mistaking it. The mark he had chipped upon it that night was there, faded by moss, but unmistakable.

Klaus stopped, his chest heaving as he gasped for breath, his heart racing as he tried to contain his excitement. He patted the rock, a sign of permanence in his unsure world. Nearly there. The clearing was off to the right, the clearing in which stood the tree that had guarded the secret of the mirror these past four years. The small saplings that had grown in those years tried to bar his path, but he brushed them aside with new-found energy. Briars tried to cling to his legs, but he shook himself free.

Then he saw the tree. Ten yards across the clearing. The trunk reached up into the canopy of the forest; at its feet, the roots dug deeply into the earth, protecting their secret. Klaus raced forward, his hands embracing the trunk. His fingers began searching for the moss, the moss on the north side. He fell to his knees, his hands moving furiously, delving at the earth beneath the leaves, scooping it aside. Nothing. He paused. What if someone had already found the mirror? His hands grasped at the earth urgently, his fingers clawing at the soft, damp soil, his nails digging desperately.

Metal. His fingers felt metal. The case that held the mirror. He tugged at the case, but it would not come free. Klaus cried out in frustration, but he was not to be denied. He scooped away the earth, his hands going deeper, under the case. At last it came free. A sob of triumph escaped his lips as he pulled it out of the earth. He opened the case and pulled the mirror from its protective felt bag; the face was a little tarnished, but otherwise the mirror was in perfect condition.

"Es ist schon, ya?"

Klaus turned quickly, startled by the German voice. His mouth gaped open in horror. It was Dressler. He looked different without his black uniform, but the menace was still there in his cold blue eyes. And in the Luger pistol leveled at Klaus's chest.

Klaus leapt back, holding the mirror to him as he pressed his back against the tree, his eyes fearful as he watched the thin smile on Dressler's face broaden. There was no escape; Dressler would gun him down before he could move. Why didn't he shoot now? Was it another of Dressler's evil tricks, to make him suffer before dispatching him?

"You are surprised I am here, Schmidt?"

Dressler's pistol did not waver, the muzzle still pointing at Klaus's chest as he spoke.

"Schneider told me you had hidden something in the forest after you had torched the ships. He saw you, but could not find the exact spot. Our move to Poland did not allow me to confront you then. Unfortunately, Schneider did not survive the war."

Klaus's eyes scanned urgently for some way of escape, but there was none; only the small path led from the clearing, and Dressler stood athwart it.

"So I had to be patient. I had you watched."

Klaus's astonishment seemed to amuse Dressler, who smiled perversely.

"Despite what you may think, there are still many of us left, Schmidt, many who still believe in the Fuehrer and National Socialism. We shed our uniforms, but we are still here. The stupid Americans needed people who could run things in Germany after the war and we stepped forward, some with new identities, to fill the positions. Even in the universities."

Klaus's mind reeled as the full import sank in. There had been a Nazi in his university – perhaps a colleague – who had been watching him.

"So I waited. And when I learned of your proposed trip to Italy, I had you trailed and followed close behind. A few bribes here and there – perhaps you have forgotten what a treacherous race the Italians are, Schmidt – and I received a phone call this morning in my hotel. From your inn."

The news of the betrayal somehow did not trouble Klaus. His whole mind was focused on escape. He edged forward, slowly, as Dressler spoke, his hand tightly grasping the handle of the mirror. If he could get close enough....

There was a crack from the muzzle of Dressler's Luger and the leaves at Klaus's feet danced violently.

"Do not be foolish, Schmidt. I could kill you here and now, but you can live. If you help me get that magnificent treasure out of Italy."

He waved his gun at the mirror in Klaus's hand. Klaus knew he could not trust Dressler. He was lying. If he went along with his plan, the bullet could come at any time. Why was he lying? Another of his depraved games?

"I am surprised, Schmidt, that you do not ask about your Italian trollop."

Dressler's uneven teeth showed as he leered. Klaus's heart sank. So that was Dressler's game. More torture, another pound of flesh to be exacted; he had to deliver the ultimate insult.

"She amused me. She fought like a tiger. However, as you probably know, Schmidt, that is the way with most women. But I tired of her. I tossed her out when I was posted to Treblinka."

The coil within Klaus became taut, then tauter still. Dressler had taken Rosanna, forced himself upon her, used her as his plaything. The lips that were now leering at him had.... Perhaps the child....

A shout came from Klaus's throat, a primeval roar, the cry of a wounded beast. He lunged forward, the mirror raised above his head. For a moment, he saw Dressler's eyes widen with alarm; then they narrowed and a flame spat came from his pistol, followed by the thwack of the report.

Klaus felt that his chest had been hit with a huge hammer as the bullet tore into him. The force threw him backward and upward. Everything appeared in slow motion. His body arched in the air, turning. He saw the tree and the saplings float by as he was turned in the air by the force of the shot; he saw the mirror slip slowly from his hand, twisting and spinning lazily in the air, once, twice, as it fell, then bounced off the ground, hanging for long moments before it nestled back into the carpet of leaves.

He fell heavily alongside the mirror, the breath crushed from his wounded body. He lay face down in the leaves, the mirror inches from his head. He thought he saw her face in it, the image he had seen when Paolo had shown them the treasure. His eyes looked down; a leaf clung to his eyelid. His mind asked his hand to brush it away, but the hand did not answer; he asked again, demanded, but still the hand did not obey.

Why didn't Dressler finish him off? The pain was beginning to hit him, the waves spreading from his chest, screaming through his body. He wanted to turn, to look back at Dressler, but his left arm was useless. He felt the warmth of his blood run down under his shirt.

Thwack. The noise again rang around the clearing, but Klaus felt no further pain; there was no rip of a bullet into his flesh. Klaus coughed and tasted the blood in his mouth. Thwack. Still no bullet. What was happening? With a superhuman effort, Klaus rolled over.

Dressler was on the ground, his head a bloody mess. Rosanna stood over him, a stout branch held above her head. Thwack. It came down on Dressler's skull. Blood poured from his head, his arms twitching uselessly. Klaus saw Rosanna's arms and hands as she raised the branch again. Her muscles were taut and hard as the branch fell again, the wood splintering the bone. Thwack. And again. Thwack.

Dressler made one final heave, then his body quivered and laid still, his face and skull a bloody pulp. Still Rosanna's arms rose and fell, her face and eyes afire with hate. Thwack. Down came the branch again as the frenzy continued to seize her. Thwack.

Klaus tried to call out to her, but he choked on the blood coughed up from his lungs. At last the rhythm of the blows slowed; Rosanna tossed the blood-bespattered branch aside and fell to her knees.

Still her hatred was not vented. She leaned over Dressler, her fists flailing at his lifeless body. A cry came from her throat, like no other cry Klaus had heard, a cry that startled the birds, filling the canopy of the forest with the sound of frightened wings. The cry continued, as if she were trying to cast out all the grief and torment that had been inflicted on her life.

The cry stopped suddenly. She breathed deeply for a few moments and got up. Her whole body was still shaking, but she turned and hurried to Klaus's side. She knelt by him, looked briefly into his eyes and began to open his jacket.

"I came when Gianni told me you were here. I saw. . . " she nodded toward Dressler's body ". . . him following you." Her breath came quickly, and Klaus could see the tremor in her hands.

Her trembling fingers wrestled briefly with the buttons of his blood-soaked shirt, then pulled violently, ripping the cloth away. Her eyes fell for a moment to the icon she had given him, hanging at his neck, and a pained smile briefly visited her face. Then she saw the extent of his wound; she winced and drew back.

"We must get you to a doctor, a hospital, at once, Klaus."

Rosanna tore at the hem of her dress, ripping it away for a bandage, pressing the torn cloth over Klaus's wound. With her coat, she made a pillow and eased his head onto it, leaning him against the trunk of the tree. As she did so, he caught the glint of light on the fallen mirror. He tried to turn to it, but cried out with the pain. He looked at Rosanna and motioned his head; she retrieved the mirror and brushed the leaves away. She rubbed the surface with her skirt and then held it, as she had done those years ago, so they could see each other.

At first, Klaus saw a different Rosanna. Her hair was short, cropped of the tresses he had fondled. There were lines at the corners of her eyes and beneath the eyes a hint of darkness, as though the years had cast their shadow prematurely. But her eyes still shone as she looked at him, still full of the fire that had consumed him; and, below them, a trace of a smile came to her lips and the dimple beneath them.

Klaus wondered what she could see of him in the mirror, how passing time had wrought the metal of his face. She did not look at the wound on his cheek, but held his eyes with hers. She put the mirror down and leaned over him, her gaze invoking another time, another place. He slowly lifted his hand to his neck, his bloody fingers searching and finding the amulet. He looked up at her, searching for its mate. Her head fell and she began to cry.

"It was sold. Things were difficult after the war. There was the child."

She sobbed, her body shaking. Klaus took her hand and placed it, with his, around the icon. He tried to speak, but coughed, blood running from his mouth. She stopped sobbing and kissed him softly on his forehead, but the anxiety soon returned to her face.

"I must hurry, *mio caro*. Rest still. I shall soon be back with help."

She went to get up, but his hand clamped around her wrist, surprising her with his strength.

"The child?"

"He is well."

Her fingers eased away his grip. She came closer to him, cradling his face in her hands, looking intently into his eyes. Her lips spread warmly into a smile.

"Your son is well. His name is Carlo."

She saw his smile, then broke from his grip and stood up.

"I must go for help, *mio caro*. Now."

"Your mother. See your mother."

She smiled again and nodded.

"Later."

She reached the edge of the clearing and looked back briefly at him before turning away. Klaus listened as her feet raced down the path. The sound died away, leaving him in the silence of the clearing, a silence broken only by the wind-stirred leaves.

He looked across at Dressler's body, slain like the ancient King of Diana's Forest, dispatched by one of the boughs of her trees. Perhaps the past was dead now, too, the ghosts laid to rest. He saw her eyes again and felt the huge burden begin to lift from his mind, felt the specters of the past that had haunted him vanishing. He held the mirror to him, despite the pain stabbing in his chest.

His head fell back again against the tree. The past was dead and he could see the future. With Rosanna. With their son.

Klaus felt very tired. Where was Rosanna? He closed his eyes and it was May again. But a different May. He saw himself standing, proudly, on the prow of one of the great ships, looking out across the lake. The sun shone, but it was night, and he could see the three moons, each caressing her face. The lake parted before the ship. Ahead, on the shore, was the temple of Diana. He looked, and saw she was waiting for him there.

AFTERWORD

The perched village of Nemi, and its beautiful lake nestled in a crater, can be found just off the Via Appia about twenty miles south of Rome. Caligula really did ferry his magnificent ships across the lake to Diana's sacred temple, which, at the time of his reign, was already several centuries old and one of the grandest of antiquity. And, according to legend, the King of the Forest, Diana's protector, did acquire his sovereignty by killing his predecessor with a bough from a tree in the woods surrounding the lake, as described and analyzed in Sir James Frazer's classic, *The Golden Bough.*

In 1928, after centuries of dreaming of the treasure at the bottom of the lake, engineers found a way to bring the ships out. As described in the book, they ingeniously drained the lake through a tunnel, built by the ancient Latins, then improved by the Etruscans, that was even more ancient than Diana's temple. A triumphal ceremony, Mussolini attending, was held in 1940 to inaugurate the lakeside museum that had been built to house the ships. But for only four more years. On May 31, 1944, the ships, which had endured twenty centuries below water, were reduced to ashes. Whether their funeral pyre was lit by retreating German troops, partisans, or even an American artillery shell, remains to this day pure speculation.

The surrender of the Germans in Italy took place, in late April 1945, at the Palace of Caserta, near Naples; ironically, at the end of the Palace's magnificent gardens, there is exquisite statuary depicting the legend of Diana and Acteon, the legend sculpted on the mirror.

All of the above is known history. Everything else is the product of the author's imagination.

ACKNOWLEDGEMENTS

I would like to acknowledge the following books, which enabled me to grasp the history of Caligula's ships, and the legends surrounding them.

Le Navi di Nemi by Guido Ucelli (Instituto Poligrafico e Zecca Dello Stato); *The Goddess of the Lake* by Margaret Stonehouse (Press Time, Rome); *Mysteries of Diana* arr. by A.G. MacCormick (Castle Museum, Nottingham); *The Golden Bough* by Sir James Frazer (Simon & Schuster); and *The Green Man* by Mike Harding (Aurum Press).

In addition, a visit to the Palazzo Massimo alle Terme, part of the Museo Nazionale in Rome, where the surviving treasures are displayed, enabled me to see the magnificent relics recovered from the ships. A similar visit to the Castle Museum, Nottingham, England, provided me with details of the artifacts of the Temple of Diana taken to England by Sir John Savile Lumley in the late nineteenth century.

I am deeply grateful to the following people:

Rosario d'Agata, who is Director of the Project to rebuild one of the ships (www.nemiship.multiservers.com), gave me much advice and information, not to mention friendship and kindness.

Laura, and the staff of the Diana Park Hotel in Nemi, whose superb service made research a pleasure;

Lia Becherlin and her friends, who took my wife and me around the site of the Temple of Diana, and told us of future excavations;

Canny, Rose and Kimberley, from Charlie's in Tenafly, who read the first draft and made valuable suggestions;

Lou Stanek, Nancy and Kelynn, who had the courage to allow me to read the book to them, and who provided constructive critiques of the developing work;

And, of course, my darling wife, Carol, a gifted artist (the cover design is her work) whose idea gave birth to this book. Above all, her patience and love supported me throughout the whole project.

.

Breinigsville, PA USA
14 October 2010
247374BV00002B/146/A